Praise for Jessica James' Books

"Very engaging. Hard to put down." — BILLY ALLMON, U.S. Navy SEAL (Retired)

"Sweetly sentimental and moving… An endearing page-turner." — PUBLISHERS WEEKLY

"A tapestry of emotion deeply set inside the bravest of Americans: the soldier." — MILITARY WRITERS SOCIETY of AMERICA

"Reminds me of *American Sniper* and *Lone Survivor*, but accompanied with a beautiful and epic love story that is completely unforgettable." — LAUREN HOFF, United States Air Force

"A heart-rending, white-knuckle journey into the courageous lives of our nation's heroes. Shows us the meaning of commitment—to country, and to love." — JOCELYN GREEN, Award-winning author

Other Books by Jessica James

Romantic Suspense

DEAD LINE (Book 1 Phantom Force Tactical)

FINE LINE (Book 2 Phantom Force Tactical)

FRONT LINE (Book 3 Phantom Force Tactical)

Meant To Be: A Novel of Honor and Duty

Historical Fiction

Noble Cause (Book 1 Heroes Through History)
(An alternative ending to Shades of Gray)

Above and Beyond (Book 2 Heroes Through History)

Liberty and Destiny (Book 3 Heroes Through History)

Shades of Gray: A Novel of the Civil War in Virginia

Non-Fiction

The Gray Ghost of Civil War Virginia: John Singleton Mosby

From the Heart: Love Stories and Letters from the Civil War

www.jessicajamesbooks.com

JESSICA JAMES
HONOR COURAGE LOVE

FRONT LINE

A Phantom Force Tactical Novel (Book 3)

Jessica James

#WarriorReader

"

"I am not afraid…I was born to do this."
– Joan of Arc

Prologue

F ernando Enrique Ortega pushed the cleaning cart down the hallway toward the men's restroom, nodding and smiling at everyone he passed.

It was a game day so everyone was in a good mood. Even the ones arguing over their teams were doing so in a good-natured manner—for now. Fernando knew by the third quarter, with a few bad calls and too much alcohol, sentiments would undoubtedly change.

As far as Fernando was concerned, it didn't matter which side won. He was here for a mission that had nothing to do with football. Today was his last chance to finalize the timing and exact route he would take during the big game a month from now—and neither team would claim victory in that one.

Fernando concentrated on counting the steps from the janitor's closet to the men's bathroom on the lower level, and then pretended to check his phone. Leaning against the wall, and attempting to stay out of the way of fans, he took notes on how many minutes and footsteps it had taken him to make his way through the throngs of people crowding the corridor.

Although Fernando made sure to keep a smile on his face, anyone looking closely would have seen that his eyes carried no humor. A former member of the Mexican military, he'd been cleaning toilets in this stadium for the past eight months—and he could truthfully say he'd hated every second of it.

But today was different. This mission made all the previous demanding and demeaning work worthwhile. Fernando basked in the glory of this role and felt a strange, numbed contentment, despite the adrenaline rushing through him. The intelligence he gained during this shift ensured that the *El Soldado* cartel he belonged to would become a well-recognized name. Soon, they would not only be taken seriously in the United States—but be feared more than any other terrorist organization in the world.

Just as he reached the restroom, a security officer appeared, seemingly out of nowhere, walking swiftly toward him. Fernando raised his hand in greeting. "How are you today, sir?"

The man simply nodded and continued toward the food court, but Fernando felt an undeniable sense of satisfaction. They had made eye contact with one another, exactly as Fernando had wished. Next time, even if things were tense and chaotic, he would be accepted as part of the natural landscape.

As the security officer disappeared into the crowd, a man pushed past Fernando in the doorway of the restroom, knocking into the cleaning cart and almost tipping it. Fernando had the impulse to lash out, but successfully controlled the urge.

Instead he began humming to calm himself, and went about his normal cleaning duties. The restroom had cleared out somewhat by the time he finished, leaving only a few occupants at the urinals.

Trying to appear as inconspicuous as possible, Fernando removed a security uniform shirt and badge from a canvas bag attached to his cart and placed them in the end booth. Then he attached an *Out of Order* sign on the stall door and wheeled his cart back into the corridor, whistling as he went.

Once in the hallway, Fernando squinted down at his timer to see how long it had taken, and made the notations. As he turned to go back in to retrieve the shirt and credentials, his phone vibrated. He was tempted to ignore the interruption—it would throw off his calculations—but recognizing the number, he answered. "Go ahead."

"We have a problem." The voice, though quiet, carried an ominous tone.

Fernando did not respond, but walked swiftly to a place where he could find a little more privacy. He knew without asking what was coming next, so he waited.

"It will require the services of you and your men."

Fernando smiled. *Of course, it will* is what he was thinking. "What are the terms?" is what he asked out loud.

"Before we get to that, I need an update."

"On what? I am busy. Please hurry." Fernando scanned the hallway. He didn't want to be seen talking on the phone when he was supposed to be working.

"On our friend with the gambling problem."

Fernando felt a nerve twitch over his right eye. He hated being micromanaged. "He will receive another call in two days, and he will make contact—just as we discussed."

"Are you sure?"

Exhaling loudly, Fernando replied, "I am certain." The man's condescending words sparked more anger in him. "Now, what is the reason for this call?"

"As I said, I need your services."

A clicking sound echoed through the receiver, causing Fernando to envision the man pacing in his extravagant DC office.

"And the terms?" Fernando asked again.

"One million dollars on satisfactory completion of the assignment."

Fernando stopped walking, causing the people behind him to almost run into him. That was a large sum of money for one job. He knew there must be a catch, so he tried to sound casual. "And what does the *satisfactory completion* of the mission entail?"

"Remember I mentioned a thorn in my side?"

"*Si.*"

"I want it taken care of."

"Do you mean eliminated?"

"Eliminated. Once and for all." There was a short silence. "Do you have paper and a pen? Write this down."

Fernando grabbed the small tablet he had in his back pocket and a pen from his shirt. "Go ahead." He wrote down a date, time, and address and then read it back. "Wait. This is tomorrow. That is impossible."

"Why is it not possible?"

"I have no time to do reconnaissance on the site or formulate a plan."

The man laughed but there was no trace of humor in it. "You will have to figure that out, my friend."

"This is a large undertaking." Fernando did not try to conceal his anger. "With preparation, the job would only take two men. With this type of turnaround, I will need five to ensure nothing goes wrong."

"What are you saying?" The caller's voice hardened.

"I'm saying I need more money." Fernando knew he was pushing his luck, but this man had a way of getting under his skin, making him feel more like a servant than a partner. Just because he held a high position in the U.S. government didn't give the caller the authority to push him around.

Plus, Fernando could sense the urgency and tension in his voice, indicating the importance of the mission. With the close timing, there would be no time to find someone else to undertake the assignment. "Two million."

"One and a half. Take it, or leave it."

Fernando sighed. "Very well… I think I will leave it." He started to hang up.

"Wait! All right! Two!"

"Thank you for being reasonable," Fernando said, calmly. "Back to the business at hand. You say you have a *thorn*, but I need a name."

"I will send you the information. You will perhaps be surprised by the person's photo, but do not underestimate the threat."

"*Si.*" Fernando frowned and shook his head. "My men are not in the habit of underestimating the threat."

"It is imperative this be taken care of once and for all. Completely. And at this point, no matter the cost."

"No matter the cost in money, *señor*?" Fernando wanted to be clear about the instructions. "Or lives?"

"This person must be eliminated no matter the cost," was the reply. "*Period.*"

Chapter 1

Saturday

Nicholas "Colt" Colton stood beside his truck outside the dilapidated office building on the outskirts of DC and studied his surroundings. He liked to trust his gut, and right now, his gut was telling him something wasn't right.

Sliding his sunglasses to the top of his head, he watched a fast food wrapper bounce and tumble across the muddy parking lot before getting lodged between the links of a rusty construction fence. Two large bulldozers and a truck sat idly beside porta-johns, indicating major renovations were taking place.

From the appearance of the neighborhood, it needed a facelift. The building in front of him stood twelve stories tall with an apparent mix of retail and commercial office space inside. Colt's gaze moved to the structure on the south side, which, judging from the broken windows, was abandoned. The building on the other side still had windows but was only in slightly better shape.

Colt continued to scan the area. A large banner on the building read *Office Space Available*. Even though a few dozen cars were parked in the lot, there didn't appear to be any security measures in sight—no cameras, no doorman, no guards. Maybe that was a good thing. Colt was pretty sure the high-powered rifle and other tactical equipment he intended to take inside with him would not pass a checkpoint screening.

Although he had planned to leave his equipment in his vehicle, he didn't want to take the chance now. Hell, from the looks of the neighborhood, he didn't even feel comfortable leaving his truck unattended.

At least by taking his gear inside with him, he could help relieve the sensation of foreboding roiling through his body. He had no idea if this meeting was a setup or the real thing, but he was at the point where he'd do anything to catch a lead on the suspected terror plot against the United States.

Leaning inside the vehicle to grab his bag from behind the seat, he winced at the pain the position caused. The wound he'd received during a hostage rescue operation four days earlier had been stitched, but it still hurt every time he moved. He'd spent every waking moment since then responding to tips about the possible infiltration of terrorists from the Mexican border, but so far had come up empty-handed.

Colt checked his watch and saw it was time to get moving. Carrying his equipment in a duffel bag to look inconspicuous, he relaxed a little when he entered the building and discovered the lobby was deserted. The muted sound of a filing cabinet drawer being slammed shut—and then a phone buzzing—reached his ears, providing the only evidence the offices on the first floor were occupied.

He contemplated taking the stairs for a little exercise, but the elevator door was open, and the cab was empty. With two dozen stitches holding his abdomen together, he decided the elevator appeared more inviting than the stairwell.

The fewer people that see me, the better.

As the doors started to close, Colt rested his head against the wall and breathed a deep sigh of relief. He hated encounters with anonymous people—"blind dates" as they called them in the intelligence community. He was glad for the few minutes of solitude the elevator ride would provide to focus his mind on the task at hand.

But suddenly, a toe—and then an entire high-heeled red shoe—appeared in the crack of the closing door, causing the safety mechanism to engage, and the door to reopen.

"Sorry." A tall blonde stepped in without bothering to look up from her phone. Wearing a just-above-the-knee, black pencil skirt with a white blouse tucked into it, she carried a cup of coffee in one hand and had an oversized purse slung over the other shoulder. A pair of dark, reflective sunglasses sat snugly on her nose, concealing her eyes.

Glancing over the top of her shades at the panel of buttons and apparently seeing it was going to the twelfth floor, she lifted her foot and pressed the >|< button, as if using her feet and legs to operate the elevator was a common occurrence for her.

Even though Colt kept his gaze downcast, he couldn't help but notice the thin ankle that turned into a shapely calf, and then the leg that disappeared beneath the hem of her skirt.

He cleared his throat and lowered his head even further, so all he could see was the laces of his own shoes.

When she retreated to the other side of the elevator, he leaned his head back again—and concentrated on not banging it repeatedly against the wall. The only thing worse than riding all the way to the top floor with someone was when that someone was female with long legs. *Damn, why didn't I just take the stairs?*

To make matters worse, the elevator groaned and vibrated and moved so sluggishly, he could barely tell it was ascending. Colt concentrated on the numbers above the doors as they blinked off the floors, intent on not looking at, or making eye contact with, the blonde standing four feet away.

For one thing, it was about business—he didn't want her to get a good look at him. But the second reason was personal. He had formed a vivid picture of the face that belonged to those legs, and he didn't want to be disappointed by the reality. It would be comparable to opening a big, brightly wrapped package at Christmas and discovering that it wasn't at all what you imagined it to be. And there was no way the real thing was as good as what he had pictured in his mind right now.

Let a man have his dreams.

He watched floor number three light up.

Can this thing move any slower?

The view of the woman on the other side of the elevator continued to tug at the periphery of his vision like a magnet, but Colt refused to turn his head.

Well, maybe it won't hurt to take a quick peek.

That's when Colt thought he heard a gunshot.

The woman must have too, because out of the corner of his eye, he saw her slide her sunglasses onto her head and stiffen as if on high alert.

Not taking any chances, Colt casually removed his jacket and reached down to unzip his duffel bag almost in one movement. He glanced at the woman after he had finished assembling and loading his modified M-4 and saw no fear—only a calm, disconcerting curiosity on a face that was so stunning, it caught him off guard. A Christmas package that was even *better* than he'd imagined? He didn't want to look any closer. Things like this didn't happen in real life.

"You're a cop, I hope," she said with a faint smile as she stared at the gun. Her voice was soft and had the same effect as a warm sunbeam settling upon his shoulders on a cold day.

"Something like that." He lowered his gaze and caught the breath she had taken away, then slung the rifle over his shoulder and clipped some extra equipment to his belt before hitting the button for the ninth floor.

The initial gunshots sounded as if they were coming from the first floor, but they were getting louder and more frequent. He wanted to give himself room to escape to an upper level if necessary—especially since he now had a civilian to protect.

"Here's what's going to happen." He put his hand on the woman's shoulder and maneuvered her to the far corner of the elevator, causing him to look at her again. Her hair was pulled back and piled on her head in a simple, old-fashioned bun that brought to mind the image of a school librarian—prim and proper and probably prudish.

Strike that—never met a librarian with legs like that.

He cleared his throat and his mind and returned to the task at hand.

"When the door opens, I'm going to step outside. Don't move until you hear me say, 'clear.'" He leaned forward to make sure she understood, and stared into the most brilliant green eyes he had ever seen. Not wanting to stare, his gaze inadvertently dropped to her lips, all glossy and red like she was going out on a date. *Geezus.*

He noticed she was nodding, waiting for him to continue, so he took a step back to put some space between them. "When I say, 'clear,' come out, grab my shoulder, and hold on. Got it?"

The elevator bell dinged, indicating they had reached the eighth floor, so he moved into position. Glancing over at the woman, he gave one last command. "Leave the coffee and the suitcase behind."

When the light for the ninth floor lit up, he raised his weapon and went on full alert. "Get ready."

Standing to the side as the door opened, he swung his gun out, left and then right. "Clear."

He felt a hand grab his shoulder just as he'd instructed, but as the elevator doors rolled shut behind him, he was pulled backward, and sharp fingernails dug into his skin.

"What in the hell are you doing?" He turned around and saw that her purse had caught in the door, and she was trying to dislodge it. "I thought I told you to lose the suitcase."

"It's not a suitcase." She kept tugging on the strap firmly stuck in the door. "It's my handbag."

He grabbed her hand and physically pried her fingers away,

just as more shots echoed from a floor or two beneath them. The elevator had apparently been built as an afterthought and stood right in the middle of the building. They were sitting ducks from every direction. Colt pushed her back against the elevator block and stood in front of her as they inched their way around to the opposite side.

"You see that?" He pointed toward a room with a long counter running across the entire length.

She nodded.

"When I say 'go,' run across the hall and dive behind it. You understand?"

She acknowledged that she understood, but kept her gaze intent on the office doorway.

Colt stepped out and aimed his gun toward the stairwell in case anyone breached it. "Go!"

She took off running and disappeared over the top, followed by a loud thump when she hit the floor on the other side. Colt sprinted right behind, but instead of diving, he placed one hand on the counter, and threw his legs over, landing on his feet. He crouched down beside her as she sat rubbing the top of her head. One shoe was still on, but the other lay on the floor beside her. "Show off," she muttered. "You said *dive*."

Colt just shrugged, pretending the vault had been easy—and under ordinary circumstances, it would have been. But his gut felt like it had ripped open again. He hoped it wasn't bleeding, but he was too busy dialing his phone to worry about it.

"Fury One here, you read?" He forgot he was on the phone, not a radio.

"Yeah, I got you."

Colt heard the calm voice of Blake Madison, a former SEAL teammate and now co-owner of Phantom Force Tactical, a private security business they'd opened together. Blake was his closest and most trusted friend, and was the one who had arranged the meeting in this building.

"Hey, man. What's going on here? You hearing anything?"

"Yeah," the woman said from behind him. "What's going on?"

Colt shot her a look over his shoulder that made her lean back and bite her lip.

"We're getting reports that the building you're in has an active shooter or shooters," Blake said.

"I knew *that* much." Colt glanced at his watch and saw he was now late for his appointment. He wondered if the guy he was supposed to meet had been caught up in the chaos. "Is it related to anything we're working on?"

"What *are* you working on?" The woman inched closer.

Colt stood but remained low behind the counter and moved a few feet away so he could have a confidential conversation. As he did so, he could hear a muffled discussion as if Blake were receiving an update.

"Okay. Not much coming across on the local scanner, but Twitter is saying five shooters and possibly some hostages." Blake paused a moment as if reading more. "Some witnesses are saying the hostiles appear to be Hispanic."

Colt tried to keep his face from showing any signs of emotion, but his mind was going a million miles a minute. Was this a coincidence? Or the prelude to something much bigger?

"What floor are you on?" Blake interrupted his thoughts, and before he could respond, his friend spoke again. This time, Blake's voice conveyed much more urgency.

"Wherever you are, head—" The phone crackled and then went silent.

"Head where, buddy? You still there?"

The lights in the office flickered once and then everything went dark.

"That's not good." The woman spoke the words quietly, but in the sudden silence, they sounded thunderous.

Colt had been thinking the same thing but didn't want to say it. He didn't offer any words of comfort, and he didn't tell any lies. The darkness and his silence would confirm her suspicions of the seriousness of the situation so why waste his breath?

Glancing down at his phone, he saw it had no signal. *Shit.* He rolled his eyes upward. *Seriously?* Another two seconds of service so Blake could have finished his sentence would have been nice. Head *where?*

"What's going on?" The woman didn't sound fearful, but she inched nearer, sliding her rear end across the floor so that now he could feel her leg against his.

Colt was busy listening to the sounds coming from below them and trying to figure out his next move. The door of the office they were in was hanging by one hinge. From what he'd seen when they'd exited the elevator, none of the other offices on this floor even *had* doors.

"Not my job to tell you." He reached into his bag and pulled out another magazine for his gun, which he tucked into one of his leg pockets within easy reach.

"What *is* your job?"

He turned his head to glare at her, but since he couldn't see her in the dark interior room, he pretended not to hear.

"Okay. Let's try something easy." She sounded irritated. "What's your name?"

Colt didn't answer, and this time didn't bother to look at her.

"Guess I'll just call you Fury One. That works, right?"

He growled in disgust and turned his head toward her. "What are you, a reporter or something?"

"Umm, yeah."

Colt felt his heart drop. He couldn't help it. It was like sitting down beside a good-looking woman at a bar and then finding out she's married. Actually, it was worse. It was like sitting down beside a beautiful woman at a bar, one you hoped to get to know intimately, and finding out she's a lesbian.

He turned away to make sure she couldn't read the disappointment stamped on his face. "And *your* name is?" He spoke into the darkness.

"Who wants to know?"

Geezus Lord. What did I do to deserve this? Note to self: Take the stairs next time.

"Never mind."

Colt checked his phone again. Still no signal. Blake must have meant head *up* to the top of the building. Judging from the sound of gunfire and screaming below, there was no way he could go down. With a little better than a fifty-fifty chance of being right, Colt grabbed the woman's hand and helped her up. "Follow me. We need to move."

Chapter 2

"You ready?" Colt stood facing the door, his gun in position, waiting for her to move in behind him."

"No. Wait. I lost a shoe."

She had apparently dropped back down to her hands because he could hear her groping around in the dark.

"You need to be able to run." He grabbed her arm and pulled her to her feet again in one swift movement. "Barefoot is better than heels."

"You've obviously never seen me run in heels."

The vivid image of her long legs in nothing but a pair of red heels made him stop what he was doing, but the mental diversion only lasted a second. "You've got me there." He reached all the way down, lifted her ankle with one hand, and removed her remaining shoe—none too gently—with the other.

"Maybe we'll try that sometime for kicks when there isn't a chance it could get both of us killed." He flung the shoe so it fell out of reach. "For now, no shoes."

"Your call," she said, seeming to take his sarcasm in stride. "By the way, it's Josephine."

"What's Josephine?"

"My name, dummy."

Colt nodded, but his thoughts were focused on an escape plan. They were on a floor that contained empty office space, with no place for concealment. He had to find something that provided better cover.

He glanced over his shoulder at her. "We're going to run up the stairwell, take one floor, and see what's up there." He didn't bother to tell her he was hunting for something that would offer some protection—like a room with a door that would lock. "Got it?"

He switched on a small flashlight and saw her nod.

"Keep your hand on my back so I know where you are."

Again she nodded.

"And be aware of what's behind you. Give me a squeeze if you see or hear anything. Let's go."

They both hopped up on the counter backwards and swung their legs around to the right in unison, almost as if it were a practiced move. Colt felt her hand on his shirt as he made his way to the stairwell, and took the steps rapidly with his gun aimed up.

Tearing open the door on the next level, he saw in a glance that it was clear of targets. The walls had been knocked down between the offices so only a few supports and piles of debris remained. Colt barely paused. "Let's take another floor."

Back to the stairwell they went. Josephine kept up with his stride but was breathing hard by the time they reached the next landing. Colt charged through the door, rifle ready, and saw that, again, it was mostly under construction. But this time, there were large stacks of plywood and lumber, as well as assorted equipment strewn throughout.

As he was analyzing the defensive qualities, a barrage of gunfire echoed from below, helping him to make his decision. It sounded close—no more than two floors down.

"This way." With Josephine's hand still holding onto the back of his shirt, he sprinted to a pile of plywood and heavy lumber that provided adequate cover as well as a view of the doors. They both collapsed with their backs leaning against the wall, sucking in air as the sound of sirens—and now even a helicopter—reached them.

There was no doubt in Colt's mind that Blake had located a nearby chopper and sent it here to assess the situation. Within seconds of losing comm, Blake had undoubtedly been ordering up the cavalry, too. Help was on its way.

Nice job, guys.

"How much ammo do you have?" Josephine interrupted his thoughts.

Despite the fact that she was still trying to catch her breath, her voice sounded casual, as if she were asking if he'd brought an umbrella in case of rain.

Colt peered down at her sideways. "Enough for a while. Why?" He knew something was wrong because up until now, everything she'd said had been with a smile and a sense of humor. Now her brow was creased, and her eyes were serious.

He started to rise, but she grabbed his forearm and stopped him.

"Because if things go to shit, I'd appreciate it if you'd save one for me. Okay?"

Colt stared again into her green eyes. They were expressive, stunning, yet seemed to reflect a trace of sadness he hadn't perceived before. His gaze reflexively darted to her lips again before locking on to those emerald orbs that seemed to turn from solid to liquid beneath his stare. They were, without a doubt, the most beautiful eyes he'd ever gazed upon—and they belonged to a woman who had just politely asked him to put a bullet through her head if the shooters came through the door.

For a moment, he wasn't sure he could answer. He cleared his throat. "We're going to get out of here. Don't worry."

"I don't need a pep talk." He'd never beheld such a serious expression on a woman's face before. "Just promise."

Colt stood and eased his way to a window. It resembled a war zone out there. Police were staged everywhere, but they were behind their cars—taking defensive stances, not moving. Meanwhile, the firing below them continued to move closer. From the looks and the sounds, it didn't take a rocket scientist to see there was a pretty good chance that things would go to shit—and soon.

He sat down again, put his head against the wall, and closed his eyes. "Here's the deal." He lifted his head and studied her expression. "If things go south, I'm going down fighting."

She gazed up at him with a confident, hopeful look as she brushed a strand of loose hair from her eyes. For the first time, his eyes fell on the wedding band on her left hand, and he came to a conclusion. She was somebody's wife—maybe even a mother. She deserved a fighting chance to survive this—or to end it on her own terms.

He pulled his sidearm from a holster under his shirt and

handed it to her, grip first. "You ever use one of—"

She grasped it confidently, pulled back the slide and checked the chamber for a round, never bothering to answer his question. "Thanks. I feel better now."

Colt turned his head away, and gazed upward in silent appeal. *I don't.*

Chapter 3

S uddenly, a great rush of noise and loud footsteps
reached them, echoing in such a way it was hard to tell
from where it came. Colt stood and readied his gun
as three women and two men—one of them elderly—came
bursting out of the stairwell, tripping over one another.

Gunfire could be heard, as well, but the way the sound
was magnified and distorted in the confines of the building, it
played tricks on Colt's ears. He was unable to determine if the
clamor was coming from above or below, who was shooting,
and from where. It was a gigantic mishmash of noise and
concussion with seemingly no point of origin.

"Over here." He stood up from behind the pile of wood
and waved at those who had entered, but the women screamed
as soon as they saw his gun. They all turned to run in the opposite direction, and ended up pushing and tripping over each
other in their haste.

Josephine climbed onto the pile and waved her arms. "No,
this way. He's a good guy."

The group stopped and then barreled toward them as if
they'd made a collective decision without speaking.

"Get behind the wood," Colt ordered. "Keep your heads

down low and stay quiet."

As Josephine helped them, he walked toward the stairwell and listened. It was silent for the moment, but sometimes that could turn out to be worse than noise.

"We were trying to go up the stairs, but there was a masked guy with a gun," the one man told Josephine.

"What floor?" Colt went back to the group and jumped in on the conversation. "Was he above or below us?"

"He was right behind us." The man stopped to catch his breath. "From below, but he didn't stop on this floor. I think he kept going...up."

Great. Now I've got men with guns above and below and a bunch of civilians. What next?

A blaze of gunfire answered his question. One of the shooters burst out of the stairwell door with his gun firing straight ahead of him. Colt whirled around and pressed the trigger twice. *Tap. Tap.* The firing stopped.

Walking over the prostrate body, he tried to make out features in the dim light. The man was dressed in black, and, just as Colt had suspected, wore body armor—which is why he had aimed for the head. Unfortunately, that made any type of identification difficult, but he didn't have time to worry about that.

With a quick motion, he reached down and grabbed the weapon lying on the floor. Before he could turn around, one of the women was standing beside him with her long fingernails digging into his arm. Her other hand covered her eyes so she couldn't see the body. "What are you going to do?" She shook his arm. "You've got to help us find a way out of here!"

Before Colt could respond, Josephine spoke in a voice that

conveyed an end to her patience. "He's not a first responder, ma'am. He's your last resort. Stay out of his way, and let him operate."

Colt shot her a look of appreciation as he mechanically handed her the shooter's gun. "Hold onto that in case I need it." Then he motioned for the rest of the group to gather around.

"We're going up to the top floor." Colt had been listening to the sound of the helicopter and knew for sure it had to be a Phantom Force operator signaling for him to go *up*. Once they got to the rooftop, he would have to fend off the bad guys for as long as it took to fly everyone out. The chopper could take three at a time tops, so that would mean two trips before they got to him.

"What if they have explosives? A bomb?" Josephine sounded unconcerned, as if she were just analyzing the situation and wanted to figure out how to react.

Colt had been wondering the same thing but didn't want to reply with the possibilities that had gone through his mind. The best-case scenario was they would all be killed instantly, but there was the possibility of getting crushed when the building fell—or worse yet—surviving the initial blast and living long enough to die of smoke inhalation. "You watch too many movies," is all he said.

He slammed a fresh magazine into his gun and turned to the group. "Everybody ready? We need to stick tightly together."

They all nodded.

"Get in a line and hold onto the shoulder of the person in front of you. Josephine positioned the older gentleman as the third one in line before she went to the back, making her the first one to be hit if someone approached them from behind.

She had the gunman's AR-15 slung over her shoulder, and Colt's pistol tucked into the waistband of her skirt within easy reach, but she seemed more intent on helping the others up the stairs than taking any defensive action. The expression on her face was one of worry—not fright—evoking an image of strength and stamina that was completely at odds with her feminine persona.

Colt's eyes scanned the group. "Listen up. I'm going through the stairwell door. When I say 'clear,' everybody move forward. Got it?" When he saw the nodding of heads, he turned and swung open the stairwell door with ferocious energy, pointing his rifle up and then down. "All clear."

As a hand grabbed his shirt, he began climbing, but he was moving much faster than the line, so he broke away and reached the landing door when the rest of the group was only about halfway up. Not wanting to take a chance and open the door, he removed his ball cap and held it near the small window—causing an instant barrage of gunfire.

"Everyone down!"

One woman screamed, and the other civilians whimpered as they flattened themselves against the stairs. Colt stood behind the concrete wall and shook his head, counting the shots and waiting for the pause when the gunman had to reload.

"Stay calm, everyone." He heard Josephine whisper to the group. "And stay low until you hear him yell 'clear.'"

The moment the gunfire stopped, Colt lunged through the door. The terrorist was so sure of himself, he stood with his head down, slamming another magazine into his rifle. Colt double-tapped him, and he dropped.

Taking no chances, Colt turned and swung his rifle left and right, seeking other targets. This floor was nearer completion than the one below; at least here, the walls were studded out. Not seeing or hearing any other threats, Colt yelled "clear" to the group behind him. He wanted to get them out of the stairwell as quickly as possible.

The sound of the helicopter sweeping down was loud on this floor, but so was the sound of shooting from below. Colt had taken out two gunmen, so if the reports were right, there were still three loose in the building, probably heading this way now that they had heard the return fire.

He put his hand into his bag and felt around, his eyes still scanning the room. He was down to two magazines of ammo for his rifle, plus another one for the Glock he'd given to Josephine.

Thinking of Josephine, he caught a glimpse of her as she came through the door. Her tattered blouse was half in and half out of her skirt now, and her hair was mostly loose and in complete disarray. Her face showed little signs of strain, but he assumed that was just an act to keep the others in the group calm. He wouldn't be surprised if she collapsed into a weeping mess when this was over, and for a fleeting moment, he hoped he'd be there to catch her.

Suddenly, one of the women yelled and fell to the floor, holding her arm. "Oh, I'm bleeding!"

Josephine ran over and inspected the injury while Colt raised his gun back to the ready position and tried to figure out what had happened. After a few seconds, he realized the woman had been in such a hurry to squeeze through the door first, she'd sliced her arm on a nail sticking out of the wall.

There was a large amount of blood, but the injury was minor. When Colt's gaze met Josephine's, he could have sworn she rolled her eyes before kneeling down and trying to calm the woman.

"It's not that bad," she said soothingly while searching around for something to stop the blood. Finding nothing, she ripped a strip off her own torn blouse and made a makeshift bandage. "All better." Then she peered up at Colt.

"Looks like you need a nurse, too." She nodded toward his stomach.

"Dammit." Colt noticed his blood-soaked tee shirt for the first time.

"Let me take a look." He didn't resist when she lifted his shirt, but he watched her face as she ran her eyes over the large slice on his stomach. He wanted to think it was his six-pack abs that made her eyes burn brighter, but he had a feeling it was the copious amount of blood seeping out of the wound. When she ran her finger over the torn flesh, he pressed his lips together— not from pain, but from the gentleness of the touch.

"You've got a couple of ripped stitches." She gazed up at him with humor in her eyes again. "You pick a fight with a barbed wire fence or something?"

"I'll live." He pulled his shirt back down.

"Here's a first-aid kit," one of the men said, pointing to a shelf.

"Great." Josephine walked over and rifled through the

dusty box. "Let me throw a bandage on so you don't bleed to death on us."

The others nodded in agreement. "Yes, we *need* you."

Colt grudgingly nodded. He didn't want to rip any more stitches if he could help it. A bandage would be better than nothing.

"Here's some antiseptic spray. Probably going to sting."

Josephine didn't give him a chance to respond before sticking the bottle near the wound and giving it a squirt. Colt closed one eye and suppressed the swear word on the tip of his tongue when the liquid hit the wound.

When he looked down to verify that she hadn't actually thrown acid onto the exposed skin, she was pulling the sides of the laceration together by crafting butterfly sutures from medical tape. Then she pulled out a roll of gauze and held it in place with one hand while unrolling it around him with the other.

Colt raised his eyes and stared at a bare light bulb, trying to concentrate on something other than the sensation of her arms wrapped around him. He hated to admit it, but this was the closest he'd been to a woman for quite some time—and the electric current he had been trying to convince himself didn't exist when in the presence of *this* one, now jolted through every nerve.

She finished with a piece of tape to secure the ends and then stepped back to examine her work. "There." She met his gaze with a gleam of satisfaction in her eyes. "That should keep it from getting any worse, anyway."

"Thanks, Doc." He pulled his shirt down. "Now, get the others ready to move."

Chapter 4

Colt positioned his gun and began to survey the floor. Behind a wall that was partially studded out, he found the ladder that led to the rooftop. "This way, everybody. We need to go up."

There were some cries of dismay as the tired group saw that they would have to scale a metal ladder. "I'm injured. I can't climb that," the woman whined.

"Sorry to hear that." Colt didn't bother to convey any empathy. "Because that's the only way out."

At the sound of gunshots, the woman pushed her way to the front of the line. "I can do it. I'll go first."

"Hold on." Colt turned to Josephine. "Cover me. Use the pistol. It's got a full magazine."

She nodded and pulled the handgun from her waistband as she took a position behind a pile of wood and concentrated on the stairwell about fifteen feet away from her.

Colt turned toward the ladder and began climbing. When he reached the hatch, he ran his hand around it to check for booby traps then readied his gun as he lifted the trap door. He was a sitting duck if anyone was up there, but when he popped his head over the top, he saw nothing but the ventilation system and air conditioning units.

Giving a quick wave to the helicopter hovering over his head, he flashed them six fingers so they knew he had six civilians to evacuate. The man sitting with his legs hanging precariously out of the chopper nodded and gave him a thumb's up. Colt could have sworn that man was Weston Armstrong, who had just been on the op with him in New Mexico, but he didn't have time to do a double take.

Half climbing and half sliding back down the ladder, Colt hurried the group toward its base. "Get in line. Climb as fast as you can." He sent one of the men and the strongest-looking woman first so they could help the others up.

"They're one floor below us." Josephine spoke just above a whisper. "I heard at least two different guns."

Colt nodded and glanced over his shoulder to assess the progress the others were making. Two of them were still standing at the bottom of the ladder—and one of them was the older man. Colt swiped away the sweat rolling down his temple but kept his eye trained on the door, his rifle at the ready.

"I don't think I can do it," the man said when it was his turn to climb. Colt turned his attention to Josephine, who was on her knees behind the pile of wood with a two-handed grip on the Glock, the barrel aimed at the door. With her face set in iron determination, she seemed to sense his dilemma but never removed her eyes from the stairwell. "I'm fine. Take care of him."

Colt didn't have time to hesitate or decide whom to save. He helped the man up the first two rungs and then placed the senior citizen's backside on his shoulder and climbed until the group above was able to pull him up and clear.

Just as the weight was removed from his shoulder, Colt heard gunshots, and at the same instant, felt a slight ping in his ankle. He let go of the ladder and dropped the eight feet to the floor, whirling around before he had even touched the ground, and spattering the entry with gunfire.

When the shooting stopped, two bodies lay sprawled in a heap by the doorway. Josephine had apparently hit the first one as he'd burst through, but not before he'd gotten off one round in the direction of the first target he'd seen, which was the ladder and a pair of legs. Colt was glad the man was a poor shot. There was no blood, and the pain was already forgotten.

"Up! Up! Up!" Colt motioned for Josephine, who shimmied up so fast she was to the top by the time he'd even gotten to the second rung. He didn't know if the urgency was necessary. The sound of gunfire had stopped. But he had no way of determining if there were still shooters in the building until the police moved in to search it.

On the rooftop, the helicopter was preparing to take off with the first three civilians. Colt walked over to the corner of the roof where the remaining ones were huddled, and saw Josephine leaning down to fan one of the women with a piece of cardboard.

"Everybody okay?"

The woman, who appeared pale and shaken, nodded. "Yes, thanks to you."

"Good." Colt turned to Josephine. "You're on the next chopper out."

Instead of thanking him, she straightened and cocked her head. "Really? Is that an order?"

From the defiant tone of her voice, and the way she stood staring at him with her hands on her hips, Colt got the impression she'd taken offense to the way he'd told her she was being evacuated.

He allowed his gaze to slide from her tangled hair to her dirty, tattered shirt, then lower to his pistol sticking out of the waistband of her skirt, which was shredded and covered in grime. Her knees were scraped and bloody from kneeling on the plywood floor, and, strangely enough, the hue matched the color of her toenails almost perfectly. He feasted his eyes on the image of perfection for a moment because he knew there was very little chance he would ever see her again. She would go home to her husband and live happily ever after.

"Yes, ma'am." He nodded. "That's an order."

Colt turned abruptly so he could keep his eye on the hatch, as well as monitor what was happening below, when he felt a sharp twinge of pain in his ankle. He limped over to the wall that lined the rooftop and sat down.

"You okay?" Trin, one of Phantom Force's best marksmen had roped in from the helicopter, and was standing watch while helping provide coordinates to the pilots.

"Think so." Colt started unlacing his boot. "Just got something jabbing me here."

The moment Colt loosened the lace, blood started gushing over the top of his boot onto the rooftop, and everything started moving in slow motion. He lifted his head and watched Josephine move toward him, sliding her belt from her waist with one hand as she walked.

He closed his eyes—he thought it was only for a moment—but already, she was kneeling beside him, her knees in his blood as she wrapped her belt around his ankle and pulled it tight. "Is that too tight? Can you hear me?"

She framed his face with her hands and leaned in close. "Fury One. Can you. Hear me?" Colt couldn't tell if the words were said with alarm, anguish, or anger. All he could think was: *She doesn't even know my name.*

For a brief moment, Colt wished he had a business card he could hand her with his contact information, but in his line of work, there was no such thing. His eyes fluttered open, and he was startled by what he saw. For the first time all day, he saw fear in her eyes, heard panic in her voice.

"Hey," she yelled, apparently to Trin. "How far out is the chopper?"

Colt never heard Trin's reply. Perhaps the man didn't know.

"Hold on, Fury One." He felt her shake him. Hard. "That's an order, dammit."

Colt supposed she was trying to be funny. He wanted to study her face to see if she was smiling, but his eyes were focused straight overhead at the dark cloud that appeared to be descending upon them. *Did she see it, too?*

He heard her speak again—or maybe it was the chopper. Either way, it sounded like it was coming to him through a thin tube, or maybe from a thousand miles away. He tried to focus his eyes, to find her, but he couldn't. He was floating one moment, and lying on a hard, unforgiving rooftop the next. It was completely dark, and then eye-blinding light. *This is wonky* he thought to himself, and then wondered if there was such a word as wonky and if he had ever used it before in a sentence.

Those thoughts disappeared as a wave of nausea swept over him, causing his hands to curl into fists as he fought getting sick. In desperation, his eyes searched for hers again—and this time, he found them. They were hard to miss, so close and anxious-looking that it made his heart feel strange.

He smiled—or thought he did—but her expression did not change. She was talking, yelling maybe, the way her lips were moving, but now there was no sound. Silence, absolute and complete, surrounded him. He felt the wind from the chopper blades, and the sandblast from the dirt and debris on the rooftop, but he could not hear it.

Wait. Stop. He tried to get the attention of the Phantom Force crew. *She's on the next chopper out—not me.*

No one paid attention. Maybe they were watching the same swirling veil of darkness that he was. He wanted to point to it so everyone could get away, but before he could lift his hand, the cloud hit him hard, and everything went black.

Chapter 5

Sunday

"I think he's waking up."

Colt recognized the voice, but couldn't quite place to whom it belonged. Soft and feminine, it expressed deep concern, inspiring him to fight his way out of the darkness.

"Nick. Are you awake?"

Colt smiled. Now he knew it was Caitlin. Blake's wife. She was one of the few people who called him by his given name of Nick—but that was usually when she was upset or angry. He wondered what he'd done to piss her off. Maybe got drunk at the house and kept her husband up all night. *Oh, well, she'll get over it. She always does.*

Finally getting his eyelids to comply, Colt blinked and stared at the fluorescent light overhead. No, he wasn't at Hawthorne, Caitlin and Blake's home that they used as the headquarters for Phantom Force Tactical. He turned his head slightly and saw Caitlin leaning over him with an anxious look on her face.

"Yo, bro. Nap time is over."

The next moment, Blake was standing where Caitlin had been.

Colt shifted his attention to the bag of fluids hanging from a hook on the side of the bed, a conspicuous clue that told him he was in a hospital. Now, all he had to do was figure out why. "Fill me in," is all he said.

"You saved my life in New Mexico. Remember?" Caitlin had moved to the other side of the bed. "I wanted to have a party to celebrate, but you had to go to DC for something first."

That was all he needed. Everything started to come rushing back. Colt tried to sit up, but Blake apparently anticipated his reaction and held him down by the shoulder.

"What day is it?" Colt tried to blink away the haze.

"Sunday. A day of rest—and you need it."

"What I *need* is for you to get me out of here. Give me my phone. I need to call the President."

"He's been briefed."

"Then *I* need a briefing. What in the hell is going on? Was that attack related to—?" He stopped when he remembered that Caitlin was still in the room.

"Okay. I can take a hint." Caitlin, a former newspaper reporter, was well aware of the classified work Colt did with her husband through Phantom Force. "But don't you even *think* about leaving here before the doctor says it's okay to go." She shook her finger in his face for emphasis and then kissed him on the cheek. "Thanks for saving my life, Nick. I can never repay you for that."

His eyes slid down to her stomach and then back up as his memory continued to return.

"And you checked out okay?"

Caitlin smiled, and her face glowed as she put her hand

where his eyes had been. "Thanks to Uncle Nick, yes. Baby Madison and I are both doing great."

Colt smiled at the thought of his best friend being a father again, and his eyes drifted to the joyful expression on Blake's face. Colt wasn't a blood relative, but he doubted there were any family bonds closer than what he shared with this couple.

As soon as Caitlin turned to leave, Colt locked eyes with Blake, but he waited until he heard the door click shut to speak. "What's the status of the investigation? Anything new?"

"First things first. How do you feel?"

"Are you effing kidding me? I feel fine. I'd feel even better if I knew what the fu—" He stopped himself, put his head back on the pillow and closed his eyes. "Okay. You win. I don't even know why I'm here."

"Let's start at the beginning. You remember the operation in New Mexico, right? Killing Carlos?"

Colt stared at the ceiling as the images of that night circled through his mind. Caitlin had been kidnapped, and he and Blake had tracked down her abductor—the drug kingpin, Carlos Valdez—in New Mexico. He nodded. "Yes. And then I was sent to DC."

"Right. The President wanted you to lead a task force."

Colt closed his eyes and concentrated on the last time he had talked to his friend Patrick Calloway, who was now commander-in-chief. He'd saved the President's life almost a decade earlier when Colt was a newly retired Navy SEAL working for a private security firm abroad.

Back then, Calloway was just a senator from Colt's home state of Texas. Colt had been in the right place at the right time to rescue him during a hostage crisis. Their friendship had continued through the years and even strengthened since Calloway had been elected to the highest office in the country.

Colt nodded as he recalled the conversation. "Because he's received intelligence that DC is the target for something big. A dirty bomb or something."

Blake nodded. "Right. Do you remember going to meet a contact outside the city?"

Hazy images began to form of the dilapidated building he'd entered, and then a pair of alluring green eyes came into focus. Colt's gazed darted up to Blake. "That woman. Josephine. Did she make it out okay?"

"I don't know anything about any particular woman, but everyone with you got out."

"Are you sure?" Colt lifted his head off the pillow.

Blake studied his face before replying. "Yes. I'm sure."

"Apparently, I didn't make out so well." Colt laid his head back down and exhaled with exasperation.

"It's nothing major, really," Blake said, "except you had a good chance of bleeding out on that rooftop."

Colt tried to remember the events that had unfolded, but the images that appeared in his mind's eye were hazy and muddled at best.

"The doctor thinks a bullet ricocheted off something and then pinged you pretty hard. Lost most of its steam by the time it made it through your boot, but it was enough to penetrate the skin and nick an artery."

Colt stared at the ceiling as Blake talked, and concentrated on picturing what had happened. He vaguely remembered the shots fired when he was standing on the metal ladder, and the twinge of pain he'd basically ignored.

"Your tight lacing evidently kept enough pressure on the wound to hold back the bleeding, but when you loosened your boot. *Boom.*"

Colt blinked because all he could see or remember now were brilliant green eyes. He turned his head toward Blake. "The tourniquet...the belt. It was hers. Did you see her?"

"No-o-o. By the time I got word, you were here alone, playing sleeping beauty in a bed."

"She must have left after I did," Colt said to himself.

"Yeah. Sure. Whatever you say." Colt shook his head. "Anyway, the fact that you'd gotten sliced a few days before in New Mexico didn't help your red blood count, so if not for the tourniquet and direct pressure on your ankle, you'd undoubtedly be six feet under right now."

"Okay, well then thanks to Josephine, I'm alive and well. When can I leave?"

Blake cocked his head. "I'm not sure now. It sounds like you're hallucinating about some kind of guardian angel."

"I'm not hallucinating. Ask Trin. She's the one who put a belt around my ankle."

"If you say so, boss. Trin never mentioned any hot chick to me."

"That's because you're an old married man who wouldn't be interested. Now quit trying to change the subject and tell me when I can get out of here."

"Okay. Calm down." Blake took a deep breath of exasperation. "Last I heard, they'd given you some fluids and a couple pints of the red stuff. I'm sure after a few days of rest, you'll be good as new."

"Ha. Ha. That's a good one." Colt threw the blankets off and started moving his feet to the side of the bed. "A couple of days, my ass."

He felt a strong hand on his shoulder.

"You heard my wife, right? Pretty sure that was a direct order."

Colt groaned. "Don't do this to me, bro. Something is brewing. Something big."

Blake pulled a chair close to the bed and sat down. "You're right. The team found some new intelligence at Carlos's house—what was left of it."

"And?"

"There is definitely reason to believe that the drug cartel has teamed up with Islamic extremists—or at least they're using their tactics."

"What do you mean?"

Blake rested his arms on his legs, and spoke barely above a whisper. "Wes and some guys went through the rubble and found hundreds of fake security guard uniforms."

"Mexican?"

"Yeah. But it shows they're attempting to carry out false flag attacks and other crimes in the name of Mexican authorities."

"Tactics that have been used by radical, militant groups in Iraq and Afghanistan for a long time." Colt closed his eyes and squeezed his temples. "But what about a specific incident here? Anything new on that?"

"They're still going through communications and files. Nothing yet to corroborate what the authorities heard from one of the drug runners about a specific raid."

"So there may not be an attack planned?"

Blake shrugged. "The President wants to proceed as if there is. He doesn't want us to let our guards down."

Colt stared straight ahead. "I guess not. Especially if we're talking smuggling a dirty bomb with radioactive materials across the border."

Blake nodded. "Yeah."

"What about the contact I was supposed to meet. Did he show?"

"No one with that name did. Might have been an alias."

"And no Josephine," Colt murmured to himself.

"You sure you didn't hit your head and dream this chick up?"

"I'm not sure of anything right now except that I want out of here." Colt glared at Blake.

Blake stood and stretched. "That a fact?" The look on his face showed he didn't really care what Colt wanted.

"When can I talk to the President?"

Blake consulted his watch. "How about fourteen hundred hours? Gives you some time to clear your head, and maybe get a nice sponge bath." The way Blake smiled deviously should have been a warning to Colt, but with those green eyes still in his mind—the idea seemed enticing.

"Now that would be—" Colt stopped mid-sentence when a nurse walked in. His mouth clamped shut when he saw her plump, bulldog physique and threatening scowl. "Get me out of here, brother," he said, his eyes locked on the nurse. "And that's an order."

When he heard no reply, his eyes darted back to where Blake had been standing. His *friend* was already at the door, waving goodbye, his whole body shaking with the laughter he was trying to suppress.

Chapter 6

Monday

Caitlin Madison woke up with a startled jerk, fighting through the cobwebs of nightmare-filled sleep. She relaxed when she saw where she was—her own bedroom. In her own bed. The traumatic events of being kidnapped by the drug kingpin Carlos Valdez were behind her. He was dead. And she was safe.

With a smile on her face, she put her hand on her stomach, remembering she had double the reason to be happy.

She heard a tap on the door. "Breakfast in bed for my lady?"

Then the door sprang open, and Blake strode through it carrying a tray with both hands.

"Am I dreaming?"

"Thought you might wake up hungry." He sat the tray of food down beside the bed. "Eating for two, you know."

Caitlin rubbed her eyes. "What time is it? How long have I been asleep?"

"It's nine o'clock on Monday. We visited Colt in the afternoon and then you went to bed around eight o'clock."

"Wow. Who's feeding the animals and cleaning the stalls?"

"I had Paula come over. She loves hanging out with the horses."

"I'll go help her."

Blake put his hand on her arm to stop her before she could get her feet on the floor. "*After* breakfast."

Caitlin scanned the food and grinned. Two fried eggs stared up at her, and a piece of bacon positioned like a mouth, smiled from the plate. "I can hardly believe you did this."

"I remember a time when I made eggs, and you said they were the best you'd ever eaten."

"That's right, I did." Caitlin remembered the meal more than a year earlier when they were on the run together—not yet husband and wife. "I have a feeling this is going to be even better than thrown-together scrambled eggs."

"Well, I didn't have much to work with back then."

She laughed as she picked up the fork. "How's Colt? Is he out of the hospital?"

"You know Colt."

"I'll take that as a *yes*," she said, sampling a piece of toast. "How is he, though? I worry about him. He pushes himself too hard."

"He's fine." Blake hesitated. "He's…Colt."

Cait nodded. Colt was definitely one of a kind. Even though he'd officially retired from serving his country as a Navy SEAL and then as a private security contractor, he was still sought after by intelligence agencies for his experience and tactical abilities. Special operations soldiers frequently requested his expertise as well, and her husband often marveled that it was a miracle Colt had escaped death so many times, on so many dangerous missions.

But Caitlin knew another side of him.

She'd watched him hold young children in those big strong arms as if it were second nature to him, and console grieving widows with gentle words of comfort and support. His smile, when he showed it, was captivating—but those occasions were rare these days. Only his closest friends knew he'd lost the love of his life a few years earlier, and he hadn't been the same man since.

"I wish he would at least take it easy here for a while." Caitlin talked while eating. "I could take care of him. Why don't you make him stay over for a few days?"

When Blake remained quiet, she stopped what she was doing and studied him. "You two working on something?"

"Yes. And, ah, now that you mention it, I might have to leave for a little bit, too."

Caitlin dropped her gaze to what was left of her bacon and eggs. "Hence the breakfast in bed."

Blake sat down on the side of the bed with a remorseful look on his face. "Sorry. I wanted to soften the blow. I wouldn't leave if it weren't important."

"Are we talking hours?" She gazed into his steady blue eyes. "Or days?"

"I'm not sure about that yet."

"Okay." She wrapped her hands around his neck and gave him a kiss. "I know you wouldn't go unless it was important."

"It is. Sorry I can't say more."

Caitlin forced a smile to her face. When she'd met Blake, she had been a journalist, and he a homicide detective. Now, she worked from the house as a freelance writer, and he was the co-owner of Phantom Force Tactical Security with Colt.

Even though the company was new, it already had hundreds of contracts with Fortune 500 companies and government agencies both domestically and abroad.

Both men brought years of experience to the business, so they were well connected within the intelligence community and possessed high-level security clearances. Much of what they did was beyond top secret. Caitlin never asked about things she knew they couldn't—and wouldn't—tell her.

"I guess that will give me time to get some work done in the barn," she said, trying to find something positive to say.

"As long as you don't work too hard."

She scrutinized her husband's concerned expression. "Don't tell me you're going to treat me like I'm going to break for the next six months."

"I'm going to worry about you every minute if that is what you're asking."

Caitlin was just about to respond to that when a face appeared in the doorway.

"Hey, pumpkin." Cait patted the bed for Blake's four-year-old daughter, Whitney. "Hop up here."

Before she knew it, *two* youngsters ran into the room and jumped onto the bed.

"Whoa. Be careful." Caitlin handed the tray to Blake before the dishes tumbled to the floor.

"You guys be careful," Blake warned. "Caitlin is…"

"Caitlin is what, Dad?" Blake's eight-year-old son, Drew, asked.

Blake's jaw tightened and his eyes reflected a rare apprehension, indicating he hadn't planned to have this conversation right now.

"I think your dad has something to tell you." Cait shot Blake a look that said *I can't wait to see how you handle this one.*

Both sets of eyes jerked toward their father.

"What is it?" Drew sounded indifferent, as if he didn't think the news would be anything of great importance.

"What is it?" Whitney echoed with a tilt of her head.

"Well…you see…" Blake stopped, his lips compressed as if not sure how to proceed.

"I've never seen you at a loss for words before." Caitlin began to laugh.

"Why don't *you* tell them, then?"

"Tell us what?" Whitney began jumping on the bed like a frog.

"Yes, tell us *what?*" Even Drew appeared curious now.

Caitlin stopped laughing and took a deep breath. "Okay, what your dad is trying to say is that by this time next year, you are going to have a baby brother or sister."

Both kids' eyes widened as they regarded Cait suspiciously.

"How?" Drew appeared completely confused.

Now it was Cait's turn to be speechless. "Ask your father."

Both sets of eyes jerked up to their dad. "It doesn't really matter how." He clapped his hands together. "It only matters that we take care of Miss Cait."

"Is that why the men took you away?" Whitney had witnessed Cait being kidnapped by members of the drug cartel. "To get a baby?"

"No," Blake corrected her. "She already had the baby."

"Where is it?"

"Okay, enough questions." Blake hustled his children toward the door. "Let's let Cait get dressed. I'll meet you downstairs."

"When will it come out? Can I hold it? What's its name?" Whitney was still asking questions when the bedroom door closed behind her.

"Okay, that went well," Blake said.

"You should have planned it out a little better. You should have known they would have questions."

"I'm kind of new at this. It's been a while."

"I'm even newer. My first time. Remember?"

He sat down on the side of the bed and picked up her hand. "We'll figure it out. How are you feeling anyway?"

"Believe it or not, I feel terrific."

"No morning sickness?"

"Not at the moment."

"Good." He kissed her, but lingered. "Remember, don't work too hard in the barn."

"I won't." She gave him a reassuring squeeze. "When are you leaving?"

"I have a quick meeting in DC at noon. I'll know more after that."

"Okay. Be careful."

"I will." He stood and headed for the door but stopped with his hand on the doorknob.

"Hey, baby." He turned his head back to her, a big smile on his face. Then they both said the same words at the same time. "Don't miss me too much."

Chapter 7

Wednesday

Colt left the hospital late Monday and studied intelligence reports most of that night. He'd talked to the President briefly, but the conversation had ended up being more about Colt's health than the threats at hand. After a day of trying to take it easy, he was back on his feet, having agreed to help a friend evaluate security measures at a large concert and sporting event venue in DC.

"What are you looking at?"

Colt moved closer to the monitors he was watching, his hand automatically moving to his injured stomach as a jolt of pain erupted there. "Did you see that?"

"No. What?"

"I just saw movement. Like someone was there and sat down just out of sight of the camera."

"You must have been seeing things. The cameras give us coverage of every seat."

Colt picked up the seating chart and examined the screen. "Above the Loge Level." He pointed again. "Section 422."

The man sitting at the controls leaned over and squinted at the monitor as if he were trying to see something that wasn't there. He ran his finger across the screen, his lips moving as he counted the seats. "You're right. There *is* another row above this one."

Colt shook his head and left the control room, walking as swiftly as he could toward the seating area. His ankle barely hurt anymore, just felt like a bruise, but the slice in his abdomen was still tender—and at times, even painful.

When he entered the upper balcony section through a side corridor, he stopped a moment to get his bearings then turned all the way around and looked up. Sure enough, there was a figure up there, sitting in one of the uppermost seats.

Wanting to come in from behind, Colt went back through the hallway and took the inside stairs to the top. This time when he made his entrance, the figure was in front of him. The blond ponytail sticking out from the back of a ball cap indicated it was a woman. He attempted to move quietly behind her, but when he was a few feet away, she turned her head as if she possessed a sixth sense. "Hey," was all she said.

Colt recognized the voice before he even saw her face. But when his gaze locked on a pair of familiar green eyes, it took his breath away. He was staring at the woman he'd convinced himself had been a figment of an overactive imagination, enhanced by blood loss and exhaustion.

Josephine appeared to recognize him at the exact same time because her eyes swept over him, as if not believing he was standing in front of her. "Wow. You bionic or something?"

"What are you doing here?"

She angled her head questioningly and held up the credentials she wore around her neck. "I'm a journalist. Remember?"

"But what are you doing *here*." He pointed to the seat she

was sitting in.

Colt thought he saw a slight twitch in the muscle of her cheek, but he couldn't be sure.

"What do you mean?" She blinked her eyes innocently.

"Here. This venue. This seat."

"Why are you being so interrogative?" She sat back and crossed her arms defiantly.

"Why are you being so evasive?"

She shot him a laughing smile as if that would make him forget his line of questioning, and truthfully, it almost did.

"Since when is a journalist not allowed to pick a seat?"

"Since a friend of mine asked me to do a walk-through and give him an assessment of the security measures here."

Her hands moved slightly in an effort to cover up the tablet she held in her lap, and her face lost all its playfulness. "I hope you're not saying you suspect *me* of something."

He leaned close, ignoring the pain the action caused. "I'll put it this way, then. When someone is diagramming the layout of security cameras and sitting in one of the few seats they don't cover, I get a little suspicious."

Her mouth dropped open and then snapped shut.

"And when that person mysteriously shows up a few minutes before a terrorist attack at a location I was sent to—and then just as mysteriously disappears…" He straightened back up, stiffly, making an effort not to wince, and placed his hands on his hips. "Let's just say I'm not a big believer in coincidences."

"By the way,"—he pointed down and to her right after catching a glimpse of the diagram she held on her lap—"you missed that camera over there."

"I saved your damn life, you know." She sat, glaring straight ahead now as if trying to figure out her next move.

"Thank you. Now, who are you?"

"I told you." She brought her gaze back to him. "Don't you remember? Josephine."

"Josephine, who?"

"Summers. But everybody calls me Joey."

Colt nodded and pursed his lips. "Oka-a-y, Joey—I'm sure it's just another coincidence that the contact who lured me into that building in the first place was a person named *Joey*. So, did you *save* my life or try to *take* it?"

"I didn't *lure* you. I wanted to talk to you."

"There was ample time for talking if I remember correctly."

She frowned out of the side of her mouth. "Once I realized who you were, there just didn't seem like a suitable time. And then you…" Her eyes lowered to his ankle and lifted again. "You know, you left kind of suddenly."

"Okay, so tell me now." Colt crossed his arms and shot her a threatening look. "What's going on?"

"I can't."

He raised his eyebrow and glared. He didn't say anything, but he was pretty sure the look he discharged in her direction said plenty.

"Not here."

"Why not?"

"Just because." She stood and shook her head. "If someone sees me…I can't."

He thought he saw real fear in her eyes—or at least anxiety—but she was so mysterious and elusive, he couldn't be sure.

Colt pulled out his phone and pushed a button, but never removed his eyes from her. While the call was connecting, he tilted the phone away from his mouth to talk. "Still carrying a suitcase, I see." His eyes motioned to the large canvas purse that sat on the seat beside her, but he didn't have time to see her reaction.

His call went through, so he put the phone back to his mouth. "Hey, do you have a trailer in the back I can use for a meeting? Great. Unlocked? Perfect. Talk later."

He turned back to her. "Follow me, princess."

Chapter 8

"Where are we going?"

"Somewhere secure. Where the big, bad wolf won't get you." He took her by the arm, firmly but gently, and escorted her to the same corridor from which he had entered.

"By the way, I never got your name." She smiled at him again with a look that was playful and teasing.

Colt walked fast, his eyes focused on the hallway straight ahead. "That's because I never gave it to you."

She moved faster. "So...what am I supposed to call you?"

He kept walking. "I don't care."

She ran a few steps to catch up. "Okay, I-don't-care, where are we going?"

"This way." He directed her down another hallway that was too narrow to walk side by side, so he let her go first. He tried not to stare at her rear end—which was no easy feat—and focused his attention on her feet.

She wore a pair of jeans and, what appeared to be, men's work boots. They weren't the fashionable, wannabe type boots like some women wore to be trendy. They were real boots, scuffed and splashed with mud. The contrast in her attire from the last time he'd seen her was stark, but her ap-

pearance now in faded jeans and a bulky sweatshirt seemed to
more naturally fit her character.

When she came to the end of the hallway, she stopped, and
Colt almost ran into her.

"Which way?" She turned around to face him, waiting for
an answer while he stared down at the top of her ball cap that
read, *God Bless America*. She seemed shorter than he remembered, but then again, she'd been wearing three-inch heels
when they'd first met. Sidestepping her, he pushed on a door
leading outside and held it open. She looked up and smiled.
"Thanks."

It was just a simple word and a simple look, but the combination made Colt's heart slam into his chest. He scolded
himself for reacting this way. He had a job to do. Just because
he was standing beside the green-eyed, enhanced version of
the woman of his dreams, didn't mean he could slack off.

He scanned the row of trailers, most of which were either
used as command centers for different aspects of security for
the stadium or to provide eating and sleeping quarters for the
core team currently working on an upgrade. "Number four is
available."

She pointed helpfully. "There it is."

Walking ahead of her, he opened the door and offered his
hand to help her up the steps, which she didn't accept. Once
inside, he pulled out one of the chairs pushed up against a
small table. "Have a seat, *Joey*."

She threw her purse on a bench that ran along the wall and
took a seat while he went to the fridge.

"Something to drink?" he asked, purely out of politeness,

not really expecting to find anything.

"An ice-cold Bud bottle would be great."

A wide grin spread across his face. "Ask, and you shall receive." He sat two bottles on the table. "So you're psychic, too."

She twisted off the cap. "I wish." She held up the bottle and said, "Cheers," before taking a swallow.

All of a sudden, Colt felt way too comfortable with this woman. The quarters they were in were close; their arms were practically touching. Yet she seemed as relaxed and casual as if they were long-time drinking buddies.

"So," he began, not sure where to start. "What are you doing here?"

Before she could get any words out, he stopped her. "And don't tell me you're a journalist. The truth."

"But I *am* a journalist." Even though they were alone, she said the words quietly as if someone were listening.

"So, why did you set up the meeting with me?"

She took a deep breath and stared at her beer. "It had to do with a story I've been working on for almost a year."

"About what?" He twisted the cap on his bottle.

"A drug cartel."

Colt tilted his head. "I'm listening."

"Well, something's going on. Something big."

"Why do you think that?"

"I don't *think* it." She looked at him as if insulted. "I *know* it."

"Wait. Back up." He rested his arms on the table. "So you're telling me you sat down, face-to-face, with someone from a drug cartel? Is that how you know something's going down?"

She rolled her eyes as if exasperated. "No. Not exactly."

"What then?"

"Let's just say I know someone who knows someone who thinks they're preparing to launder a great deal of money."

"What's the money for?"

She bit her lip and concentrated on the label of her beer as if it held something of interest.

"What's the money for?" He asked the question a little louder in case she hadn't heard. "Who's paying the cartel, and for what?"

"I'm not sure."

"Are you trying to be evasive again?"

"No. I mean I'm really not sure, and I don't want to raise alarm bells if I'm not right."

"But let me guess. You have a theory."

"Yes. I have a theory."

"Which is?"

"Okay. I did some digging, connected the dots—which are pretty unclear—and came up with a few possibilities."

"Which *are?*" He put his beer down on the table, hard, to let her know his patience was running thin.

"I'm sorry, but it sounds pretty crazy."

"Turns out, I'm in the crazy business," he said. "Go ahead. Nothing much surprises me."

He brought the bottle of beer to his lips to take a swallow but never removed his eyes from her.

"Okay. Just based on things I'm hearing and seeing and reading about, I think a Mexican drug cartel is working with members of an Islamic terrorist group."

Colt almost spit the beer he had in his mouth across the table, but then tried to keep from showing any emotion—despite the fact that his mind was racing. Was it just a coincidence that her information lined up with everything they'd been hearing through official intelligence channels?

"And?"

"I think the cartel is going to get paid to do something, and they're looking for a way to hide the cash."

"They're going to do something for the terrorist group? And that's who's going to pay them?" He knew he sounded skeptical, but it all seemed just a little too convenient. *What is she hiding?*

She nodded.

"What do you think this *thing* is?"

"I'm not sure about that."

"But I'm guessing you have a theory about that, too."

"Okay, this is where it gets to be a very *imprecise* theory."

"I'm listening."

"I've seen the stories about Islamic terrorist groups coming across the border, and I've read the reports that say some of them are in possession of radioactive material..."

Colt blinked in surprise, but otherwise tried to keep his face impassive. Yes, the information was out there for the public to find, but most Americans probably weren't aware of it. "And?"

"I believe they want us to think they're bringing it across the border.

"But they're not? There is no threat?"

"That's not what I said." She leaned forward and became businesslike and serious. "Why would they expend the time and energy to come across the border when they can acquire everything for a dirty bomb right here?"

"I don't follow." Colt knew where she was going but wanted to hear it from her.

"Cobalt-60, for instance. Hospitals. Food processing plants. There are lots of industries that use it."

Colt nodded indifferently, but his mind was racing. She was right. Cobalt-60 was widely used at hospitals for cancer patient radiation therapy, sterilization of medical disposables, and for food irradiation everywhere. He wasn't sure which bothered him more—the fact that what she was saying made sense, or the fact that she knew so much about it.

She must have read the look on his face as being confusion, because she kept going. "The U.S. has forty food sterilization centers and thousands of hospitals. It isn't logical to take the chance of getting the material across the border and then transporting it halfway across the United States when they can get their hands on it locally."

"So you think they're trying to throw the authorities off track by leaving some pretty big clues at the border." He stroked his chin as he mulled it over, but he already knew she was right. The materials to make a dirty bomb were so easily accessible, no police force could hope to contain or limit the threat. The possibility of such an attack had been unthinkable a generation ago, but now many of those in the intelligence field considered it to be inevitable.

Colt put his fingers to the bridge of his nose and squeezed

as he recalled a report he had read a few weeks earlier. Nearly four out of five hospitals across the country failed to put safeguards in place to secure radiological material that could be used in a dirty bomb, and the U.S. Nuclear Regulatory Commission estimated that approximately one radiological source is lost, abandoned, or stolen every day of the year.

Joey must have read the same report.

"Only three hundred or so of the fifteen hundred hospitals that possess high-risk radiological sources have set up security upgrades—and dozens of hospitals have serious security lapses."

Colt nodded, recalling that one of the facilities listed in the report had a device containing potentially lethal radioactive cesium stored in a room with a combination lock—but the combination was written on the door frame. And at another medical facility, a machine containing almost two thousand curies of cesium-13 was stored just down the hall from a loading dock near an unsecured window.

"So what do *you* think?" Joey studied him intently as if to get his attention.

Colt stared into her eyes and then jerked his gaze away. He had no trouble reading most people's thoughts or measuring their sincerity, but he couldn't rely on that technique with Joey. She had a way of pulling you in and resisting you all at the same time. And despite the easygoing smile she usually wore on her face, her eyes reflected a hint of seriousness and sadness all at the same time.

"I think you've spent a lot of time thinking about this. Which, frankly, seems a little strange."

She lifted her hands, palms up. "It's my job."

Colt's cynical, wary side kicked in again. "Really? It's your job to worry about national security?"

Joey sat her beer bottle down hard. "It's my job to worry about the safety of my friends and neighbors. If I find something that has to do with national security while researching a story, I'm going to share it with authorities. Not sit on it."

Colt massaged his temples at her tone. He'd come here to do a quick sweep to check out security measures as a favor to his friend, Todd. This day was not turning out as he had planned, and he had a pounding headache to prove it. He probably should have taken the day off and laid low like the doctor had instructed him to do, but it was too late to worry about that now. The silver lining was that the mysterious Josephine had corroborated some of the information he'd already had, and provided new insight to help substantiate the leads he had been following.

Everything she'd conveyed to him coincided with what had just happened on the border with Caitlin's kidnapping. The cartel leader Carlos Valdez had lured him and a large assembly of other counter-terrorism groups to the border. Once there, Colt and his men had discovered evidence that implied the kingpin was trying to smuggle radioactive materials into the United States.

Thinking back, the clues had been just a little too convenient and obvious. With eyes and resources looking to the south, who knew what could be going on right under their noses?

And Joey was right. It would be hard to transport the material without severe radiation damage and maybe even death to those involved. And alerting the authorities would make traveling with the device that much more difficult.

"If you feel so strongly about this, why didn't you go to the authorities?"

"I did."

He cocked his head and waited for the explanation.

"I got the response I expected: 'When a law is broken we'll investigate.'"

He sat back in his chair as the tension between them began to melt. "Their hands are tied to some degree."

"It does sound pretty far-fetched, but would be worth looking into."

"I'll see what I can do."

Joey nodded and then seemed to remember something. "Oh, by the way." She reached around to the small of her back and retrieved something from under her sweatshirt in one smooth move. "This is yours. Mine was in the purse that you wouldn't let me take out of the elevator."

Colt blinked at the sight of his gun, then slammed the palm of his hand against the table. "How did you sneak that past security?" He looked into her eyes again and knew the answer before he'd even finished the sentence. *That* smile on *that* face was a free pass anywhere.

She acted like it was nothing out of the ordinary. "They checked my bag, but not me."

"I want you to point out the security guard that let you in." His voice was loud and demanding.

"I don't think I remember what he looks like." She looked

away, obviously lying.

Colt leaned forward and punched the table with his finger as he spoke. "This is serious shit. We can't have security guards letting people into a venue just because they're drop-dead gorgeous."

She did not acknowledge his compliment. "I'm credentialed." She held up her pass again. "I'm sure he figured I'd already been through a background check—which I *have*."

Colt shook his head and stared at her with half-closed eyes, wondering how many other weapons she had hidden under that bulky sweatshirt. Then, after picking up the gun and tucking it under his own shirt, he put his arms casually on the table again. "One more little question."

"Okay. Shoot." The words were indifferent, but he noticed that her lips tightened and her eyes turned a darker shade of green.

"What reason does a reporter have to diagram the security cameras at a large concert venue?"

She fingered the label of her beer, shredding it with one nicely manicured nail. If he remembered correctly, it was the same color of polish as her toes. "I'm working on a story on security and I wanted to try writing it from a different angle."

"You're working on a story on security flaws at one of the largest public venues in the area?"

"No."

"What then?"

"I wasn't looking for flaws necessarily…" She paused a moment as if to think. "I just went into it trying to think like a terrorist would—to see what I could find. Not something to use directly in the story, just to use for my own background knowledge."

"I don't follow."

She shrugged indifferently. "I don't know what I don't know, so I wanted to dig down, figure out every little nugget of information I could."

Colt took his last slug of beer. "And?"

"By diagramming the cameras, I found that seat."

"So you found a seat not covered by security cameras. What good is that? What do you think a terrorist would do with that information?"

"I'm not sure I can think like a terrorist, but seems to me, it would be easy to put an explosive under a seat no one is watching—or maybe even locate a sniper there."

"Geezus." Colt sat back as images raced through his mind of the chaos a shooter could cause. Once security realized people were being shot and the direction it was coming from, they would be looking at the camera feeds for help in pinpointing the shooter. The seconds and minutes that would be lost would be crucial to saving lives.

The package scenario was equally as terrorizing because the person watching the security images wouldn't see the suspicious behavior. "You trained for this sort of thing?"

Colt thought he saw something flash in the back of Joey's eyes, but before she could respond, someone knocked on the door, and then a head appeared in the doorway. "Hey, buddy. You about done?" The man's gaze landed on Joey, and his eyes grew wide before he winked at Colt. "Oh, never mind. Sorry to interrupt."

From the look on his face, he may as well have said, "you still have your clothes on, you're obviously not done."

"We were just finishing up." Joey spoke at the same time as Colt said, "Give me another twenty minutes."

"Another twenty, huh." The young man's eyes twinkled with humor. "I'll give you thirty so you don't have to hurry. But try not to drink all my beer, okay?"

He didn't give Colt time to respond. The door slammed shut, but Todd could still be heard as he walked away. "Take your time, bro!"

Joey cocked her head. "Friend of yours?"

"Acquaintance."

"I see." She said the words in such a way as to suggest she did not see at all.

"Back to business." Colt tipped the chair onto its back legs and crossed his arms. "How did you find me? What made you set up that appointment in the first place?"

Joey scraped what little was left of the label from her empty bottle of beer. "I saw a blip on the news about a hostage rescue that Phantom Force did. I checked out the website, and thought you might be able to help me fill in the blanks—just enough so I could go back to the authorities with something tangible."

When Colt didn't do anything but nod thoughtfully, she continued. "So, I sent an email and someone named Blake replied, asking where and when to meet." She looked up at him. "We set it up, but he never gave me your name. Which, by the way, I still don't know."

He ignored the question about his name because his phone

was vibrating. After glancing at the screen, he scrolled through the text message and then put it back down.

"Bad news?" She had a way of frowning with her mouth and smiling with her eyes, which was confusing and enchanting all at the same time.

"Not especially. Just alerting me that at least three of the dead terrorists from that building came from Mexico. They're still trying to identify the other two."

"Open borders," she mumbled.

Colt looked up. "It's a mess, but President Calloway is trying to clean it up."

"But it's going to take time. The floodgates were open for years."

"Well, at least Homeland Security did a decent job of manipulating the press to cover up the incident outside DC so the word 'terrorism' wasn't used." Colt sighed. "Called it gang-related violence."

"Well…it *was* a gang, by definition. And it *was* violent."

"Should have known you would take the side of the press."

"I'm not part of the group." Her eyes narrowed. "I don't twist the truth and mold my stories into the version that fits the publisher's—or the government's—narrative."

"Whoa. Sorry." Colt held his hands up in feigned innocence. "Touchy subject, obviously."

"As a matter of fact, it is."

"Well, what do you think that whole deal was about?"

"I'm not sure." Her brows drew together, and he could have sworn he saw that twitch in her cheek again. "Maybe a dry run for a future hit? A training run of some sort?"

"They needed some training, that's for sure. It definitely wasn't a sophisticated group as far as technique goes in taking down a building."

"Well, they most likely thought their target was just civilians. They had no way of knowing *you* would be there."

"Which brings us back to you. I was only there because you set up the meeting."

She jerked her head up. "You don't think I set up the appointment there because I knew *that* was going to take place?"

"I don't know anything." He crossed his arms and placed them on the table. "You tell me."

"I chose that building because it's isolated—which I thought you would appreciate."

"Isolated? More like dilapidated. Ghetto. Crime scene central."

"Next time, I'll pick a barroom. How's that?"

"Speaking of *next time*, do you have a card or something so I can contact you?" Colt didn't want to let her get away without having some way to contact her again. Not for personal reasons…but in case he thought of any more questions.

"Do *you*?"

He frowned at her attempt to coerce information out of him. "You can contact Phantom Force just like you did before. They can get in touch with me."

She sighed and dug through her purse. "Here."

He skimmed the card to make sure it had a phone number. "This is a real number, right?"

"Of course. What do you think it is? A phone booth or something?"

Ignoring her, he stood and headed toward the door. "You know your way back to the parking lot?"

"I think I can find it." She picked up her purse and followed him. "You're going to look into my theory, right?"

He waited until they were both down the steps before answering. "I'm going to look into it, yes." He leaned down and stared straight into her eyes. "But if you think I'm going to give you updates on what I've found…no."

Colt expected to see a reaction to that, but her expression remained impassive.

"Okay. See you later." She walked away, gave a quick wave without turning around, and then she was gone again.

Chapter 9

Thursday

Forty-three-year-old Frank Clayton couldn't speak. He just nodded with the cell phone pinned to his ear. When the man on the other end of the line said, "Did you hear me?" He realized he needed to say something. "Yes, sir, I heard you...but if you could just give me a little more time—"

"You've been given all the time you're going to get." The words and the tone conveyed a serious threat. "Pay up by the first of the month, *señor*, or someone is going to die. Perhaps you...perhaps your wife."

Click.

Frank winced when the phone call disconnected.

"Honey. Why are you sitting here in the dark?"

Frank looked up at his wife of twenty-two years as she flicked on a lamp. "That's not good for your eyes. I hope you weren't trying to read."

"No." Frank tried to keep his voice from shaking. "I was just on the phone."

"With who? Charlie?"

"No." Frank got up and walked over to her. "No one important." He bent down and kissed her.

"What was that for?" She laughed.

"Does a happily married man need a reason to kiss his wife?"

"I guess not. What do you want for dinner?"

"Let's go out."

"Are you kidding me?" She gave him a serious look. "Can we afford to?"

Can we afford not to, is what he wanted to say. Instead, he just shrugged his shoulders. "We deserve it. I work long hours. You're working two jobs." He wrapped his arms around her.

"But I can throw something together. We don't have to—"

"No. Let's go out." He held her at arm's length. "We always eat in. We need to spend some quality time together."

"I don't understand what's gotten into you, but if you say so." She laughed. "It would be nice to get out of the kitchen for a night."

"And you deserve it."

"Give me a minute to put something on." She turned and practically ran from the room.

Frank dropped into his chair and raked a hand through his hair. *What am I going to do?*

He'd never been a very religious man, but right then, he felt like praying. His wife didn't know he'd lost next month's mortgage, plus money he hadn't even earned yet on some bad bets at the track. He'd put off the bookie for as long as he could, but the debt was due, and the threats were real. He needed money, and he needed it fast.

Frank had never admitted to himself that he had a gambling problem, but now it was staring him right in the face.

He had a beautiful wife and a marriage that was better than most. His job was endurable and even paid pretty well. Driving a truck that made deliveries to and from hospitals was not that bad of a gig. It was boring at times, but at least he didn't have a boss watching his every move like a lot of guys did. His hours were flexible as long as he made his deliveries and pickups on time.

That's why the gambling had started in the first place. He'd stopped by the racetrack one day at the invitation of an acquaintance he'd met at a bar. He'd made a few bets over his lunch hour—and had won. It felt wonderful to have some extra money in his pocket, so he'd gone back… again and again.

The winning streak had lasted for most of the month, and before he knew it, he was able to get ahead a little. He'd paid off some bills, and even surprised Annette with a few trinkets.

But then he'd started losing. Rather than just quit like his friends told him to, he'd kept thinking he could start winning again. Even Fernando, the acquaintance who had taken him to the track in the first place, insisted it was only a matter of time. "You can make it all back and more, *señor*," he had told Frank. "You just need to keep going until another lucky streak hits."

Anyway, giving up would seem like giving in. Frank hated being a loser—or a quitter. But before he knew it, the hundreds of dollars he'd lost had turned into thousands—and then, tens of thousands.

And now, it seemed, there was no way out.

Frank pulled open a drawer and dug around for the piece of paper he had stuffed in the back almost three months earlier.

It was the phone number for a man he'd never met, given to him by Fernando. He'd never thought he'd ever need it, yet he hadn't thrown it away. Now, it looked like it might be the answer to his prayers.

Fernando had assured him it was all on the up and up—and the way he'd flashed money around, buying drinks and betting on horses, Frank believed him.

Fernando was a janitor at a football stadium, but apparently lived like a king. He'd convinced Frank that he only kept his janitorial job so the IRS would see that he was working and leave him alone. The money he made doing side jobs for this unnamed man was all cash.

This one job, according to Fernando, would pay at least half a million dollars. All Frank had to do was pretend he'd been robbed during a delivery.

What in the world would someone want with hospital waste?

Frank didn't linger on the question. With a half-million dollars in his bank account, he could pay off his debts, and his wife could stop working. That was reason enough not to care what they did with it.

He picked up the phone and dialed the number.

Chapter 10

Saturday

Colt hadn't expected a call from the White House, so he assumed new intelligence must have come in to warrant a gathering of the commander-in-chief's advisors. It was a little before noon when he pulled through the gates.

"Mr. Colton." An aide greeted him at the security checkpoint. "Follow me, please."

Colt followed, but soon became confused. "Wait. Aren't we going to the Situation Room?"

"No, the President wishes to speak to you in the Oval Office."

"Okay," Colt said, instead of voicing what he was thinking, which was, *Oh shit*. Calloway often brought Colt into his innermost circle of confidences on security matters, so Colt had expected to be sitting in on a briefing with all the other agencies involved in fighting terrorism. But the President wanted a private meeting. This couldn't be good.

The aide hustled Colt down the hallway at a rapid pace, even for him. They passed the secretary's desk with barely a nod, and then Colt entered the iconic room he'd only visited a few times before. He found the President sitting on a sofa, not at his desk. "Colt. Come in. Good to see you."

The words were spoken with a sincere tone as Calloway stood and shook Colt's hand, but the creases on his brow showed the tremendous pressure he was under. "I'm sorry to call you in here. I know you're still recovering, but I—"

"That's not a problem," Colt interrupted. "I'm fine."

"Well, I'm not." Calloway ran a hand through his graying hair. "I'm out of options, Colt. I need your help."

"My pleasure, Mr. President. Just tell me what you need me to do."

"Have a seat." Calloway pointed to a chair and sat down again on the couch. He let his breath out slowly as if trying to decide how to continue, then leaned forward with his hands clasped, arms on his knees. "There's no one who's opinion on security I value or trust more than yours."

It was said as a statement, not a question, so Colt didn't say anything other than, "Thank you, Mr. President."

"The problem is that Homeland Security hasn't taken this threat seriously enough."

Colt wasn't sure how to react to that. He knew Homeland Security had turned into one of Washington's largest bureaucratic bungles—which was saying a lot. Even with a large budget and the resources that other agencies would kill for, they just couldn't seem to get out of their own way.

Part of the problem, according to gossip within the Beltway, had to do with the people that the former administration had appointed to key positions. Politically correct allies were now so firmly entrenched that rules had been re-written and common sense no longer dictated protocols.

"I've heard it's a bit of a mess over there," Colt finally said.

"That's putting it mildly." President Calloway shook his head. "You probably don't know this, but they even squelched someone from TF2 who laid out the possibility of this entire scenario months ago."

Colt cocked his head at the mention of Task Force 2, a highly classified unit that was rarely alluded to and never discussed outside secure areas. It was so secretive that only those with top authorizations even knew it existed—and most of them weren't sure what the task force did.

Even with Colt's rank and clearance, he knew only that it consisted of some of the best and brightest minds of the CIA, and some of the most highly trained and daring individuals from the military. It was financed by the government, but no line item on the budget existed to say so. There was no list of members or what they did—or how they did it—but Colt knew they worked under deep cover to infiltrate suspected terrorist cells in the United States.

"Do you mean about an attack here?"

The President nodded. "An operative acquired information that involved a drug cartel teaming up with some members of a local mosque, but it was deemed too controversial by the agency's civil rights lawyers to pursue."

Colt clenched his teeth. "What in the hell do civil rights have to do with terrorists trying to kill Americans?"

"That's why you're here." Calloway stood and began to pace and gesture with his hands. "I'm done with the games. I'm done listening to the lawyers and politicians."

"What do you mean, exactly?"

"We need to stop this thing. By any means, and at any cost."

Colt nodded and breathed an inward sigh of relief that someone with military experience was leading the country. This was a commander-in-chief who understood that fighting terrorists meant things could get messy. "I agree completely."

"You're the only one I know who can take this and do what is necessary." The President stopped and turned to Colt. "But *no more* than is necessary."

"And what does *that* mean?" Colt's heart dropped.

"It means that I fully understand the necessity for ferocity and violence in wartime. It's never nice. And it's never neat. But nevertheless, it's necessary."

Colt nodded.

"But I don't want to see collateral damage."

Colt's eyes glazed over. So he was going to be like all the rest. Establishing Rules of Engagement that would make it impossible to fight the enemy on even terms.

"Look, Colt. I know you've been challenged and tested. You've proven what can be done against impossible odds and demonstrated that you'll keep fighting no matter what..." The President took a deep breath and let it out slowly. "You saved my life. I haven't forgotten."

"That's just part of the job." Colt felt uncomfortable with the direction of the conversation. They had never discussed the event after it had occurred. Never.

"What I'm trying to say is that what I'm asking you to do is dangerous."

Colt started to speak again, but Calloway held up his hand.

"So, when I say I don't want to see collateral damage...I'm talking about *you*. I know the chances you are willing to take—

and I'd truly like to keep you around."

Colt half-smiled at the off-handed compliment, and felt a surge of relief that he was being given free rein to do what needed to be done. "Just tell me what you want me to do."

"First, I'd like you to meet with the agent from TF2. Compare notes. Put your heads together and get back to me with a summary and a contingency plan."

"Okay."

"I'm going to be honest, Colt. I'm worried."

"Why? You know something I don't?"

"Nothing black and white. But the daily briefings mention talk of an RDD."

Colt's heart skipped a beat. A Radiological Dispersal Device was exactly what they had feared—a weapon intended to cause panic and economic damage by dispersing a radioactive substance over a wide area. Even though the actual lethality might be low, the chaos and terror it would elicit made it dangerous. "That would line up with everything we've been observing and hearing at the border."

"That's what has me worried." The President sat down again. "This type of thing was a goal of Osama Bin Laden's, and one he referred to as a 'religious duty.' We have to take it seriously."

Colt nodded. He knew well the implications of such a scenario, and that it was a method of terror that appealed to Islamic terrorists. Making a device to scatter dangerous amounts of radioactive material required limited technical knowledge to build and deploy. And since the radioactive materials were widely used, the ingredients would be easy to obtain.

"Do you think they're going to target DC?"

Calloway relaxed back into the cushions and sighed. "Let's put it this way. Terrorists like to focus on prominent economic infrastructure, and political targets. Their goal is to produce mass casualties, visually dramatic destruction, and fear among the U.S. population." He inclined forward, studying Colt with careworn eyes. "What do *you* think?"

Colt lifted his head and stared at the flag beside the window. He merely nodded in agreement.

"The latest report from the Justice Department shows that a major route has been established to bring illegals from the Middle East and Africa to Honduras, then to Guatemala, and finally to Mexico and into the United States."

"So we basically don't even know who or what we're dealing with." Colt didn't state it as a question, but rather as a fact.

"That's it in a nutshell." The President turned to his desk and picked up a card. "This TF2 agent is a friend of mine, and risked a lot to bring this to my attention. I don't need to tell you how sensitive this information is."

Colt nodded. "Of course

"And time is of the essence."

"I'll call as soon as I leave here."

"Great. This business card is for a front operation to disguise the agent, but the number is secure. Once contact is made, you can decide how and where to meet—but it will have to fit within the confines of the agent's cover story." He looked up, his brow creased with concern. "That's important. I can't have an identity blown because of an operative going to a clandestine meeting that is outside their usual routine."

Before Colt could acknowledge that he understood, an aide knocked once and then appeared in the doorway. He gave a quick nod and left.

Colt took that as a sign that it was time to go. He placed the card in his wallet without looking at it and held out his hand. "I'll be in touch, sir."

President Calloway gave his hand a strong squeeze. "It's good to see you, Colt. We need to get together soon... on a social level when I don't need your services."

"I'll hold you to that. The beer's on me."

Colt headed for the door where the same man who escorted him to the Oval Office stood waiting to take him back to the lobby. He could see out of the corner of his eye that Calloway was being rushed out another door toward the Roosevelt Room, apparently late for another engagement.

He'd known this wouldn't be a social encounter, but still, he wished he'd have had more time to talk to the President. *Maybe in about three years he'll have some time—or with any luck, seven.*

Colt waited until he was back in his truck to pull the card out of his wallet, and immediately started dialing the number. He'd sensed the urgency in Calloway's voice, and knew this was something he wanted taken care of immediately.

In the midst of punching in the numbers, he noticed the name on the card, and he froze.

JOSEPHINE SUMMERS
Freelance Journalist

He blinked twice as if the name would somehow change,

then rolled his eyes and shook his head. *Nice job, Nick. You blew off a freaking TF2 agent, and never gave her your name. This is going to be awkward.*

He finished dialing the number. What did it matter? She'd probably known who he was from the first day they met.

"Hello?"

"Hey, it's Nick Colton."

There was no hesitation. No surprise. No change in tone or urgency. "What's up?"

"Just met with a mutual friend and he suggested we get together." He cleared his throat. "As soon as possible."

"Okay. I'm tied up with an event all day." She paused. "It's not something I can get away from."

"How about I come to you?" He grabbed a pen from the console. "Go ahead with the address."

"Just follow Route 50 to Aldie and take a right on Windsong Road. It's the second farm lane on the left. Valhalla Manor. You can't miss it. There's a horse show today."

"Got it."

"You'll see a big, new barn—but I'll be in the old, stone one off to your right."

"See you in less than an hour, I hope."

He clicked off the phone and snapped on his seatbelt. This get-together was going to be a bit uncomfortable, to say the least. The woman he'd pretty much treated like a common criminal had skills and expertise in counterterrorism that were beyond the comprehension of most people.

To belong to an exclusive and elusive group like TF2 would require experience and proficiency in everything from spy

craft and evasion techniques to combat training and operation of advanced weaponry. Just like being a SEAL, a position
in TF2 was one of high achievement. It would necessitate a
tough-as-nails physical and psychological profile, as well as
the ability to engage and deceive some of the most dangerous
men on the planet.

Well the deception had worked on him. Colt had been
completely fooled, never guessing that the woman he believed
he'd met by chance, was part of one of the most secretive and
elite counterterrorism organizations in the world.

Chapter 11

The stop-and-go traffic signals on Route 50 eventually thinned out and then ended altogether, making the drive westward an enjoyable one. Colt loved leaving the sprawl that surrounded DC and traveling to this part of Virginia.

Old stone walls appeared and disappeared over the rolling hills, stretching out as far as the eye could see. Historic landmarks, like the Mount Zion Church he had just passed and the old mill in Aldie he was approaching, had been sites of cavalry skirmishes involving the legendary Confederate officer John Singleton Mosby during the Civil War.

Hard to conceive now, but this land in every direction had been fought over and bled upon by troops from both the North and South. Even the houses themselves were historic, many being owned and preserved by the same families for generations.

Colt's business partner Blake had that connection with this part of Virginia, being a descendant of the celebrated cavalry officer, Colonel Alexander Hunter. On both sides of the road and for miles on end, lay the long-forgotten locations of desperate clashes, where the revolver of that mythical cavalryman had blazed away at the head of his men. And about twenty miles west sat Hawthorne—Colonel Hunter's home

during the Civil War, and now headquarters for Phantom
Force Tactical.

According to family lore passed down from Blake's ances-
tors, Hunter's wife had been a Union spy at the beginning of
the War Between the States—proof that love can conquer
anything.

Colt half smiled and half frowned. It was hard to imagine
Confederate troops riding down this very road now, especially
considering the hustle and bustle of everything that lay less
than fifteen miles to the east. But here, at least, time had stood
still so that signs of the past could be seen and felt if one took
the time to notice.

As he came closer to his destination, Colt wondered what
the proper attire was to attend a horse show, and hoped he
wasn't overdressed. For his appointment at the White House,
he'd worn a pair of khaki trousers with a dark blue, collared
shirt, and a tweed blazer. Hopefully, that would not make him
stand out in the crowd where he was heading. He wanted to
be as inconspicuous and unmemorable as possible.

After making the right-hand turn onto a gravel road and
driving about a mile, Colt spotted the property long before he
arrived at the entrance. On the rolling hills to his left, horse
trailers and trucks were parked in rows for acres. His eyes
scoured the landscape while he drove, and focused on a barn
off to his right. It didn't look like he was going to be able to
park very close, and judging from the number of four-legged
animals, it was going to be a treacherous walk.

When the elaborate front entrance to the property came
into view, Colt put on his turning signal and pulled in. A

decorative wrought-iron gate, embellished by stone walls on each side, was swung open, but Colt slowed down to read the bronze plaque inset that read *Valhalla Manor, 1783*.

Putting his foot back on the gas, Colt rolled down his window for a group of young, freckle-faced girls who stood right inside the gate, waving him to a stop. One of them, who had two long braids hanging down on each side of her head, held up a man's type work boot—the kind he'd seen Joey wear. "We're collecting money for BootCamp." She pushed the boot through the window.

Colt pulled his wallet out of his pocket and stuck a twenty-dollar bill in the boot. "I don't know what that is, but you look like you're working hard."

"Thank you, mister." She turned and jumped up and down with her friends, all of whom began squealing and laughing the way young girls do.

Colt waved and put his foot back on the gas, but veered off the dusty path into the field to avoid the deep ruts and dust of the lane. As he looked around, he noticed he was not going to be overdressed, after all. He glimpsed women in dresses and heels walking beside men in sports coats and ties, mixed in with those in jeans and jodhpurs—and even bib overalls.

He was beginning to see the brilliance of this meeting. It was the perfect place for a clandestine get-together—hiding in plain sight.

Colt eased his truck in beside a Volvo and a late-model Ford truck and turned off the engine. Cracking the door open, he looked down to make sure it was safe to step out, then stood and stretched. After driving for almost an hour, including stopping and backtracking to make sure he wasn't being followed, it felt good to get out and stretch his legs.

He inhaled and recognized the scent of horses and sweat and leather. All mixed together, it smelled sweet, and reminded him of his youth growing up in Texas.

Scanning his text messages as he began his walk to the barn, Colt kept one eye out for any road bombs along the way. The grass was tall in the field where he'd parked, so he moved over to a well-trampled path where he could see more clearly.

It wasn't until he rounded an outcropping of trees that he spotted the house that stood on a small rise beyond the barn. Six tall, white pillars graced the wide front porch of a mansion that looked like a painting from the Old South.

He'd never seen the house before, hidden as it was by the trees, even though he often drove this road as a shortcut to get to and from Phantom Force headquarters. He stopped a moment and took in the scene. In front of the mansion was a sprawling yard that ended where the fields and paddocks began. Neat lines of fences created a pattern of rectangles that held dozens of grazing horses, seemingly oblivious to the chaos of the event happening around them.

Colt turned his attention back to his destination and continued walking. The sign at the entrance said the house had been built in the seventeen hundreds. The barn, though well-kept and in pristine shape, appeared to be just as old.

When he got to the wide doorway, Colt paused before entering to allow his eyes to adjust to the low light. Particles of dust hung in the sunlit entrance, creating the effect of a misty haze. He could hear talking and then the familiar sharp crack of a hoof hitting a stall door.

"Cool it back there," someone yelled.

Taking another step, Colt made out bales of hay stacked to his right, and a line of stalls in front of him. The floor was dirt, and the smell of freshly oiled leather was strong.

"Okay. Up you go."

He turned to his left and sighted Joey helping a young girl into the saddle. Since she appeared busy, he didn't announce his presence. Instead, he stood quietly near the doorway, studying the mysterious Josephine Summers. Wearing a tank top with a blue flannel shirt tied loosely around her waist, she stood with her hands on her hips. Her stance revealed well-defined arms and a sinewy, lean figure that conveyed a noticeable strength. Yet she also exuded a femininity and gracefulness that contrasted with what he knew of her secretive persona.

"You're going to do great. Just have fun." Joey squeezed the rider's leg. "Okay?"

The girl nodded but looked scared to death.

"I'll be right there watching you." A woman with a worried look on her face patted her hand.

"And Daddy will, too?"

"Of course. Daddy will, too," the woman said.

As if sensing his presence, Joey looked over her shoulder, and walked toward him with her hand extended. "You must be Mr. Graves. Thanks for coming on such short notice. My editor moved up the deadline at the last minute, and I hate doing phone interviews."

"No problem." Colt played along, shaking her hand politely. He hadn't been sure what to expect from her, but he could see now she played her role with skill and ease. In neither her mannerisms nor facial expression, could he detect any indication that they'd ever met before.

"Mrs. Davis, this is the gentleman who agreed to help me with my article. He's an expert on the subject."

The woman looked over at Colt and nodded, but he couldn't help but notice a perplexed look—or maybe it was surprise—cross her face when she ran her eyes over him. "Nice to meet you."

Colt's eyes darted from the woman to Joey to see if he could get any indication of what he was an expert on, but she had turned back to the girl.

"Let's go, honey." The woman spoke to her daughter, who urged the gray horse forward.

Joey and Colt followed behind as they walked out of the barn into the sunlight.

"I need to watch this class," Joey said, "but we can talk ringside if that's okay with you."

Colt nodded, but when the mother and daughter got a few steps ahead, he talked under his breath. "But first, what exactly is the article I'm helping out with about?"

Joey picked up her pace and waved her hand in the air. "Oh, I don't remember. I just made something up in the spur of the moment."

He grabbed her arm and stopped her. "Think about it. I'm curious."

Her eyes sparkled with humor, even though she was biting her lip as if not sure she should say.

When she continued to hesitate, Colt started walking again. "Maybe I should ask Mrs. Davis." He was joking, but she apparently didn't perceive that.

"No, wait. I'm remembering now."

Colt slowed down to give her a chance to catch up.

"I told her I'm doing an in-depth article on men who—"

"You know what?" He held up his hand to stop her. "I changed my mind. I don't even want to know."

Joey breathed a sigh of relief as she matched his stride.

"But next time, how about you make it a story on staying fit after forty or something like that?"

She turned her head toward him, her vibrant green eyes assessing him slowly from his head to his feet and back up. A smile seemed to hint at approval, but before she had a chance to comment one way or the other, an excited voice spoke from behind them. "Here she is. Hey, Joey!"

Colt turned to see another young girl dragging her mother by the arm toward them. She broke loose and ran to Joey, wrapping her arms around her waist.

"Hello, honey." Joey returned the hug and looked up at the mother. "You made it."

"Are you kidding me? Do you think she'd miss seeing you at a show?"

Joey laughed. "I'm only in one class. Wish I had time for more."

"We'll be cheering for you," the little girl said.

Joey got down on one knee. "Thank you. It means a lot to have you watching. Next year, *I'll* be watching *you*."

The little girl beamed and looked up at her mother. "We'd

better go find a seat."

"Good luck!" The mother waved as the girl led her toward the grandstand.

Colt started walking again, but only got a few steps before someone else yelled. "Hey, Joey. Good luck later!"

She just waved and kept walking.

"You're a pretty popular person."

"This used to be my world." She sighed. "Not so much anymore."

"And you're going to ride today?"

"I wasn't planning to, but my best friend broke her ankle yesterday, and she wants me to ride her horse in a jumper class."

"I might have to stick around for that."

She looked up at him, her eyes serious but dancing. "There's a good chance I'm going to crash and burn."

"I'm not sure what that means, but it sounds a little dangerous."

"Yeah, but in a fun-as-hell way…" Her attention turned to the horse and rider ahead of them. "Good luck, Lucy!" She signaled the girl with an enthusiastic wave of her hand. "Go get 'em!" The next moment, she had her tanned arms propped on the fence that lined the ring, her arm carelessly close to his. "So, I assume you've been briefed on the basics." Her voice was suddenly low and serious.

Colt could hardly keep up with her changing conversations. One minute, she was enthusiastically talking about horses; and the next, she was discussing highly classified national intelligence. "Yeah. I just came from the White House."

"It never should have gotten this far."

"So I hear."

She looked up at him. "You were my last hope. I'm afraid I waited too long."

"They haven't won yet. We just have to figure out what they're going to do and when."

"What are you thinking?" She kept her gaze fixed on the action in the arena. "Any thoughts on what they're planning?"

"Not sure. It could be as simple as an IED. That's been the weapon of choice in the war zones. It could be crude or sophisticated, depending on the targeted environment, the resources, and the skill of the bomb maker."

She cocked her head as if thinking. "True. They're pretty simple to make, and their effectiveness doesn't depend solely on the volume of explosives. A device could be tailored specifically to suit the attack scenario."

"So if an IED *is* the scenario, we'd have to think about what could do the most destruction. Do they want to take down a building from the blast with a large explosion?"

"Or just cause destruction by using high-velocity fragmentation for the additional collateral damage," she finished for him.

Colt let out his breath. "And then add the possibility of radioactive material into the mix."

Joey shook her head. "Pure chaos."

"Right. Even though it's unlikely to cause many deaths from radiation exposure, it would still create mass panic, and terror."

"A weapon of mass disruption." She paused and looked up at him. "The sad fact is that more people would die trying to escape the area than from the actual device."

"Exactly. And then add in the time and money it would take to clean up—especially in a place like DC. It would put a huge dent in the economy, making the suffering long-term."

They both remained silent for a moment. "No matter what tactic they use, we have to assume they're looking for a soft target, a place where people aren't prepared or are vulnerable," Colt said. "And they obviously want to produce as much widespread terror as possible."

Joey nodded in agreement.

"DC is pretty tight security-wise, but there are plenty of soft targets. Shopping centers. Hospitals. The Metro."

"Those are all definite possibilities." Joey waved at one of the other riders, gave them a thumb's up, and then continued as if there had been no interruption. "But I'm thinking even bigger. They understand this is their chance. They have to go big. Like a large-scale event or something."

"Like at a sports or concert venue?" It finally occurred to Colt why she had been at the stadium and what she had been doing. Her cover story of being a journalist had succeeded in fooling him even though he'd found it suspicious.

She nodded, still deep in thought. "There's always the Mall area, which is crowded pretty much all the time, but I was thinking a site with a widely-publicized event would create the fear and panic they're after."

Colt nodded, seeing her point of view. "True. But there is an even bigger venue nearby."

She looked up at him with a questioning expression. "There is?"

"Football."

The look in her eyes went from comprehension to concern to fear as she grasped that he was talking about FedEx Field, home of the Washington Redskins.

"When's the next home game?"

Colt pulled out his phone. Caitlin Madison was a diehard Steelers fan, and the last time he was at the house, he remembered her telling Blake that Pittsburgh was going to be playing the Redskins. He couldn't remember if the game was home or away. "Looks like the day after tomorrow." He looked up from his phone. "A Monday night game."

Chapter 12

They were both silent for a moment as they analyzed and evaluated the possible magnitude, scenarios, and impact of a potential terrorist attack at a Monday night game.

"One of the most-viewed football time slots by two of the most popular teams in the region." Joey let out her breath as the full force of the implications hit her. "So you'd have your eighty-five thousand or so onsite, plus a television audience of millions."

Colt nodded. "Live coverage. And football is watched by men, women, and children—just the demographics they want to target with terror."

"Wow. That's a scary thought."

"And we still don't have any idea who we're dealing with. Drug cartel? Hamas? al-Qaeda?"

Joey cocked her head and looked up at him. "Or all the above. That's what has me the most concerned. It's a matter of us figuring out who is working with whom before an event happens."

"Believe me, I hear the clock ticking every waking moment." Colt pretended to be watching the riders intently. "I think you're right about getting sidetracked by what's down South."

She looked up at him with a curious expression. "You do?"

"Yes. I don't think they'd undertake the expense and risk of moving the weapon across the United States when all the key ingredients are here. Plus, the clues that were left at the border are just a little too obvious."

"I agree." She nodded. "And as far as assuming their target location is in Washington, it's a logical choice. It has it all—economic prominence, complex infrastructure, political targets, the probability of mass casualties, *and*, perhaps best of all from a terrorist's point of view, visually dramatic destruction of landmarks."

"Any of which would cause significant fear and economic aftershocks."

"A perfect scenario."

Colt sighed. "Have you detected any activity at the local mosques? Do you think they're linked? Should we be looking there?"

"Yes. I do." She shook her head in disgust. "Absolutely. But we would need surveillance to prove it."

"I can take care of that."

She snorted. "I don't think so. Even the TF2 lawyers won't sign off on that without substantial evidence—like dead bodies." Her voice dripped with both sarcasm and frustration.

"The President is done with them. My orders come from him, and I'll take responsibility if there is a problem. Phantom Force will do the surveillance, not a government entity."

"That's what I was hoping to hear from you." Without missing a beat, she straightened and clapped her hands excitedly, making Colt realize she had been watching what was going on in the show ring the entire time she was having an in-depth conversation about matters of life and death.

"She just did a flying lead change." She bumped up against him like they were old friends, and her features became more animated. "Did you see that?"

Colt hadn't seen it—or if he did, he didn't know what it was. He'd done a fair amount of riding as a youngster in Texas, and even a little in Afghanistan, but flying lead changes weren't in his vocabulary. Anyway, he was too busy staring at the girlish enthusiasm of a woman who had successfully gotten him to believe she was nothing but a freelance reporter.

The next minute, she was all business again. "I've got my contacts with the drug cartel. I'm going to have to start leaning on them a little harder. Maybe induce them to move or at least show their hand."

"That could be dangerous. Don't do anything risky."

She started laughing, then covered her mouth with her hand. "Sorry. If you think *that* is risky, wait until you see me ride. "

"So I guess I definitely need to stick around. Someone needs to be able to report to the President about how one of his best agents went down."

Her eyes suddenly grew serious. "No, don't do that. I told him I wasn't riding today."

Colt grasped from both her tone and the graveness of her expression that she had done more than have a casual conversation on the topic. "*Told* him? Or *promised* him?"

"Why?" She looked up at him with inquisitive eyes. "Did

he say something to you about it?"

"No. Of course, not. I didn't even know you were you until after I'd left."

"Oh, yeah. Sorry about that."

"But you knew who *I* was."

She nodded, but it was clear her attention was focused once again on what was taking place in the arena.

"Sorry I was such a prick and didn't give you my name."

That caught her attention. "You kidding me?" She jerked her head toward him. "That's why I insisted that the President bring you in as an outsider to TF2."

"Because I was a prick?"

"No. Because no matter how much I flirted and evaded your questions, you stayed focused and didn't veer from the information you wanted." She turned her head back to the ring. "Highly unusual for a man."

Colt stared at the cloud of dust enveloping the horses as it began to sink in that his prior encounters with this woman had all been a test of his character. He was a little taken aback that he'd been manipulated so easily, but he tried to sound indifferent. "I don't know about the flirting, but I do remember the evasive part, definitely."

"You must not be in the company of females much if you don't even notice when someone is flirting with you."

She said it good-naturedly enough, but must have noticed when he winced a little. "Sorry." She looked up at him. "I didn't mean to get personal."

"I can take it. I'm a big boy."

"I know, but that was below the belt. Seriously. I'm sorry."

He tried to look away, but his eyes rested on the wisps of hair that had escaped from the French braid she wore and curled around her face. Then his gaze drifted down to her left hand, to the wedding ring, causing him to turn his attention back to the action in the arena. *I wonder if her husband is here. And how much he knows about what she does for a living.*

Suddenly, an announcement came over the loudspeaker. "The judges have reached a decision in Class 23, Equitation Under Saddle."

Joey grabbed Colt's arm with one hand and covered her eyes with the other. "I'm afraid to watch."

"Okay." Colt kept his eyes on a well-dressed gentleman walking toward the lined up contestants with an armful of ribbons. He found the innocent, emotional display from one of the country's most elite intelligence experts intriguing. "Don't look now, but a man holding a blue ribbon just handed it to the girl on the gray horse."

"Are you serious?" She opened her eyes and started jumping up and down, clapping her hands. Joy bubbled in her laugh and shone in her eyes. Suddenly, the woman he'd met earlier was there, crying and laughing and hugging Joey. And then they were both crying and laughing and jumping up and down.

"You gave her her life back," the woman said. "How can I ever repay you?"

Just then, the girl trotted up from behind them with the ribbon in her hand and a huge smile on her face.

"Are you kidding? That smile is payment enough."

Other people walked over and patted the girl, and the

horse, and the mother, and Joey, on the back. Some of them were laughing, but most of them were crying.

Joey backed up from the crowd then and just stood and observed the scene, her eyes dancing, her face beaming as if she were a proud mother, while others stepped up to congratulate the girl.

"That a relative of yours?"

"No." She shook her head. "She was in a car hit by a drunk driver two years ago. Killed her father—an Iraqi war veteran."

Colt contemplated the smiling face of the girl.

"They told the family she'd never walk or talk, but she's doing both—thanks to Penny, her horse." She turned to Colt as the announcer called the next class. "I'm sorry, I have to go get dressed. I should be done in an hour at the most. Then we can really talk."

Colt tried not to stare into her eyes, but he couldn't help it. Although, at times, he detected an undeniable glint of sadness in them, they had a way of twinkling in the sunlight like sparkling pools of water—the kind of water that pulls you in and crashes over your head. "Okay." He looked away. "Good deal."

"If you see a big, black, out of control horse, you'll know it's me."

As Joey walked away, Colt's gaze swept over every inch of her, from her ripped blue jeans, down to her work boots, and back up. There wasn't much to see from this angle. She'd put on the large flannel shirt that covered most of her backside, and rolled up the sleeves that had hung below her hands. The shirt was well worn—a little tattered, even—like it was a favorite of hers, or perhaps her husband's.

It seemed to take Joey forever to reach the barn because every couple of steps, someone stopped her to talk. Despite the interruptions, she carried herself with confidence and grace, seemingly unperturbed by her lack of progress and apparently unaware of the many appreciative glances from men. She smiled and talked to everyone as if they were long-lost friends, bestowing hugs and kisses on most of them in a way that was completely contradictory to the bold and brazen operative he knew was hiding inside.

As Colt was learning, Josephine "Joey" Summers was a popular—and perplexing—woman.

Chapter 13

Colt made his way to the food truck on the east side of the grounds and ordered a cheeseburger and a cup of coffee. Amazingly enough, the burger was one of the best he'd ever eaten. The coffee was terrible. He dumped it on the ground and threw the cup into the nearest trash bin.

When he noticed everyone heading toward the arena, he started walking that way, too. But on the way, his gaze was drawn to a practice area where horses were jumping back and forth over a few low fences.

Out of the corner of his eye, he spotted a large, black steed come into view from the field where the trailers were parked. Joey walked beside him, holding the reins while pulling on a pair of gloves.

She now wore polished black boots up to her knees and tight, tan riding breeches. Her hair was neatly braided again and tucked up under a black velvet helmet with not so much as a strand out of place. When she was done with the gloves, she thrust one arm through the sleeve of a black jacket, and then the other while trying to keep the animal under control.

Walking beside her was a woman on crutches, who sported

a bright pink cast that covered her foot and ankle. She kept stopping and moving her hands as if explaining something in deep detail.

Joey nodded and turned to mount while the woman held onto the reins—no easy feat, apparently. The horse pranced and sidestepped in anticipation, and as soon as Joey hit the saddle, it laid its ears back in obvious disapproval and snorted.

Colt had a penchant for danger and loved a good rush of adrenaline, but this seemed just a little on the crazy side. From what he could tell, this type of riding involved trying to control a fifteen-hundred-pound animal with your thighs and four fingers.

He turned his attention back to the ring and studied the vast array of colorful jumps that, to him, were set willy-nilly throughout the showground. The jumps were of varying heights and widths, including one that was two fences together with a spread of about four feet. *No way*, he said under his breath.

When the announcer started the class, Colt inched his way closer to the action and found a spot to stand ringside. He looked to his left as the first contestant trotted through the gate, and noticed that the brunette on crutches had ended up standing right beside him. She wasn't watching the action. She was gazing behind them, at the black horse backing up and doing tight turns in the grass.

"That your horse?"

She looked up at Colt and nodded. "Yeah. He's crazy."

"I can see that. You win a lot of ribbons with him?"

She laughed. "None yet. Success with him is measured by

finishing the course in one piece."

He looked down at her ankle. "Any chance he had a part in that."

"You bet he did. Sideswiped me right into a fence rail. He loves to jump, but he gets pissed off easily. You know the type—kind of like a woman—you need to *ask* him to do something instead of *tell* him." She chuckled. "That's what Joey told me anyway. She told me asking works a lot better."

Colt nodded as if he understood.

"Hi, I'm Bev by the way." She held out her hand. "You a friend of Joey's?"

The question caught Colt somewhat off guard. "No, not exactly. She asked me to come here for an interview so she could finish up a story she's working on." He squeezed her hand. "Colt. Pleased to meet you."

"That sounds like Joey. Always working." Bev shook her head. "Sorry if this class is interfering with your interview. I'm glad you didn't try to stop her, though. She needs this."

"She needs *this*?"

"Riding. Competing. It's her way to relax."

Colt glanced doubtfully back at the horse doing tight pivots behind them.

"Doesn't look real relaxing—but it does look interesting."

"Oh? You've never seen a jumper class?" The woman seemed amazed. "The object is to get over the fences without knocking anything down. There's a time element, too, but in the first round, it's usually more about faults so long as you finish in the allotted time."

"Faults?"

"Faults...the number of jumps knocked down, refusals, rider errors."

"Gotcha." Colt nodded as a rail got knocked hard and fell.

"You ride?" The girl looked up at him.

"Not like this."

She laughed. "It actually looks easier than it is. Some people think the horse does all the work—but believe me, it's the rider, too." Her gaze shifted and her eyes signaled a look of scorn. "Unless you have one like that one."

Colt turned his head and took in the sight of a woman sitting on a sleek, dappled gray that was groomed to perfection—right down to the tidy little braids in its mane and tail. The rider was twirling a crop in her fingers as if she were bored to tears and already knew the outcome of the class.

Even though he caught the obvious twinge of dislike in Bev's voice, Colt didn't comment. The sharp sound of a horseshoe hitting a rail brought his attention back to the ring. The animal landed from the jump awkwardly and then ran sideways away from the next fence, causing the rider to almost fall off.

"That's called a refusal," Bev said.

"So that's a fault."

She looked up at him and smiled. "Actually, it's four faults."

Colt shook his head as he tried to understand the rules.

The following competitor had two refusals, and the one after that knocked down three rails. The next rider to enter was the woman on the dappled gray. As she cantered before the first jump, she looked as if she had just ridden off the pages of a high-society magazine. There was not a hair out of place on either horse or rider, and the jumping round was almost boring to watch. They sailed over the first line of fences in an easy gallop without touching or hitting any of the fences.

"This show is billed as a *training* event to give experience to young horses and inexperienced riders." Bev's voice dripped with scorn as she nodded toward the woman who was finishing up the last line of jumps. "That's Suzie Wells, one of the top riders on the circuit—and that's a fifty-thousand-dollar animal."

"Wow," Colt said, as the rider completed the course with no faults.

As soon as Suzie exited, another participant entered and headed for the first jump. It took that one and the next with ease, but the rider seemed to have trouble once they turned and started to canter across the arena on a diagonal.

Colt took a step back and said, "Whoa," when the horse refused the next jump at the last moment, and the rider flew over its head—and the fence—landing in a heap on the ground.

"*Shit. Dammit.* That *sucks.* Oh, sorry." Bev looked up at him as if embarrassed at having sworn.

"That's okay. Is that what you call crash and burn?"

"Yep. Big time."

The girl, who looked to be about sixteen, got up, dusted herself off, and started crying.

"Oh, shee-it!" Bev practically yelled the words before covering her face with her hands and shaking her head.

Colt looked around to see what the woman was swearing

about now.

"Here comes the wrath of Joey," Bev said from between her fingers. "I don't want to watch."

That's when Colt noticed Joey walking into the ring with a riding crop in her hand, her boots creating a rising cloud of dust in her wake. She had an intense look on her face—not angry exactly—but determined. She waved her hand toward a member of the jump crew and pointed at the fence. "Lower it to two feet." Her voice was loud and commanding, a tone Colt had never heard before.

"What's going on?"

"The number one rule around here is you can't give up. You have to get back on."

"Sounds like a beneficial thing to teach." Colt kept watching with interest.

"Well, it's important for the kids, and it's necessary for the horse, too. If the horse thinks it can stop and get away with it, he'll keep doing it."

Joey turned to the young rider. "Hop on."

The girl shook her head. "No. I don't want to."

"You know the rules. Back in the saddle after a fall."

Bev nudged Colt's arm with hers and whispered, "Let me tell you something. *That* horse is going over *that* fence with *that* rider, even if it takes the rest of the day."

Seeming to understand there was no way out, the girl reluctantly walked over to the animal. Joey leaned down and talked to her with one arm over her shoulder. The teen nodded and let Joey hoist her onto the saddle.

"Just the one fence." Joey's voice was strong and

authoritative. "Don't let him win."

The girl cantered in a circle, and the entire crowd grew quiet, seeming to hold a collective breath.

"Look up. Look ahead." The commands sounded loud in contrast to the hush of the spectators. "Relax. Relax."

The girl did as she was told, but as they approached the fence, the horse appeared like it might duck to the side again. When they were just two strides away from the fence, Joey commanded, "Leg. Leg. Leg!"

The animal seemed surprised at the sudden pressure from the girl's legs and sailed over the fence with a foot to spare as the crowd erupted in applause.

"Since when do they allow riding lessons in the middle of a show?"

Colt turned around to see the woman named Suzie standing just behind him. She rolled her eyes expressively and turned back to her own mount. "Can't we get this class over with already?"

Bev's face turned red with anger. "Teaching a kid to get back in the saddle after a fall is a little more important than another blue ribbon for your wall, don't you think?"

"Whatever."

The woman walked away, which was a relief to Colt. He didn't want to be standing in the middle of a catfight if one erupted—and he could sense that Bev's claws were out and ready to rip.

Chapter 14

Colt watched intently as the jump crew put the fence back to the proper height. After a few minutes delay, Joey entered the arena.

"Here come Joey and my Bart." Bev stood on one foot and rested her crutches against the fence so she could clap.

Colt didn't need for her to tell him because, all a sudden, there was a crowd—two and three deep—surrounding the perimeter of the ring. Whether they were there because they wanted to see *her*, or they were anticipating a crash, he didn't know. But he did recognize that she was having a hard time keeping the animal under control. Then again, maybe that was just his imagination because the beaming smile on her face made it appear as if she were enjoying herself immensely.

"When I signed up for this class, it was just a way to give Bart some experience." Bev nodded toward her horse. "He's retired from the racetrack, so jumping is new to him."

"He looks like he wants to run," Colt commented.

"Yeah, he doesn't understand anything but full speed ahead. Not exactly helpful when you're in a jumping class."

But even with his fast pace, Bart cleared the first two fences with room to spare and headed down a line of three jumps with his ears pricked forward.

"This is the hard part right here." Bev pointed to a

combination of fences right in front of them, and covered her eyes as if afraid to look. "If they don't get into it right or aren't going the right speed, they can crash."

The horse sailed over the fences with ease, making it look easy. Another sharp turn and they were on their last line of fences. Bart went clean until the last jump when he just nicked a rail with a hind hoof. The crowd went wild.

"Is that a fault?"

"No. As long as the rail doesn't fall."

"So who won?"

"We don't know yet. Two more contestants have to go, and then they hold a jump-off for the ones that are tied."

"A what?"

"You'll see." Bev stood quietly as the final competitors completed the course. One of them knocked down a rail, and the other hit two rails, but nothing fell. As soon as that horse exited, a crew ran into the stadium.

"Wait. Are they making the fences *higher*?"

"Yes. Now is where the timing comes in. Since this is a small show, they'll just do one jump-off, and if it's a tie as far as faults, they'll go on time."

"That should give your Bart an edge," he commented.

She shrugged. "It could. But there's a fine line between being fast and being clean. It's hard."

She didn't have time to say anything else because the first challenger in the jump-off entered to loud applause. The horse started the round clean but seemed to tire on the last line and knocked down two rails on two different fences before completely refusing the final one.

Bev and Colt watched silently as they left the arena, and
Joey and Bart entered.

Colt noticed that this time, Joey's face was more serious.
She was concentrating. Even from this distance, he could see
her green eyes intensely studying the course as she circled in
front of the first jump.

"She's pretty popular around here," Colt commented as
the volume of the crowd increased.

Bev nodded. "Oh, hell yeah. Everyone loves her for what
she's done."

"What do you mean?"

Bev looked up as if surprised and then seemed to remember
that he was a newcomer. "Hmm. How do you explain Joey?"
she said as if to herself. "She's kind of a combination horse
whisperer and soul healer."

"A what?"

"She's fixed more broken animals and broken people than I
can even count." Bev nodded toward her own mount. "Like I
said, he was off the racetrack, on his way to the slaughterhouse
when she told me about him. I've seen her literally take horses
off the meat truck and give the driver cash out of her own
pocket." She took a hopping step forward and leaned on the
fence. "And believe me, when she first brings them home,
they don't look like they're worth ten cents."

"You said she heals people, too?"

Bev looked over at him suddenly suspicious. "Where are
you from? Do you seriously not know about Joey?"

"No." Colt repeated his story. "She's on a tight deadline and
asked me to stop by so she could interview me for a story."

"Oh. Well, she doesn't like any recognition, but this show is a fundraiser for her charity."

"*Her* charity?" Colt looked around.

"Yeah. It started small as a way for her to give back to military families. She would give their kids free riding lessons, help them find the right horse, that sort of thing. Then, when so many guys were dying in Iraq and Afghanistan, she started a summer camp for kids who had lost a parent."

"Oh, is that what the BootCamp thing is?"

Bev laughed. "Yeah. Joey has worn those horribly ugly men's work boots the entire time I've known her. And she's as strict with the kids as a military drill sergeant. So, it became BootCamp."

Colt didn't say anything, but he found the fact that Joey would ignore negative comments from other women and keep right on wearing what she wanted was just another example of her character. As for the drill sergeant part, he'd pretty much witnessed that today.

"Well, the charity just kept growing." Bev waved her hand around at all the people. "She never turned anyone away. Everyone here has a story now. Drug abusers, ex-convicts, veterans with traumatic brain injuries, cancer survivors, car accident victims. You name it. Joey has a gift for matching up horses and riders—and this is the result."

Colt looked around at the different ages, different races, different sexes, all milling around—all of them with big smiles on their faces.

"How long has this been going on?"

Bev cocked her head up toward the sky and scrunched

her face as if in thought. "Geez, ten years now, I guess." She frowned, and her eyes turned noticeably sad. "It started as a way for her to get over her own grief…but I'm not sure that ever worked."

Colt wondered what that meant, but sensing it was a personal and painful topic, he didn't ask any more questions. As it turned out, he didn't need to.

"He's been lying in Arlington for ten years, and she's still living in that big house all alone. Says she's happy." She forced a laugh. "Did you ever look into those eyes?"

The question hung in the air. Colt assumed Bev didn't really expect an answer, and he didn't want to give one. How could one look into those serious, somber eyes and *not* notice the flicker of pain there?

"Worst part of it is that it was his last deployment and they were planning to start a family." She looked around. "This is her family now."

Colt looked around too. "It takes a strong person to make such a lasting legacy out of such a tragic loss."

Bev nodded. "Sometimes I think she should leave here. Too many memories. You know?"

"Memories aren't always a bad thing." Colt cleared his throat. He hadn't expected his voice to crack like that.

"True, but the house was his, and now she's in debt up to her neck—as if she needed another thing to worry about. Scott would be telling her to get rid of it and get on with her life."

Bev turned and looked Colt up and down. "Maybe *you* could help in that department."

Colt held up his hands, palms out. "I'm not in the market…

Anyway, she's married."

"But he's gone." She threw her hands up in the air in exasperation. "All these years later and she won't take that wedding ring off. Says she's still married in her heart."

"It takes time."

"Time? Ten years this fall he's been dead. I think that's time enough."

Colt didn't know what to say.

"I wish she'd at least quit that job."

"Writing?"

"Yes. Sounds like a great job, but it stresses her out. She's always running here and there on deadline. Gone for days—sometimes weeks—at a time. That's why the bills are piling up."

Colt didn't respond, but he could see why she made the perfect TF2 agent. She was well respected and well liked, with a profile that no one in a million years would think twice about. She was soft-spoken and appeared placid—yet he had no doubt she could kill if the situation warranted it.

His gaze drifted to the crowd surrounding the arena, and he could see it truly was a wide assortment of people. There were women in dresses and fancy hats—probably donors—as well as those in jeans and ball caps who were leading horses around as proudly as if they were kings.

As Joey continued the course, Colt felt an adrenaline rush of both fear and anticipation—he could feel the same surge in everyone around him. It was like a force of energy of well-wishers, joining together to send positive vibes to the rider.

She must have gotten into the next fence in a bad way

because Bev swore under her breath and put her hand over her eyes. Somehow, Bart managed to clear it, and they cantered to the next jump. At the speed they were going, even Colt felt the need to close his eyes, but he forced himself to watch.

Even with his inexperienced eye, he could tell Joey was trying to slow the animal down when they got to the three-fence combination, but to no avail. A collective groan came from the crowd when a hoof hit the second fence, followed by a loud cheer when the rail didn't fall. But with the third fence, they were not so lucky. The loud clunk of a hoof hitting the rail, and then it falling to the ground sounded thunderous.

Bev whistled and clapped. "Pretty super for an animal that was bound for the meat market."

Colt laughed. "You mean you didn't pay fifty thousand for him?"

"Joey never told me what she paid," Bev said. "I'm sure it was no more than a few hundred dollars—and I guarantee you she put the fear of God in that guy buying horses for meat."

Colt smiled. Despite her calm exterior and quiet demeanor, he could sense that Josephine Summers could be a fireball when necessary.

"Oh, well." Bev bent down with her arms relaxed on the railing. "Made it to the jump-off round and had one knockdown. That's an unbelievably successful day in my book."

"So she didn't win?"

"She's in first place now, but Suzie will go clean." She looked around as if to see if anyone were listening. "To tell you the truth, if it would have been any other rider behind her, Joey would have steered Bart off course just so the next person could win. But Suzie,"—she nodded in the woman's direction and then shook her head grimly—"she does this for a living. She could do this course with her eyes closed. Her mount runs on autopilot."

Very few people clapped when Suzie entered the ring. Colt could see how effortlessly the horse moved, and there was very little concentration on the face of the rider. It was like a baseball player who had hit a home run. Confident and no need for speed. Just run the bases.

"She can take her time as long she is within the set time limit." Bev spoke as if reading his mind when he turned his head to see the large clock on the other side of the stadium. "A clean round wins."

Colt tried not to wish for something to happen as the duo continued through the maze of fences. The horse cantered at a steady, relaxed pace, taking each fence with ease, as if this were just an easy practice round before something much bigger. Joey had done the course in about half the time.

As they began the last line of fences, they still had forty seconds left on the countdown clock. Bev pushed herself off the railing and gathered her crutches. "I'm thrilled with second place. Probably the only ribbon Bart is ever going to win." She turned and started walking away. "Nice to meet you," she said over her shoulder. "I'm going to move closer to the center of the arena so I can snap a picture of Bart getting his—"

A loud clank interrupted her sentence. Colt had taken his

eyes off the course, thinking it was over, but the rider had apparently relaxed a little bit too much. Seemingly in slow motion, the rail of the last fence shook in its brackets and then fell to the ground, sending a puff of dust into the air— and the crowd onto its feet.

"No fucking way," Bev said, before hobbling swiftly on her crutches toward the gate to find her horse and the rider who had just won the class.

Chapter 15

It took quite a while for Colt to get anywhere near Joey, but he was content watching from a distance. He bought a bottle of water and sat down on a bale of straw in the shade to rest his ankle while he had the chance.

After a few minutes she walked over to him and gave him an apologetic smile. "Sorry about the delay. This event usually runs by itself so I thought I'd be free to talk." Motioning for him to follow, she walked briskly, but people still came up and patted her on the back or gave her a thumb's up from a distance.

"No problem." Colt fell into step beside her. "Good job, by the way."

"The horse did all the work."

Colt was going to respond that it didn't look that way to him, but he left the words unsaid. When they got to the barn, Joey sat down on a bale of hay and struggled with taking off the riding boots.

"Here, I'll give you a hand." Colt tugged at the boot by the heel, and it finally slid off."

"Damn that feels good. Thanks." She looked up at him. "Seriously, I'm sorry for keeping you all day. We have a lot to talk about, and time is of the essence."

He pulled off the other boot.

"You don't mind coming up to the house, do you?" She stood and walked over to a large box, lifted the lid, and pulled out her work boots. "Easier to talk up there. Fewer interruptions."

She sat down again and began putting on the work boots. After pulling them on she didn't bother to tie them, because she spotted someone she knew and stood to talk to him.

"Hey, Dan."

A tall, well-built man carrying a bucket of water stopped in the aisle and waited for her to reach him.

"You okay if I head up to the house?"

The man nodded. "Sure." Then his eyes drifted over to Colt.

"I have to finish up an interview," Joey said. "If you could lock the gate on your way out, I'll come down for a final check."

"Sure thing." The man turned and went back to work.

"Follow me." Joey walked out the door with long strides and didn't wait to see if Colt followed. But in midstride she stopped dead so that he almost ran into her back.

"How far away are you parked?"

He pointed to his truck that was now sitting alone in the field.

"Let's get it now and drive up to the house." She swept her gaze from his face to his stomach and back. "You're okay, right? It's been a long day for you."

Colt had been thinking the same thing, but shrugged it off.

His ankle throbbed in tempo with his head, and the stitches in his stomach burned. "I'm fine."

They walked in silence past the ring and the fields that were swiftly emptying. The sounds of horses whinnying and kicking in their trailers now replaced the sounds of the show.

"This is quite an operation you have here."

Joey nodded. "Yeah. It started small, and has grown over the years."

"Seemed like everyone was having fun."

"That's what it's all about."

Colt hit the door unlock button and opened the passenger side door for Joey before moving to the driver's side.

Joey pointed to a rutted lane once she'd climbed in. "Take that up past the tree line. There's a driveway on the left."

Colt followed her instructions up a winding lane and through another gate that stood open, to a circular driveway in front of the house.

Joey hopped out as soon as the truck came to a stop without saying a word. Colt followed her onto the porch and waited while she punched some numbers into a security pad. At the sound of a soft click, she pushed the door open and stood to the side, motioning him forward. "Come on in."

Colt stepped into a huge foyer with polished wooden floors and an antique chandelier hanging above. A large stairway with ornate carvings on the banister stood off to the right of a wide center hallway.

"I should have started a fire. It really cools down at night this time of year." Joey turned to the security panel and reset the alarm before setting her keys on a little table and continuing to the hallway. She pulled the clip from her hair as she walked, undoing the braid by running her fingers through her tresses. "Follow me. Want a drink?"

"If you're having one." His gaze fell upon her hair as she walked in front of him. Curled and wavy from being in a braid all day, it cascaded over her shoulders and down her back like a waterfall.

"Yeah. I need one. With a couple of aspirin on the side."

They entered a room that looked like an old-fashioned library, complete with elaborately carved bookcases that reached from the floor to the ceiling. There were two couches that looked like they were from the Victorian era on either side of a fireplace. A small table lined with bottles sat between two large windows.

"Beer?" she asked as she walked toward the table. "Or something stronger?"

"Something strong on the rocks if you have it."

"You read my mind."

She pulled two glasses out of a drawer and opened the door of a small refrigerator that was built into the unit. Ice cubes tinkled in the glasses, followed by a splash of whiskey.

"Beautiful room," Colt commented as he took the glass. That's when his eyes landed on a large, framed oil painting hanging above the fireplace, offset by a number of pictures on the mantel. It had the appearance of a small shrine. Her eyes followed his gaze. "My husband," is all she said.

Colt couldn't help but stare at the portrait of the handsome, blue-eyed man holding an M-4, fully kitted out in an Army combat uniform, his Ranger tab clearly showing. Colt squinted to read the brass plate at the bottom of the frame. It read CAPTAIN SCOTT HANSON. While his attention remained there, Joey walked over to the desk, removed something from a drawer, and pushed a button.

"That's a secure room if you need to use the computer or make a call."

As he turned in the direction she had indicated with her eyes, he heard a creaking sound, like a door being opened. One of the bookshelves moved, revealing another room that contained a row of electronic equipment, monitors, computers, and three cell phones, all on chargers.

"Take a look." She walked inside and toward a bank of eight screens on the one wall, then bent down and studied each one.

From where he stood, Colt could see they were images taken from outside security cameras, showing the front gate, grounds, and even the interior of the barn. Colt couldn't hide the surprise on his face. He was standing in a two-hundred-year-old house that was wired with state-of-the-art, twenty-first-century defense technology. Two distinctly different and distant worlds—the past and the present—sharing the same small space.

"Super." Joey's hand went reflexively to her back as she straightened, and he thought he saw her wince. "Dan locked the gate, and the horses look all snug and cozy." She turned to Colt with a tired smile on her face. "All secure, as they say."

"You sore?" Colt nodded toward her back.

"Just an old injury acting up." She seemed troubled by him asking—or maybe she was agitated at herself for showing weakness. "This and the aspirin will fix it." She held up her drink. "Let's get to work."

When they returned to the library, she sat down on one of the couches and began to rub her temples. Now that he knew a little more about her background, the look made him ache. She seemed so utterly alone and vulnerable. "I've got a bit of a headache." She took a swallow of the whiskey without a grimace. "You go first. What do you think?"

"I think you look tired." He sat on the couch opposite her, his drink making a tinkling sound as the ice cubes stirred.

She gave him a weary smile. "Just for future reference... that's not really something you should say to a woman."

"Sorry. I've never been accused of being politically correct or following the rules."

"So I've heard." She took another sip of her drink and then focused on something on the far wall.

Colt tilted his head. "What's *that* supposed to mean?"

She shrugged. "Nothing."

He leaned forward, arms on his knees. "No. That definitely meant *something*."

She was silent a moment and then returned her attention to him. "Okay, let's just say I lost my best source with your last op."

He cocked his head. "Carlos Valdez? How in the hell did you have anything to do with Carlos Valdez?"

"I've been working my way into his network for the past four years." She put her head back and closed her eyes. "He was a few days away from buying three expensive horses from me—ostensibly to launder the payout he's receiving from the terrorists to do the dirty work in DC. We were close."

"Sorry about that, but it couldn't be helped."

"I'm sure it couldn't, but…"

"But what?"

She brought her head back up and pinched the bridge of her nose. "It just created a whole host of new obstacles, that's all."

"How so?"

"Taking out Carlos left a void in the organization."

"Of course, but the next person in line just steps up and takes over." Colt stood and stretched his back, not overly concerned about the drug kingpin's empire. It was like a snake, and even with the head cut off, it would continue to live for a long time to come.

"It's not that easy, actually."

"Why not?"

"Carlos was too arrogant to think that anyone could take him down, so he never set anyone up to take over for him. He never had an official second in command. His five bodyguards were the closest to him as far as his business dealings and understanding the ins and outs of the operation, but you evidently dispatched them, as well."

"When someone shoots at me, that is the usual outcome," he said with an unemotional shrug of his shoulders.

"Nevertheless, it's created a whole new monster."

"How?"

"The *El Soldado* cartel has moved in."

Colt raised his eyebrows.

"You've heard of them?"

"Of course. They're a band of rogue commandos that deserted from the Mexican army and set up their own operation. They're like mercenaries now, offering services—mostly in the form of advanced firepower—to other cartels." Colt sat back down. "They're violent, vicious, and not afraid of confrontations."

"Well, they're not in the freelance business anymore." Joey sighed. "With Carlos's death, his entire operation broke apart, and the *El Soldado* took over the most vital roles. The merger of Carlos's cartel with this one makes it the most technologically advanced and dangerous criminal enterprise in history."

"Where are we getting our information about this merger?"

"I have my sources for the specifics." She looked up at him and tilted her head. "But it's definitely not a secret. They've got banners all over Mexico announcing that they're hiring new recruits—and they're specifically targeting the military."

Colt sat down again. "Probably offering better pay, better living conditions, and better benefits if they join the ranks of *El Soldado*."

"Exactly. And with their arsenal of weapons and their military expertise, they are a very formidable enemy."

"Wow." Colt closed his eyes and thought about it for a moment. "So, basically, we now have an organized crime network operating like a well-regulated army."

"Actually…it gets worse."

Colt tilted his head and raised his eyebrows but didn't say anything.

"There are some who think that *El Soldado* was able to move in so quickly and take over the organization so effortlessly because they had help with the planning and tactical end."

"Who?"

Joey hesitated a moment before speaking. "We're not sure about that yet."

The room grew quiet as Colt tried to assess whether TF2 wasn't sure, or if Joey just didn't want to let him in on that piece of information. He decided to dig a little deeper. "Is this based on real intel? Or just a theory?"

"A little of both, I guess. It's common knowledge that we've stepped up efforts at the border to stop terrorists from crossing, so it's only logical that some Islamic groups would pay the cartels to help them in. The drug runners have years of experience, established routes, and know how to avoid border patrol."

"And in return, the cartels would receive some innovative terrorist strategies to use against America in future operations." Colt let out his breath. He could not have thought of a worse worst-case scenario than this. Now he understood the President's urgency. "So what you're saying is, we have a group of rogue militiamen backed by groups with the technology, money, military training, and weaponry to do some real damage."

Joey took a sip of her drink and nodded. "That's pretty much it in a nutshell."

Colt stood again and began to pace. "What about the stuff my guys found at Carlos's house? Stuff that made it look like the cartel was planning to move radioactive ingredients across the border?"

"Some of it might have been old—when they truly *were*

planning to do it that way—and some of it might have been a plant to steer you in the wrong direction."

"You're probably right. My guys said the stuff was impossible to miss. Almost like it had been put there on purpose."

"I'm still hoping I can re-connect with the cartel, even though Carlos is out of the picture." Joey swirled the ice cubes in her glass and stared at it thoughtfully. "We're hanging by a thread on this. We need that connection to move forward."

"Do you think they trust you enough to do that?"

"No reason why they shouldn't." She shrugged. "TF2 has made sure that, on paper, I'm swimming in debt. Ready to go under. In desperate need of money."

"But you're not?" Colt sat down across from her.

"No. Of course, not." She must have noticed his look. "Why? Did someone tell you differently?"

He shrugged. "Maybe."

She sighed heavily. "That's the hardest part about this job. People feeling sorry for me, thinking my circumstances are different than what they are."

That's the hardest part? As opposed to getting shot at?

Colt thought back to the first time they had met, and realized now that she probably knew more about that incident than what she had let on. He wanted to ask her about it but decided to concentrate on the task at hand. "You would think that if Carlos had something in the works, they would rely on his contacts. They don't have the time to start over."

"Maybe not. But will they trust me like Carlos did? I had him believing I was financially desperate and that I'd give him a good deal. I was close."

"And now he's dead." Colt began to see that what he'd thought was a separate and isolated incident was actually very closely related and directly connected to the operation he was now tasked with.

"Evidently," she said dryly.

"It was necessary, believe me." He inclined forward as he spoke.

She didn't bother to answer with words but gave him an if-you-say-so shrug before rubbing her temples again.

Colt sat back on the couch and sighed. "Is there anything you can do to move them along?"

"I've been thinking about it, but I don't want to seem too pushy. It might look suspicious."

Colt's phone rang. "Excuse me a minute." He put the phone to his ear. "Go ahead."

"Where're you at?" Blake asked.

"Ah, Loudoun County." Colt was intentionally vague. "What's up?"

"Just wanted to give you a quick update. I've got some guys checking out the mosque on Water Street like you requested."

"Okay. Anything else?"

"That's pretty much it. You heading back here soon?"

Colt lifted his eyes to see Joey standing with her back to him, staring at the picture of her husband. "Yeah. Just wrapping things up here."

"Where'd you say you were?"

Colt smiled. He couldn't get anything past Blake. They were too close. "I'll see you in a bit, dude."

Chapter 16

Colt stuck his phone back into his pocket. "Nice place you have here," he said as a way to start up the conversation again, so she'd realize he was done with the call.

Joey turned around. "Thanks. It's my husband's family home. Has been for a couple of generations."

"So he's an Army Ranger?" Colt nodded toward the painting, pretending not to know the history so he wouldn't get her friend in trouble for gossiping—but he'd recognized the name and the image of Scott Hanson the minute his eyes landed on the portrait.

"Yes… He was."

Just three words. That's all she said. Yet still, he heard the catch in her voice.

Colt closed the gap between them in three strides and touched her arm. "I'm sorry." He swallowed hard when he witnessed the heart-rending expression on her face. "For your loss."

She nodded and blinked repeatedly, then quickly looked down, as if a tragedy such as losing your husband was a thing to be borne in silence and never spoken of. "Thanks."

But her attempt to hide the moisture that had gathered in

her eyes did not succeed. Colt saw the single tear slide down her cheek before she bowed her head, and squeezed her arm reassuringly. When she looked up, he brushed the moisture away with the back of his finger. "There is nothing wrong with mourning your husband. You don't have to hide it."

She studied him with guarded eyes that glistened unnaturally in the light. "You're the only person who hasn't told me I should be over it by now." She swiped her finger across the bottom of her eye before another drop fell.

Colt didn't bother to tell her that he could relate to her pain; understood what it was like to feel loss so intense that it physically hurts.

"Sorry to be so weak." She took a deep breath and shook her head. "Let's get back to business."

"You're not weak." Colt gave her shoulder a gentle, brotherly squeeze. "Tired maybe," he said, winking to show her he was joking. "But not weak."

Before she could respond, one of the phones on the counter behind him buzzed. Her gaze dropped to the phone, and she seemed to freeze a moment as she stared. "It's the cartel. That's the number Carlos used to call."

Joey walked over and picked up the phone but turned the volume up all the way and moved to stand beside Colt before answering. She spoke in a noticeably tired and disturbed voice. "Hello?"

"*Señora* Summers."

"Who is this?" She pretended to be barely awake. "It's very late."

"I am sorry, *señora*, but there are things we need to discuss."

"Who are you?"

There was a slight pause. "I am calling on behalf of Carlos Valdez. It is about a transaction you were working on with him."

She met Colt's gaze. "I'm listening."

"Those horses. They are still for sale?"

"Two of them are. One of them has been sold."

There was a short pause. "Do you have another of equal value?"

"Of course."

"I will take them all at the terms discussed."

She gazed at the portrait hanging over the mantle with an intense look on her face. "The value of the Meadow Skipper stallion has increased substantially in value since the price was set with Carlos."

"What are you saying?" There was a hint of impatient frustration—not anger—in the voice.

"Two of his colts have won top races in the last few months. That increases his value as a stud."

The man on the other end of the phone laughed, but it was obviously forced. "So you wish to negotiate a new price?"

Joey began to pace as she talked, as if forgetting Colt was standing there. "That seems fair."

"How much?"

"Two hundred thousand more." She sounded firm and unflappable.

Colt couldn't help but be impressed by the confidence she exuded—and the desperation inferred. He held his breath at the ensuing silence, thinking she had pushed too far.

Finally, the man spoke again. "Let me see, when I do the math…the new figure seems to add up to the amount you owe the bank in taxes and late mortgage fees."

She eyed Colt, and he nodded. So they had checked her out. It had paid off.

"You should stop buying horses you cannot afford."

"I have obligations."

"Yes, of course. Your charity. It appears that is where much of your money goes. A smart businesswoman would consider paying her own bills before helping to pay others'."

"Do we have a deal?" She was a soft-spoken woman for the most part, but when she wanted to, she carried a tone of authority.

The man on the other end of the line sighed loudly as if exasperated, making it obvious he needed to make a deal, and soon. "Perhaps you are a shrewd businesswoman after all. *Sí,* we have a deal."

"And we're still talking cash, right? Because I'm selling them at a bargain price as a favor to Carlos." She made eye contact with Colt for the first time and winked, but there was no smile involved.

"*Sí.* That is what Carlos had told me were the terms."

"When?"

"Tomorrow morning."

"Sunday?"

"A potential buyer is anxious to see the horses."

"I understand." Joey shot a nervous glance toward a clock on the wall. "What time?"

"Nine o'clock sharp. Show the transporters the horses, and

they will take care of the rest."

"And they will have something for me?"

"Yes. They will have two large tack boxes for you. Feel free to inspect the contents while the animals are being loaded. They have been instructed to unload the boxes first."

"That sounds satisfactory."

"Please be sure the papers are in order."

"Of course." Joey unconsciously ran her fingers through her hair. "I will have their bloodlines and Coggin's test paperwork ready to go."

"Very well. It is a pleasure to do business with you, *senora*. I hope the horses are all that you have promised."

"They are all I have promised and more. You can count on that."

Before he could hang up, Joey pushed for more. "Will I have the pleasure of meeting you tomorrow?"

"No," he replied sharply. "The haulers know what they are doing. There is no need for me to get in their way."

"If you are ever in need of high quality breeding stock, please keep me in mind."

"I will do that indeed."

The line went dead.

"Wow. You really pushed it there." Colt almost said, "that took balls," but successfully stopped himself.

"I didn't want them to think I don't know how to negotiate." Her smile looked more relaxed now, as if the headache had disappeared. "I'm going to run down to the barn and get things ready in case they come early."

"Can I help?"

She regarded him hesitantly but then nodded. "Sure. Wait here a sec while I grab a jacket."

When she'd left, Colt made a phone call to Blake and explained what had happened.

"Wait. You're where?"

"I'm at a farm near Aldie."

"With *who*?"

"A contact."

"A *female* contact?"

Colt's eyes drifted over to Joey, who was walking back into the room with a phone at her ear.

"Yes."

He finally realized Blake was merely ribbing him when he said, "Glad to hear you're back in the game, old boy."

"Eff you, Blake. This is business," he whispered.

"It doesn't hurt to mix business and pleasure."

"Yes, it does."

"You need to relax a little."

"Right. The nation's capital is about to go up in flames, and I need to relax."

Joey was waving him over. "I gotta go."

"I understand," Blake said, but the amused tone of his voice confirmed he didn't understand at all.

Chapter 17

C olt disconnected and walked over to Joey. She had put on a long-sleeve, white, thermal shirt and was carrying three leather, strap-like items. "Take a look at these." She flopped the leather pieces off her arm and onto his.

"What are they?" He held them up to eye-level as she walked over to the bank of computers in the tech room.

"They're halters for the horses."

"What am I looking for?"

"Just wanted to see if you see anything."

He could hear her clicking away on the computer as he looked them over.

"I don't see..." He stopped talking when he looked at the computer she had stepped away from. The monitor displayed a close-up of his face, causing him to study the halter more thoroughly. Still not seeing a camera, he waved his fingers over different parts until the image of his hand appeared on the screen.

He examined the halter again and discovered that one of the small rivets contained a camera. "Can't see it even when I know it's there." He looked up at her. "And it records audio?"

Before he'd even gotten the entire sentence out, she had turned up the volume on the computer so he could hear his voice.

"Brilliant. Podge will be envious."

"Podge?"

"Our tech guy at Phantom Force. He's got something like this, but not that small—and not with that clear of an image."

"Sometimes it pays to be with TF2."

"With the right money behind us, Phantom Force will be at that level."

"I have no doubt about that."

The way she said the words made Colt do a double take, but she was already on to her next task, jumping up and trying to retrieve a box from a top shelf in a closet.

"Here, I'll get it." Colt walked over, reached over her head, and lifted the wooden box by the handle.

"I think that's everything we need." She punched her arms through a light jacket and headed toward the door. "Glad you stayed. This one horse can be a bit crazy, and I don't want anyone else to know about this."

"Know about what?"

"Can you grab those halters?" She kept walking.

Colt fell into step behind her once she had disarmed the security and walked down the path to the barn. She wore her customary work boots, still untied, and carried herself in a way that suggested she was comfortable with, and accustomed to, making decisions on her own. Yet the way her hair spilled in graceful waves down her back and wafted gently in the breeze reminded him of an enchanted princess in a book. Somehow, her confidence and strength did not lessen her femininity.

It only enhanced it.

"And you said we're doing what exactly?" he asked again.

"We're going to inject a small radio transmitter so the horses can be tracked."

Colt stopped in his tracks. "We're going to do *what?*"

"Don't worry. It's not that complicated. It's just a little bit bigger than a piece of rice. It's kind of the same thing they do with dogs and cats so they can find the owner if they get lost."

"If you say so, boss."

When they got to the barn, she slid open the big door and turned on the light switch. There was the general sound of rustling, and a few nickers of greeting as she turned and closed the massive door behind them.

"Just hang the halters there." She nodded toward a hook. "I want to double-check them, but I'm not going to put them on until the morning."

"What if the transportation company brings their own?"

"I'll insist they take these. They're custom-made for each horse with their own silver nameplate attached. It's a gift to the new owner."

He looked at the halters again and grinned. "Yeah. Custom-made is right."

Joey had opened a large cabinet and was busy pulling out items, which she placed on the top of a large trunk.

"What time is it?"

Colt looked at his watch. "Almost midnight."

"Good. I shouldn't need anything more than a topical anesthetic for three of these guys, but the other might need an injection of something stronger. We'll see how it goes." She talked while opening a pack of four-by-fours and placing them on a tray. She dunked a few of them in a reddish substance and a doused a few in a cream. "Onto our first victim. I'll start with the tough guy."

She opened a stall door and came out with a large bay horse that snorted at Colt. "What do you need me to do?"

"I'm going to put him in cross ties, but if you could stand by his head and talk to him, that would be great."

"What do I say?"

She gave him a look full of humor. "I don't know. Tell him he's handsome." She shoved the tray into his one hand. "And hold this."

Walking to the right side of the horse, she started by pushing the mane over to the other side. Then she took the wet four-by-fours one at a time and wiped the area, followed by a swipe of a dry one. Lastly, she took the ones with the cream and covered the area thoroughly. "We'll give that a couple of minutes to numb the area while I get the rest of the things ready."

"And then what?"

"I'm going to inject an electronic IPLD—an individual position locater device—under the skin." Joey continued gathering the other supplies she would need. "It's similar to the pet locater chips put in by a vet."

"So...kind of like an electronic bracelet placed on criminal offenders?"

"That's the general idea, yes. But smaller so it can be permanently implanted under the skin. It can't be seen—or easily removed."

She bent down to the box she'd carried and opened the lid, pulling out an object wrapped in clear paper. After cleaning off the tray he had held, she opened a pair of sterile gloves and put them on, then opened the object that looked like a large needle. "Here we go."

Colt put his hand on the halter and began rubbing the horse's head, trying to keep him occupied as Joey went back to his neck. "He might jump. I'll try to make it fast."

"Easy, big boy." Colt talked in a soothing voice as Joey took the needle, stuck it into the animal's neck, and pushed the plunger. The horse's head jerked up, but by that time, the needle was out, and it was done.

Joey casually did a few more swipes with an alcohol swab and then took off the gloves. "One down." She patted it on the neck. "Good boy."

"You talking to the horse or me?" Colt kidded.

"I was talking to the horse, but you did good, too." Her green eyes were shining as she looked at him. "Whatever you said to him he must have liked—or maybe you just have a magic touch."

"So I've been told." Colt had meant the comment to be lighthearted, but for some reason, his voice no longer sounded playful.

Joey's smile faded, and her gaze locked on his with a look so intense and attentive, Colt was held captive by it. Even the horses in the barn seemed to grow quiet as if sensing the sudden current that ran between them.

But it only took a moment for the spell to break. Joey

unclipped the horse from the ties and led him back to the stall. After throwing in a flake of hay, she handed the lead shank to Colt, all business again. "The next one is in the next stall down. I'll start getting things ready."

Colt led the stallion out and clipped it to the cross ties the way he'd seen her do with the one before. The procedure went smoothly, and Colt was able to anticipate what Joey would need, making it go even faster. When the last horse was done, they tested the halters to make sure each worked properly.

"I think we've kept everybody awake long enough." Joey headed toward the door.

"Where do you want me positioned when the haulers come?"

Joey stopped and turned toward him with her head tilted. "Umm. A couple of miles away would be good. I thought you'd be long gone by then."

"This is dangerous. I think I should stay."

"No way." She continued walking again. "I have a barn crew arriving at zero eight hundred. I'm not sure how I'd explain a middle-aged man lurking around." She stood with one hand on the door, staring up at him with a look in her eyes that told him she wasn't kidding—and he wasn't staying.

"Ouch." He ran his hand through his hair. "I guess that's payback for the 'you look tired' comment earlier."

"No." She shook her head and looked sincere. "I don't hold a grudge."

Colt laughed. "Then you're different from most women."

Her eyes took on a hint of humor that made them sparkle in the light. "So I've been told."

Colt thought he saw her wink, but she'd hit the light switch before he knew for sure. Just as they stepped out into the cool, moonlit night, his phone vibrated.

"Go ahead."

"Hey. You sound wide-awake."

"Is that what you called to tell me?"

"Oh, ah, no. They've got some movement at the mosque." Colt stopped walking, and Joey did, too. "What kind of movement?"

"They've loaded two big wooden tack boxes into a van." Colt was getting ready to pull the phone away from his ear and update Joey, but she was looking at her phone and reading a text. Her eyes met his and she mouthed the words, "The money."

"Do we have video?"

"Watching it as we speak."

"What about a tracking device?"

"Wes got a device on the truck, but not on the crates."

"Wes? What's Wes doing on this?"

"He insisted, and I didn't feel like getting my ass kicked trying to stop him."

Blake didn't have to say anything else. Weston Armstrong was still active duty but was home on a short leave. He'd shown up at their last op in New Mexico, and then again on the chopper when they were being evacuated from the building. And now, here he was again. The man should have been home relaxing, but he just couldn't stay away.

Like Colt, Wes was from Texas. And like Colt, he thrived on danger and excitement. Maybe that's why they'd hit it off so well from the very first time they met. Colt couldn't think of a better man for the job. Other than the fact that he was way too willing to take risks, Wes was a man who would get the mission done.

"Tell him he needs some R and R when this is over."

"This *is* R and R for Wes." Blake laughed. "Don't you think he's enjoying crawling around on his stomach out there to put a tracking device on a van? He'll come back here for a hot shower and a warm meal instead of an MRE and a latrine. He's in heaven."

"Okay, but keep a tight rein on him. We know where those boxes are most likely going, so as long as we can keep an eye on the van, we're good."

"We do?"

"Yeah." He shot a quick look at Joey again. "I'm right up the road. I'll fill you in when I get there."

"Now? Don't cut anything short on our account."

Colt turned his back to Joey a moment and spoke in a low tone. "Thank you for the call. See you in a bit."

After hanging up, he turned to Joey. "Sorry about that. You get an update, too?"

"I have someone keeping an eye on the mosque—in an unofficial capacity. He just said there's some movement."

"My guys have full surveillance on it, so we've got video and tagged the van."

"That's great."

"I'm going to head out—"

"Okay," she interrupted him. "See ya."

"*If* you're sure you're okay here."

"I'm sure." She looked up at him. "Like I said, I've got four crewmen coming in. One of them is a big guy no one will want to mess with.

Colt remembered Dan, whom she had talked to earlier. He looked like the kind of man who could take care of things if necessary.

They stopped beside Colt's truck. "Besides, this is the easy part."

Colt nodded. "It *should* be, but you never know. Just when you least expect—"

"Look." She turned around to face him. "The men driving the truck probably aren't even aware of what's going on. They're picking up horses, dropping off two tack boxes, and they're on their way."

"Yeah. You make it sound simple."

"That's because it is."

He stared into her unwavering, determined eyes and knew there was no sense saying anything else. "Okay. I have a report to write up for the President. I'll touch base with you tomorrow about your recommendations."

"Sounds good. Night, Colt."

He turned to leave. "Stay safe, Joey."

Chapter 18

Sunday

Joey went back into the house and glanced at the clock on the wall in the library. It was almost one o'clock in the morning. She didn't feel like sleeping now but knew she should try to rest for a few hours.

Instead of going to bed, she grabbed a blanket and a pillow from a closet and headed to the couch in Scott's library. For some reason she slept better in there—maybe because it had always been his favorite room. Sleeping in their bedroom made her miss him, but here, she could feel his presence.

After checking the security cameras and making sure everything was quiet, she sat down and stared at her phone. Despite what she had told Colt, she didn't want her employees to show up too early and have the barn looking spotless by nine o'clock like they usually did.

Even though she assumed the haulers were just being hired to transport the horses, she had to make sure she presented the image of an overwhelmed widow trying to make ends meet, in case they were questioned.

Making her decision, she sent some texts, set her alarm,

and closed her eyes. But as exhausted as she was, sleep did not come. Her mind whirled and danced and would not stop replaying snippets of scenes from days' past. She rolled over and listened to the steady ticking of the clock on the mantle and wished for the ten-thousandth time that it was the heartbeat of her husband.

But it wasn't, and never would be again. Ten long years had passed since she'd last felt that steady rhythm beneath her cheek, yet not a night passed that she did not long for it. As a lone tear escaped from the corner of her eye, she thought about the changes that had occurred over the past decade. In some ways, time had flown; and in others, it seemed to have stood still.

The transformation at Valhalla was the most noticeable. When she and Scott had moved into his ancestral home as newlyweds, it had been neglected and in disrepair. Together, they had restored it room by room and built a thriving equine boarding facility.

After he'd died, Joey had concentrated on the horses and helping others as a way to deal with her pain. When she'd been recruited to serve as an operative for TF2, she'd jumped in with both feet, willing to do anything to keep her mind off her loss.

Joey listened to the sound of the furnace kick on and tried to concentrate on something else. *Anything else*, she told herself.

That's when her weary brain latched onto Nicholas Colton. She shook her head to clear the image of his haunting black eyes and crooked smile, but her exhausted brain wouldn't let go. In fact, the tighter she closed her eyes, the clearer she saw him, causing her heart to race and the thought of sleep to fade even further away.

She'd thought that her sentimental, romantic side was dead—or at least sedated—ever since Scott had died. But something about Colt stirred feelings that had been inactive and unresponsive for the past decade.

It's just a temporary infatuation, she told herself. Colt, after all, was not your average, run-of-the-mill type of guy. He exuded power. Strength. And a rare combination of intensity and calmness that Joey found both intimidating and infatuating.

Although she'd read all about his exploits and experience in his file, no amount of record-keeping could equal the real thing. She'd known within the first minute of meeting him that he was the type of man who could save your life—or take it. Yet she could still feel the gentleness of his touch when he'd wiped away her tears. His hands were tough, calloused from hard work. But rough as his fingers appeared on the outside, the feel of them was tender and kind.

He was a lot like Scott in that regard. Strong. Handsome. Kind. A man who would not flinch or hesitate to make a decision that could affect the nation for years to come. A man who would be willing to lend a strong arm to lean on if the necessity arose.

Joey didn't like where her thoughts were taking her, yet she found it impossible to think of anything else. After ten years of loneliness and isolation, her emotions were all wielding together into an overwhelming surge of confusion and yearning. This new awareness that she could *feel* again was an unfamiliar sensation that was proving to be both comforting and disconcerting.

Should she welcome it?

Or fight it?

Joey finally began to relax, and it seemed only a few minutes later that the phone beeped for her to awake. She groaned and sat up, wiping the sleep from her eyes.

After splashing her face with water and braiding her hair, she made her way down to the barn. She fed the horses and started cleaning stalls, making sure to leave a mess in the aisle. Right at nine o'clock, the gate monitor pinged, announcing that someone wanted to enter.

Joey scanned the transportation truck in the monitor and pushed the button to open the gate. Just as she expected, a large, air-conditioned eighteen-wheeler crawled up the driveway, made a slow turn in the circular driveway, and came to a stop by the front entrance.

Two Hispanic-looking men got out and went about the business of opening the storage area without so much as a good morning. "Where do you want?" one asked in broken English as he pointed to a large tack box.

"In that empty stall." Joey directed him to the stall nearest the office.

When they were done putting the first box on a dolly and rolling it into the stall, she unclipped the latch and waited for them to leave. Then she threw open the lid and stared at rows of one hundred dollar bills neatly stacked inside.

Hearing sound of footsteps drawing nearer behind her, she closed the trunk and pulled two combination locks out of her pocket. When the two men wheeled the next box in, she didn't even bother to check it. She knew the cartel was good for the money. It was in their best interests to have this transaction go smoothly. This was all part of a plan—a plan she had to stop.

One of the men suddenly approached with a clipboard of papers, which he shoved toward her. She signed for the boxes, and he gave her a receipt. Then he flipped to the next page.

"Three horses."

Joey nodded. "Which one do you want first?"

He pulled out one of the sheets of paper and clipped it to the front. "Bay colt with white star."

Joey showed them the stall, then dug through her folder of paperwork to hand to the man with the clipboard. He seemed to be checking the paperwork carefully, which Joey took as a sign that he was part of a legitimate business that had been unknowingly pulled into a nefarious transaction.

After the first horse had been loaded and signed off on, the two men headed back into the barn to retrieve the second one. Joey followed them to point out the correct stall. She was watching them lead the stallion out when the buzzer for the front gate hummed again.

Irritated at the interruption, she walked into her office and pushed the button for the speaker, while looking at the camera. "Yes?"

A handsome man—possibly in his late twenties—smiled into the camera and waved. "Hi there. We're the plumbers you called."

Joey's eyes drifted to the side of the van that read, "PFT

Plumbing Services."

"You must have the wrong address. I didn't call a plumber."

"Really?" The man pointed to the figure in the passenger seat. "Because *he* says you did."

The image of Colt appeared in the frame as he leaned over and waved. He wore a smile on his face, but his tone was serious. "Be a good girl and open the gate."

Joey's blood pressure surged. She was just about to tell him to get lost when the man with the clipboard came in and started waving it around, indicating that he needed the paperwork for the next stallion. Not having time to argue, and afraid that Colt would cause a scene, she hit the button to open the gate.

Chapter 19

"Now let me handle this," Colt said. "She might be a little pissed."

"Whatever you say, bro." Wes spit some tobacco out the window as they made their way up the long lane.

Both sets of eyes fell on the woman in the faded blue jeans when they rounded the last curve. She wore a flannel shirt and a ball cap with a single, long braid hanging out the back, and was busy signing papers when they pulled up.

"Damn, bro. You forgot to mention she's hot."

"She's off limits. Don't even think about it."

"Why?" Wes shifted his gaze over to Colt for just a moment. "Oh, I get it. This is where you spent most of last night."

"It's not what you think." Colt unclicked his seatbelt.

"What I'm thinking is I just found the woman of my dreams."

"Don't get any ideas, *son*." Colt slapped a ball cap with a PFT Plumbing logo onto his head. "She's at least ten years your senior."

"Even better. I love older women." Wes laughed, seeming to sense Colt's irritation. "How about we change places and *I* play the role of Mr. Plumber?"

Colt gripped the door handle. "Just start thinking with your big head and take care of your end of things like we discussed."

He slid out of the seat and slammed the door shut with a little more force than necessary. Then he opened the back door and grabbed a toolbox, before walking over to where Joey stood signing papers on a clipboard. "You got a leak, ma'am?"

Joey lifted her head and glowered at him before nodding toward the main door. "The bathroom on the right."

Colt nodded and walked into the barn whistling, expecting to see the workers she had claimed were coming in. But the interior was silent—and a bit of a mess. A wheelbarrow sat outside one stall with dirty straw hanging over the sides. Two bales of hay had been cut open but had not yet been put into cribs. Mud and straw lay scattered in the aisle.

Colt heard the conversation of the men outside grow louder, then the banging of doors as they got into the truck. A few moments later, Joey came walking into the barn.

Before she had time to say anything, he turned to face her. "I thought you had a crew coming in."

"I told them to come in later." She turned and began to coil a lead shank in a stiff, agitated way that suggested she was trying very hard to keep her anger in check. "I didn't want everything looking clean and organized. I'm a poor, desperate widow, remember?"

"You were here by *yourself?*" Colt's voice thundered above the noise the truck was making as it prepared to leave.

Joey swung around to face him, now holding a pitchfork in her hand. Every inch of her body spoke of agitation and defiance. "Not that it's any of *your* business, but I didn't want my employees involved in this."

"I would think making sure you don't get hurt or killed in the middle of a money laundering operation might be considered *my* business."

She stuck out her chin, and met his gaze with green eyes that flickered and sparked with ferocity. "Excuse me, but I believe I'm perfectly capable of forming my own opinion without the aid of yours. And the decisions I make about my business are *my* business—not yours."

"Aw. Isn't this cute? A little spat." Wes had walked in unnoticed as the truck pulled out. He now stood with his hands in his pockets, one shoulder leaning against a stall door as if he were enjoying a show.

"Who's the dickhead?" Joey tilted her head toward Wes without taking her eyes off Colt.

Colt had the urge to laugh, swiftly followed by the inclination to cringe when he observed Joey's expression. The calm, cool, always-in-control woman had transformed into something that reminded him of a junkyard dog snarling at the end of its chain. Even Wes, who was over six feet tall and built like a farmer's son, saw the look and took a step back to get out of range of those violent eyes—and the pitchfork.

Realizing this situation was going to require some quick thinking and tact, Colt put a seductive smile on his face and placed his hand on Joey's arm while removing the dangerous barn implement. He even gave her a little squeeze for good measure. "*Calm down*. We're here to—"

"Get. Your. Fucking. Hand. Off. Me." Joey shrugged his arm away, but at the same time moved forward, so they were now standing toe to toe and just inches apart. "If someone hired you as my babysitter, I've yet to be informed about it." She punched her finger into his chest to emphasize her words as she talked.

"*Whoa.*"

Colt heard the word escape from Wes as the man took another step back, and he knew then and there that this scene was going to be repeated and embellished for years to come at Phantom Force Tactical. It would go something like this: *Hey, did you hear the story about the time Colt got his ass whipped by a woman? Well, let me tell you about it…*

"Go wait in the van, Wes."

"Yeah. Go wait in the van, Wes." Joey repeated the words but never took her sparking green eyes off Colt.

"Yes, ma'am." Wes tipped his hat like the good Southern gentleman he was and then backed up another few steps until he was out of sight. Colt guessed he was probably running by now, and sure enough, the van door slammed about two seconds later.

"Who sent you here?"

"No one *sent* me here," Colt countered as he placed the pitchfork against the wall out of her reach. He wanted to tell her to calm down, but remembered those words hadn't worked too well earlier so he didn't. "Wes and I were just heading back to headquarters from the mosque…"

"And you decided to check up on me."

"No-o-o. We decided we wanted to make sure we knew where that truck was going."

"The horses are tagged."

"But the truck wasn't."

"But it is now?"

"Yes, that's what Wes was doing while you were in here yelling at me."

"I wasn't yelling."

Colt didn't respond other than to raise his eyebrows and cock his head to the side.

"Okay. Maybe I was." She looked up at him with a somewhat contrite look on her face. "I don't like to be second-guessed."

Colt held his hands up in the air, palms out. "Message received, loud and clear. But I wasn't second-guessing. I was going by and thought that it wouldn't hurt to know if that trucking company is legit or not."

A young girl walked around the corner just then and, noticing Joey, said, "Who's the hunky guy in the van?" Then her eyes fell on Colt. "Oh. Sorry to interrupt."

"He's a *plumber*." Joey shot Colt another dirty look. "The bathroom sink is leaking."

"Again?" The girl shook her head and kept walking.

"You really have a leak?" Colt leaned in close and spoke in a low voice.

"It doesn't matter. It's just a drip."

"No. I'll take a look."

"You don't have to do that." She grabbed his arm, as he picked up his box of tools. "It's just a leak. It's been like that for years."

"So it won't hurt to take a look." He turned toward the bathroom and glanced back over his shoulder. "Right?"

Joey shook her head in exasperation and turned to the office to gather her paperwork together. After about twenty minutes, she reappeared in the doorway.

"Do you know what you're doing?"

Colt detected a thawing in her tone, but he still wouldn't go so far as to call it warm.

"Not really." He answered while lying on his back on the floor, halfway in the cabinet. "But I think I stopped the leaks."

"*Leaks?* As in plural of leak?"

"Yes, as in plural of leak." He sat up, narrowly missing hitting his head. "It was dripping down here, too."

"And you fixed it?" She looked at the faucet skeptically, then bent down and put her hand under the spigot. "I guess you did."

Colt crawled out and started putting tools back in the toolbox. "Just a loose fitting."

"Well, thanks. Send me the bill." Her expression revealed a hint of reconciliation now, though he could sense she was still annoyed.

"I'll do that." He ran his eyes up and down her tattered jeans and threadbare flannel shirt. "Hope you can afford it."

She actually smiled when she realized he was joking about her financial situation. "Sad state of affairs around here. Other than the three and a half million dollars cash in the next stall, I'm a little short on funds. Do you take installment payments?"

Colt wanted to say he'd take it out in trade but he held his tongue. "Someone coming to pick those up?" He nodded toward the trunks of money.

"I tried to talk the government into giving it to charity, but they shot that idea down."

Colt grinned at the look in her eyes. They seemed to sparkle with humor now. "Well, it was worth a try."

"Things are going to start happening fast now." Her expression—and her voice—suddenly grew serious. "They made the transaction for a reason."

"I know." Colt rubbed the stubble on his chin. "And the President and other agencies are going to want an update. I'm going to take Wes back to headquarters and head to DC. Hopefully, intel from the transaction will start trickling in, and we can start putting together the pieces of the puzzle."

"I'm inclined to do the same. No sense in sitting here waiting for a lead. I'd rather be out looking for one." She was quiet for a moment. "You hear anything back about the van that picked up the money from the mosque?"

"It went from the mosque to a stable in Fairfax. They dropped off the trunks of money and then returned it to a rental agency. We're tracing who rented the van and who owns the farm now. There's a chance they don't know anything, but we're checking it out. I'll pass on the information we find to you and the other agencies involved.

"Good deal." She said the words strongly enough, but she was staring over his shoulder with an intense look on her face as if her mind were a million miles away.

"What's wrong?"

Her eyes jerked back to his. "Nothing. Why?"

"You look like something's troubling you. What's up?"

Joey shrugged. "No. Nothing."

"If you say so." Colt rolled his eyes and made sure his expression reflected that he didn't believe it.

"Okay." She looked up at him. "To tell you the truth, I'm a little uneasy about the information you share and with whom."

"You don't trust the President?"

"Yes, I trust the President. And I trust the President to know who I don't trust."

Colt remembered his conversation with the commander-in-chief. "He mentioned something about DHS not being on his favorites list."

"Mine either." She bit her lip and shrugged and then quickly changed the subject. "I'm sorry about earlier, and thanks again for fixing the leak. I forgot what it's like to have a man around."

Colt reached out and touched her arm. "Anything you need, you let me know." His voice was much lower and more serious than he'd planned, so he tried to lighten his comment. "We have a whole team of handy men at Phantom Force."

"Thanks." A smile broke out on her face. "I'll keep that in mind."

They started walking toward the door. "Should I apologize to your buddy?"

"Hell, no."

"I don't want him to think I'm always like that."

"Why?" He stopped and looked down at her. "There's nothing wrong with a strong woman."

"Strong women don't lose their cool like that. Did you hear what I called him?"

Colt worked hard to suppress the laughter that welled up inside him at the thought of it. "Wes has been called worse, believe me."

Before he'd even finished his sentence, Joey had walked out the door and headed toward the van. When she reached the driver's side window, she tapped on the glass. For a minute, Colt didn't think Wes was going to roll down the window.

"Sorry about earlier," she said after he'd put it down about a quarter of the way.

"No problem." Wes gave her a Texas-sized grin. "Colt's got a special knack for pissing off women."

"I'm Joey, by the way." She stuck her fingers through the window, forcing him to put it the rest of the way down so he could shake her hand.

"Nice to meet you. I'm Wes."

"So you got the truck tagged?"

"Yes, ma'am. They'll be tracking it back at headquarters."

"Great. Thank you."

Colt hopped into the van and leaned over to Joey. "We'd better get going. I'll touch base with you this afternoon."

"Sounds good. Nice to meet you, Wes."

Joey waved as Wes put the van in drive and moved forward. As soon as Wes rolled up the window, Colt turned to him. "Thanks for throwing me under the bus, bro."

"All's I've got to say is that for an old man, you are a freaking stud." Wes raised his right hand in the air and lowered it while bowing his head, three times. "I bow to your prowess. You are the *boss!*"

"What are you talking about?"

"What in the hell did you do to turn her around like that, you old dog? I need to hear your secret. She was downright cheerful!"

"What can I say?" Colt put his sunglasses down over his eyes and sat back in the seat, obviously trying not to smile. "I'm a plumber."

Wes's face beamed with boyish enthusiasm as he looked over at Colt. "You saying you checked her pipes or something?"

"Not only did I check them." Colt shot him a sly grin. "I *fixed* them to her satisfaction."

"Da-a-m-n." Wes shook his head. "You should get a new handle. You know, like...Handyman." He took his hands off the steering wheel to clap his hands together. "That's it, Old Handy—"

Colt interrupted him. "I don't need a new handle. And I don't need anything about today getting back to the guys at Phantom Force. Got it?"

"If you say so, boss." Wes became uncharacteristically quiet before talking again. "Too bad she's married. That's a bummer."

Colt spoke while looking out the window. "She's not exactly married."

"I saw the ring, dude. On her left hand. In case you didn't know, that's where they put them when they're married."

Colt ignored the comment. "You ever hear the name Captain Scott Hanson?"

"Sounds familiar."

"Army Ranger..."

"Okay, yeah." Wes nodded his head. "Wasn't he the one that went in and rescued a dozen or so wounded Marines in Iraq?"

"That's the one."

"That's her husband?"

"Was." Colt cleared his throat. "He didn't make it out."

"That's right. I remember it now. He called in air support that never came. They were pinned down for hours."

"Right. When reinforcements finally did come, he was shot up pretty badly. Died on the chopper, but the unit made it out."

The van grew quiet. "That was a long time ago. I think I was in high school."

"Ten years."

"Wow." Wes looked over at Colt. "And she still wears a wedding ring?"

Colt shrugged and turned his head again to the view out the window.

Joey went back into the barn to talk to her crew who were now standing around, looking at the mess. "Sorry about this. I was trying to help."

Dan walked by carrying a bale of hay in each hand. "I have an idea. Next time, let us do it."

Joey laughed. "Okay. You got it."

"Whose tack boxes are those?" A girl named Patricia stood by the stall door where the large trunks of money had been placed.

Joey's eyes darted to the open stall door. She'd locked both trunks, but forgot to close the stall door. "The haulers dropped them off for a farm down in Warrenton. They're coming to pick them up today." She started walking into the office. "That reminds me. They made me promise I would put them in a locked stall."

"Must be some expensive saddles in there."

"Yeah," Joey said over her shoulder. "Worth a few thousand at least." She pulled another combination lock out of a drawer and affixed it to the stall door.

"Here's the name of the man coming." She handed the girl a slip of paper. "Ask for his ID."

Patricia took the paper and nodded. "Okay."

"He's the only one who knows the combination to the lock." Joey glanced down at her phone. "I'll send you a text later and give you an idea of when he'll be here."

"Okay. You working on a story today?"

Joey nodded. "I'm going to change clothes and head out. Not sure how long I'll be gone so thanks for holding down the fort."

"Congratulations on yesterday."

Joey had to pause and think. So much had happened since the horse show, she'd almost forgotten about it. "Thanks."

Chapter 20

Colt walked into the headquarters of Phantom Force and headed toward a small kitchen area. The room was buzzing with activity and conversation in its usual pulse of orderly mayhem and organized chaos. Long rows of tables were filled with men on phones and computers, while a few men dressed in black tactical pants and shirts stood talking by a row of coffee pots.

Grabbing a Red Bull and cracking the top, Colt sat down on a comfortable chair and tried to rub the sleep from his eyes.

"Glad to see you're awake." Blake sat down beside him.

"I'm not sure about that." Colt massaged his temples and yawned.

"Well, you will be when you hear what I have to tell you."

Colt's head jerked up at the intensity of Blake's tone. "Go ahead."

"I met with one of our contacts in DC this morning. The rental van with the money from the mosque went to a farm in

Fairfax called Bismillah Stables before being picked up by the horse transportation company."

"Bismillah? That's unique." Colt's relaxed grin disappeared as he processed the information.

"That's about it. Unique."

"So did we find who the owners are and who rented the van?"

He shuffled through some papers. "The owner and name on the van rental agreement are one and the same. A Dennis Morgan."

"Doesn't ring a bell with me."

Blake nodded toward a nearby desk where a man stared intently at a computer screen. Podge has some background.

"He's an attorney in Washington and is gone most of the time," Podge said. "He's married to Donya Abbasi. She runs the horse business."

"Find anything on her?"

"Not yet. No criminal history on either of them."

"Well, I'm afraid *I* have some bad news."

Podge looked up from the computer and Blake focused his attention on Colt.

"According to one of my contacts, the elimination of Carlos Valdez created a void that has been filled by the *El Soldado* gang.

"Say *what?*"

"That's right. They're recruiting from the Mexican army as we speak. Probably stealing weapons and technology, as well."

Podge let out his breath. "Can things get any worse?" Then he held up his hands. "Don't answer that."

Blake put his hands behind his head and leaned back with his eyes closed as if to concentrate. "So we have an unknown group with radical ties, most likely with expertise in tunnel building, explosives training, and your run-of-the-mill terrorist tactics, working with *El Soldado*, who is flush with money, drugs, and violent, former soldiers who hate America.

"I guess you could say that is it in a nutshell."

"It's conceivable that we're up against a military just as strong—or stronger—than a lot of countries," Blake said. "At what point do we warn the public about this?"

"Warn them about what?" Podge said. "That something bad *might* happen, but we don't know what or where or by whom?"

"True." Blake looked over at Colt. "Didn't you say the White House has authorized patrols to check for gamma-ray and neutron detection?"

"Yeah. They're riding around in unmarked vans, but not sure how effective that will be without any real intel."

"We need a lead."

"Tell you what," Colt said. "I'm going to take a shower and maybe grab a couple minutes of shuteye."

"Really?" Blake's head went up and so did most of the others in the room. Colt's ability to keep going after most men dropped was legendary. Not only was he insensible to fatigue, he never seemed to understand how or why other men needed so much rest. Then again, it wasn't clear when or *if* he had slept since being released from the hospital earlier in the week.

Colt was halfway across the room when he stopped to pull

his vibrating phone out of his pocket. "Looks like I need to be at Langley at sixteen hundred hours."

"Maybe they have something new?" Blake sounded hopeful.

"Maybe." Colt shoved the phone back in place while reevaluating his need for rest.

"Close your eyes for a couple of minutes," Blake said, reading his mind. "You never know when you're going to get another chance. We'll keep searching for anything we can find from this end."

Colt unbuttoned his shirt and ripped it from his pants as he strode toward the spare bedroom he routinely used. "Keep me posted."

Chapter 21

———

Sunday
1500 hours

Colt picked up the phone on the first ring because he was sitting in traffic, and could barely control his pent-up energy. "What's up? Something new?"

"Yes." Blake's voice sounded strained. "It happened."

"What happened?"

"A local company just reported a missing shipment and truck.

"You're shitting me." Colt hit the steering wheel with both hands. Blake didn't even have to tell him what was in the delivery truck. "Dammit!"

"How much was taken?"

"We're not sure. It was called in literally minutes ago. The truck is two hours late."

"Two *hours?*"

"Yeah. But they talked to the driver a little over an hour ago, and he claimed everything was fine. He was just running behind."

"Okay. Where was he headed?"

"He was hauling material from a hospital in Blanford County and heading west to drop it off for transport to a waste facility."

Colt heard clicking as Blake apparently typed something on a keyboard.

"They're trying to find the truck now. It's equipped with a tracking device so it shouldn't take too long."

"What are we looking at exactly?"

"Waste from an old external-beam radiation machine system." There was a slight pause. "According to Podge's sources, enough to create a scare if used with a Radiological Dispersal Device, the RDD."

"So he's familiar with it?"

"Yes. He said it's most likely Cobalt-60, typically used in radiation therapy in hospitals."

"July like Joey predicted," Colt muttered.

"What did you say?"

"Nothing." Colt let out an agonizingly long breath. "What are we looking at here? What are the possibilities as far as the number of deaths?"

"Impossible to predict," Blake said. "The extent of contamination would depend on the size of the explosive, the amount of radioactive material used, and even the weather conditions."

"And the number of people that are in the immediate area, I guess"

"Exactly. Those closest to the RDD would possibly sustain injuries due to the explosion, but as the actual radioactive material spreads, it becomes less concentrated and less harmful," Blake said. "Whoever did this better know what they're doing, or we won't have to worry about it."

"What do you mean?"

"A person handling an unshielded single-source rod would receive a lethal dose in about a minute."

"But if they *do* know what they're doing, we're going to be facing Hell with the lid off."

"Agreed. Chaos. Terror. Pandemonium." Blake inhaled deeply. "Not to mention contaminated property, so we'd be looking at economic disruptions over a wide area and a lengthy and costly cleanup."

Colt hit the steering wheel again. "Hell, when we were just talking a simple IED, it was going to be enough to cause chaos. Now we're talking about the reality of a dirty bomb."

"I'm afraid so," Blake said.

"So, let's lay this out. The first thing they need for a bomb is a source that is sufficiently radioactive to create direct damage or at least massive disruption."

"They can check that off their list, apparently."

"Second, the source has to be transportable with enough shielding to protect the carrier, but not so much that it will be too heavy to maneuver."

"It was most likely packaged that way since it was being legally transported," Blake said.

"And third, the radiological source has to be sufficiently dispersible, so that it can contaminate the area around the explosion."

"I'll have to check with Podge on that one, but I'm pretty sure the cobalt would do the job."

"What about Homeland Security? Are they keeping it quiet?"

"So far."

Colt let out his breath as he thought about the chaos that could be caused if the media caught wind of the story and reported it without the facts, creating hysteria. "Are they going to be able to keep it that way?"

"They're working on it. If there's one thing that agency is skillful at, it's spinning a story and hiding the facts."

"I feel better already," Colt said sarcastically. "There's going to come a point when we want the press to be in on this, so they can inform the public about the implications and proper precautions."

"Agreed. I don't think we're there yet, though."

Colt pulled the phone away from his ear when it beeped with another call. "I have a call coming in from Joey. Gotta go."

"Who's he?"

Colt didn't reply. "Call me if you hear anything."

He hung up and answered Joey's call. Her voice came across as calm, but impatient. "You heard about the delivery truck?"

"Just that it's missing."

"Well, they've found it."

"Where?"

"At the bottom of a pond."

"So did the driver crash into a pond? Or was it put in the pond?"

"It looks like we're supposed to think it crashed into the pond."

"But you don't think so?"

"Let's just say it's a little too convenient."

"Is the stuff still in it?"

"They're getting divers together now. There's no other way to check. And with all the security protocols they have to go through, it's going to take some time."

"Time we don't have." Colt drummed the steering wheel with his free hand. "We have to move forward under the assumption that it's gone."

"I agree."

"Which makes everything a little more urgent."

Joey remained silent. That was a fact that didn't require any further elaboration.

"What about the media? Are they onto this?"

"From what I've been told, the usual vultures started making calls when it came over the scanner, but all they know is that a delivery truck is in a pond. Since it's Friday afternoon, I think there's a fair chance no one will follow up on it."

"Did we identify the driver yet?"

"Working on it."

"What do you need me to do?"

"I'm heading to the scene. The President is gathering his security advisors and I'm sure he wants you there. Some of them were already on their way out of town for the weekend so it may take a little longer than usual to gather everyone."

"Okay. I was heading there anyway. Keep me updated on your end." He pushed the *end* button as a feeling of dread washed over him. The clock was ticking now. The terrorists had the material. It wouldn't take much time to put it into a device.

His thoughts drifted to the green-eyed woman who had predicted this outcome. At the time, it had seemed far-fetched. Now it was a fact. And it was the first step in a much larger plot that would have lasting ramifications for generations to come if they didn't stop it.

Colt breathed a sigh of relief when the road in front of him opened up a little. He pressed the gas pedal hard and took advantage of it while he could. If the people around him only knew what was going on, perhaps they'd pay attention to their loved ones a little more instead of wasting time sitting on this road, accomplishing nothing.

Chapter 22

Arman Sassani sat down at a corner booth and ordered a cup of coffee.

Out of the corner of his eye, he caught a glimpse of his reflection in the window, and had to force himself not to stare. Clean shaven and wearing a ball cap, he looked like any number of other men sitting in the diner. Yet, just this morning he had worn a full beard and looked like an entirely different person.

Nodding at the waitress when she set his coffee down, he glanced down at his phone before taking a sip. When it rang at the same moment, he almost spilled the entire mug as he hurried to answer.

"The clock is ticking," is all the man on the other end of the phone said.

Sassani put the phone closer to his ear. "You are certain?"

"The delivery you ordered has been made."

A smile spread across his face as his gaze landed on a print of the White House, hanging above the cash register. Surrounding him were the sounds of conversation and laughter from people who had no idea what was in store for them.

"We are on schedule if you wish to proceed." The man on the other end of the phone grew impatient at hearing only silence.

"Yes. Yes. Proceed. Is there enough time to make the necessary arrangements?"

"They tell me it can be done." There was a long pause. "But there is one little obstacle I think you should know about."

Sassani leaned back in the booth, trying to appear relaxed. "What is that?"

"Nicholas Colton."

"You are wrong, my friend." Sassani laughed softly. "He is in New Mexico dealing with our brothers there."

"He is here," was the simple reply.

Sassani swallowed hard and tried to control his emotions, but the thought of his arch nemesis being in the same town made him so angry, he wanted to shout into the phone. "How do you know?"

"The President sent for him."

"The President knows something?"

"He suspects something. Nothing more."

Sassani smiled at the waitress and waved her away when she started toward him with the coffee pot. He turned his head then and lowered his voice. "If he called in Colton, he knows more than you think."

"I believe I am in a position to be aware of what the President knows."

Sassani let out his breath. "I want Colton taken out of the

picture. Do you understand?"

"So do I, but it appears that task is a little more difficult than I had assumed."

"What do you mean?"

An exasperated sigh followed. "He was with someone that I needed eliminated last week. *El Soldado* lost five men."

Sassani could feel the heat rising through his body, and knew his face must be red from the suppressed rage. "Why was I not told of this sooner?"

"Like you, we thought he was in New Mexico."

Forcing a smile onto his face and nodding as if in a light-hearted conversation, Sassani spoke low so no one could hear. "If you cannot remove him by force, do it through legal channels."

"What do you mean?"

"I'll let you figure that out. We must continue to move forward."

"I understand."

Hanging up the phone, Sassani began to drum the table with his fingers, unable to control the adrenaline running through him. It was actually happening. All of the planning and pretending was going to pay off. In just a few days, America would be brought to its knees—and the blame would be cast south of the border.

Without realizing it, he laughed out loud. Stupid Americans—believing in their government to keep them safe and secure. They lived in a bubble.

Well, my country of infidels. The clock is ticking. Your bubble is about to burst.

Chapter 23

Colt slammed on the brakes for a red light and then glanced at his ringing phone. He rolled his eyes at the name that came up. It was Kelly, a girl he had dated for a short period of time.

Everyone, including her, had known it was only in an effort to forget the real love of his life, Jennifer Griffin—Griff—who had been killed on a mission in Afghanistan. Griff's death had hit him hard—so hard that he'd since given up on trying to get over it.

When he'd returned from that deployment, his younger sister Debra had introduced him to Kelly, one of her best friends from college. Even though she was going through a hard time, too, the fling had only lasted a month or two. Colt wasn't sure why it had lasted *that* long.

Kelly was a little flighty and silly, and was probably calling him because she'd broken up with another boyfriend. He figured she wanted company, sympathy, or sex—maybe all three. He didn't have time for any of them at the moment, but he felt a little sorry for her. *And if I don't answer, she'll call sis—and then I'll have an even bigger problem on my hands.*

He pushed the button. "Make it quick, Kelly, I'm headed to a meeting."

"Hi, Colt. I ah, need you to come over."

"What?"

"Um, I think someone broke into my house."

He could tell from the tone of her voice that she wasn't kidding. She sounded strange. Scared.

"Are you there? Don't go inside. Call the police."

"I did." She stopped abruptly and he could sense she was on the verge of crying. "They umm…came and said they didn't find anything, but I think…someone was here."

Colt closed his eyes and kneaded his temples. "So you want me to take a look?"

"Would you? I mean, you're probably working."

Colt studied his watch. Traffic was light now, and he'd made up some of the lost time by being heavy on the gas pedal. Kelly lived in a quiet neighborhood no more than two miles off his route, so it wouldn't take long to swing by, check it out, and be back on his way to another security meeting.

With all her faults, Kelly wasn't the type to lead him there on false pretenses. She would come right out and say if all she craved was a little comfort. It concerned him that she might truly need his help.

"I'm heading your way. See you in about fifteen minutes—but I *can't* stay."

"I understand. I'll be waiting outside. You remember the

address, right?"

Before he had time to reply that he remembered how to get there, she said, "Sixty-six Oak Drive."

"Okay. Stay put."

Ten minutes later, Colt drove up the quiet tree-lined street and pulled into the driveway of the third house on the left, a small, blue Cape Cod. He thought he'd told Kelly to wait for him outside, but he didn't see any sign of her. *Maybe she decided it was safe and went in.*

As he got out of the truck, his gaze fell on her mailbox. It was black with her last name and the address in gold lettering. Something caused him to pause and stare at it for a moment, but a nagging feeling inside him made him turn back to the house.

With his head on a swivel, he reached down and touched the Glock he had in a concealed holster under his shirt, but didn't draw it. He walked to the back, knocked on the screen door, and then shouted. "Kelly. It's Colt. I'm here."

When he didn't hear any reply, he tried the door and found it unlocked. *Geez, Kelly, at least lock the damn door.*

Stepping into a small foyer, he called again, and then proceeded through the hallway to the kitchen. Almost instantly, he saw a foot sticking out from behind the center island, causing him to pull his pistol. "Kel? You here?"

No answer. Colt rushed forward and let out a groan when he saw the foot belonged to Kelly. He bent down to check her pulse, but he knew she was dead. A small red dot on her temple and the pool of blood was evidence enough, but the pale face and staring eyes confirmed the belief.

"Put your hands up. Move slow."

Colt automatically put his hands in the air, then turned around to see two police officers standing in the doorway with their guns drawn and aimed at him.

"She's dead," he told them.

That announcement caused both officers to yell simultaneously. "Put down the weapon!"

"Calm down, guys. I'm a friend of hers." Colt talked with his hands in the air. "She called me here to check the house."

"Sure, buddy." One of the police officers walked up and snatched his Glock while the other told him to turn around. Both of them were portly and outweighed him by a good seventy-five pounds, if not more. "Hands behind your back."

Instead of turning around, Colt backed up with his hands still in the air. "No. You guys don't understand. Let me explain."

The heavier of the two officers gave him a shove. "You'll have plenty of time to explain your story to a judge. That's not what we're here for."

Colt sidestepped again and shook his head in exasperation. "Seriously, sir. I don't have time for this."

"The law doesn't run on your time schedule, buddy. You're under arrest."

"I'll give you my name, but we're going to have to clear this up in a way that doesn't involve me sitting at the station for a few hours."

Both officers laughed. "You just killed a woman. You're going to be sitting for more than a few hours."

"Killed a…?" Colt shook his head. "You don't understand.

She called me because she was scared and wanted me to check her house. She'd called the police, but they told her the house was clear." He looked down at the still form on the floor. "She wasn't convinced."

Both of the officers looked at each other and shook their heads. "Sure, she did."

"You mean you weren't called here earlier?"

They shook their heads. "We were called here for the sound of a gunshot, and we found you standing over a body with a weapon." The taller of the two men stood with both hands on his gun and a frown on his face. "Pretty sure anybody would come to the same logical conclusion."

Colt was only half-listening now as he tried to think. He'd thought Kelly's call had seemed strange, but had assumed she was just scared to go into the house. Had she been under duress instead? Had someone forced her to make that call, hoping to lure him here and set him up?

An image of the mailbox flashed in his mind again. He'd driven here by memory, not even paying attention to the address. When she'd told him sixty-six Oak Avenue, he'd not thought twice about it because all the streets in this development were named after trees. He'd gotten lost the first time he'd visited, and had driven up and down streets named Ash and Hickory and Elm. But the address on the mailbox was fifty-five *Maple* Drive. She'd been trying to give him a clue, but he hadn't caught it.

Colt stared down at the body. *Damn. I'm sorry, Kelly.*

He looked back up at the two cops standing with guns trained on him. This was not the time for regrets or to rethink what he could have done differently. "Okay. You win." He kept his hands up and spoke calmly. "I just have to grab some identification I left in my truck."

Before either officer had time to react or object, Colt walked out the door, trying to appear relaxed. He was glad he'd been taught to always back into a parking space so he could make a quick getaway, but when he rounded the corner, he saw that tactic wasn't going to do him much good. The police car was parked in front of him.

Switching instantly to another plan, he took off running, pulling his phone out of his pocket at the same time. He didn't know if anyone from Phantom Force could get to him in time to help, but he was going to give it a try.

Just as his foot touched the sidewalk around the side of the house, a black Jeep slammed on its brakes and came to a stop. The window rolled down and Joey waved. "Hey, need a lift?"

Chapter 24

C olt didn't have time to question why Joey was there or how she had timed her arrival so perfectly. She pressed the unlock door button, and he jumped in. "Go!"

She hit the gas and looked over at him. "To where?"

Colt turned around and saw the police jumping into their car.

"Turn left here." At the same time, he pushed a number on his phone.

"I have a situation," he said as soon as Blake answered.

"Let me guess. You slept with the police chief's wife."

"No, actually, I've just been framed for murder."

"You what?"

"You heard me. Kelly Olson."

"Is she dead?"

"Yes, she's dead! What the hell do you think *murder* means?" He glanced over at Joey, who was staring straight ahead, seemingly concentrating on the road. "Take a right and head out of town."

"Okay, take it easy." Blake did not seem the least bit disturbed. "Did you explain to the police who you are?"

"No."

"Why not?"

"Number one, I didn't get the feeling they were going to believe me. Number two, I don't have time to get dragged downtown to explain it. And number three, I don't want my cover blown over something that was obviously intended to do just that."

"They're probably tracing your call," Joey said nonchalantly, not bothering to turn her head.

"Who was that? Who are you with?"

"Not important. Listen, the first place they're going to look, after my house, is Phantom Force headquarters."

"Okay. Are you heading to the safe house?"

Again Colt looked over at Joey. "I'm not sure yet."

Blake must have thought his response was intentionally evasive in case someone was listening and didn't question him anymore. "You think it's tied to the bigger picture?"

"Possibly. I gotta go." Colt turned around in the seat but didn't see any signs that the police car had seen them turn off.

"I'm starting to hear scanner activity on the situation now," Blake said. "Interesting that they will be concentrating on apprehending a supposed murderer when there are much bigger things going on right under their noses."

"Yeah. Coincidences bother the hell out of me." Colt shot Joey another sideways glance, but she did not respond or display any emotion that would reveal she knew he was

talking about her. "See what you can find out on your end. I'll
check in later."

"Roger that."

Colt disconnected and sighed. Did this mean they were
getting close? Or was it just a coincidence that would now
complicate things? How was he going to track down leads
while trying to evade police with an arrest warrant? And how
was he going to get to his meeting at the White House?

Colt turned around in his seat to see if they were being
followed. He could hear sirens, but they weren't close enough
yet for him to see any lights. At the same time, he opened up
his phone and dumped the battery out into his hand. Every
second that passed would make it harder for him to evade the
police. There would be an APB out soon—if not already—
so that even police departments in neighboring jurisdictions
would be looking for him.

He shot a sideways glance at Joey. "So, speaking of
coincidences, you want to tell me how you just happened to
be driving by?"

"You probably won't believe me."

He sat back in the seat and exhaled. "Know what? You're
probably right."

"Where do you want me to go?" Her voice came across as
strained—but more frustrated than angry.

"Straight for now. Four more blocks, then right."

Joey made the turn and kept glancing into the rearview
mirror. "You probably have a safe house, but you don't want
me to know where it is because you don't trust me."

"Something like that."

Her hands gripped the steering wheel a little tighter. "We have to work together on this."

"Do we?"

Her jaw tightened. "I could take you to Valhalla."

"And then tell them where to find me? That would be convenient."

She turned her head toward him, disappointment stamped on her face. Then she gave a suit-yourself shrug and went back to concentrating on the road. "It's your call."

Sirens continued to increase by number and volume as they approached the edge of town. He had to make a decision. Valhalla was only a few miles from Phantom Force, so it was actually a convenient location to lay low and reorganize. "Okay, but take the back roads."

She nodded and pressed the gas a little harder, apparently hearing the sirens, too. They were approaching the last traffic signal in town, and then it would be a short drive on a highway before being able to take gravel roads the rest of the way.

When they were almost to the light, it turned yellow. Joey slammed on the brakes.

"Dammit!" Colt swore, then smiled and nodded and waved at two women on bicycles as they crossed the road so as not to look conspicuous. He turned around in his seat once the cyclists had passed, expecting to see flashing lights, but there was only a small red car behind them.

"Hit it," he said as soon as the light turned green.

"I know how to drive." The words had barely left her mouth when she reached out with her hand and grabbed his shoulder roughly. "Get down."

Colt didn't wait to see what had caused the alarm. He ducked down as far as the seatbelt would allow. A few moments later, he was able to see flashing lights reflecting off the dashboard and felt Joey slow down.

"Don't stop."

"Don't tell me what to do."

Colt rolled his eyes. "They most likely called in the color and the make of this vehicle."

"Maybe not." Joey waved at someone, but kept her foot on the gas, moving slowly. "They're setting up a roadblock. I think we're going to be the last car to get through."

Colt held his breath as the lights lit up the dashboard and reflected off the windows. After another few moments, Joey accelerated. "You can sit up now."

"Thanks."

They drove in silence, enveloped in a cloud of dust at the speed they were traveling down the dirt roads. Colt saw the sign for Valhalla and then the lane, but she drove right by. "Wasn't that it?"

"I'm going in the back way so my workers won't know I'm home." Joey kept her eyes on the road. "I told them I'd be gone for two or three days."

After traveling another half of a mile, Joey took a left at the next stop sign, and then another left into a lane that looked like an overgrown tractor trail. Colt recognized the house in the distance and realized they were indeed coming in from the back. The house sat between them and the barns where the workers were, so their approach would not be seen.

A couple of hundred feet farther, they came to a stone wall

with an iron gate marked clearly with *No Trespassing* signs. Joey dug a remote out of the center console and pushed a button, causing the gate to whine and creak open. She drove at a slow speed toward the house, apparently trying to create as little disturbance of dust on the road as possible.

When they were close, she hit a button on her visor, opening the door to a garage attached to the house. It had looked large upon their approach, but once they were inside, Colt was surprised that the length was only as long as the Jeep. In fact, the fender almost touched the built-in shelves that lined the wall in front of them.

Joey didn't turn off the engine, but opened her door. When he took off his seatbelt, she said, "Sit tight a sec."

Hopping out, she went over to a small workbench on the wall, pulled out a drawer, and appeared to push a button.

The wall of shelves in front of him made a creaking noise as they opened into a secondary garage.

Joey got back in and put the Jeep in drive. "Scott built this. He was a bit overprotective."

Colt looked around but didn't say anything. It was quite ingenious. The garage had simply been split in half with a fake wall and new door. Joey opened her door to get out.

"Everybody thinks I'm out of town for a few days, so we shouldn't be bothered in here."

"That's convenient."

Joey had no response to that. She opened the door to the house and kept walking, not waiting to see if Colt followed or not.

Chapter 25

The house of Valhalla was so massive that Colt didn't even know where he was until they entered the library where they'd met previously.

"I'm up for some coffee, how about you?" Joey walked past him toward another door.

"I'm not here for a social visit." He knew she was trying to stall.

"Have a seat." She kept walking, ignoring him. "You take it black?"

Colt shook his head and put his hands in the air in resignation. "Sure. Black is fine."

He paced the entire time she was gone, trying to figure out who would have killed Kelly and framed him. Finally, Joey appeared, carrying a small tray with two mugs and a carafe of coffee. She handed him a cup. "You can sit."

"No. I'll stand."

She took a sip of coffee, then looked up at him. "Okay. Should *I* start? Or do you want to?"

"How about you start?" He eyed her warily. "I can't wait to hear why you just happened to be driving by a house in the suburbs at the exact same time I just happened to be getting framed for murder."

Joey stared up at the ceiling and bit her lip while thinking, then looked over at him. "I can't answer that. It's classified."

Colt almost spit the coffee he was drinking across the room.

"You've got to be kidding me! Should I call the President and see if it's okay for you to tell me?" Colt pulled his phone out of his pocket.

"Look, I know you have friends in high places and hold top security clearance, but this is...really sensitive."

For the first time, he thought he discerned a twinge of fear in her voice, but he was too angry to care. He sat the mug down hard on a stand and turned toward the door. "Thanks for the coffee. I think I'll take my chances on the run."

She grabbed his arm. "No. Wait."

Colt stopped but didn't turn around.

She let go and started pacing. When he glanced back at her, she was biting her thumbnail.

"Are you going to tell me or not?"

She stopped and put her hands on her hips as if exasperated. "Yes, I'll tell you."

"The truth. Right?"

"Yes. Here's the deal." She swallowed hard and looked away. "I was doing unsanctioned phone surveillance on someone."

Colt turned all the way around to face her. "What do you mean *unsanctioned?*"

"I mean, on my own." She wrung her hands together. "No one else knew about it."

Colt's eyes opened wide. "Why?"

Joey sat down and put her head in her hands. "Because it has to do with someone who's in a position of power. There was no way I would have received authorization."

Colt thought she might cry. He softened his tone, but was still skeptical.

"How did that lead you to *that* house on *this* day?"

She looked up at him. "Because the phone of the person I was tracking called that number twice. I was just driving by to check it out."

Colt sat down with his arms on his knees. "Do you have a tape of any conversations?"

"No. I didn't go that far."

"I see." He squeezed his temples. "And the person you were doing surveillance on was?"

Joey swallowed hard. "Rashad Alikhan."

"You mean the guy from Homeland Security?"

She pursed her lips and nodded.

"Geezuz. You've got to be kidding me."

"I wish I were."

"Why? What made you suspicious of him?"

She sat back on the couch, closed her eyes, and shook her head. "Every time we get a step closer to uncovering something, things turn around, and we take two steps back. The bad guys seem to know everything we're doing. I think we have a leak and that it's higher up than anyone is looking."

"Did you tell the President?"

"Yes, and he tried to help through the proper channels. But his advisors told him nothing could be done because there is no real evidence."

"So you wanted to give him enough evidence to launch an investigation."

She looked at Colt for the first time, and her eyes reflected dread and worry. "Yes."

Colt remained silent as he thought about the consequences and possible repercussions of her actions. None of them rose to the level that murder did. And if she hadn't been there at the time she was, he would undoubtedly be sitting in jail right now.

"Okay. So Mr. Alikhan—or someone using his phone—makes some calls to a location on the same day someone ends up dead."

Joey nodded.

"Back up. Did you check out every single place he called? I mean, surely he makes a lot of calls in one day."

Joey bit her lip. "Not exactly."

"Can you stop being so damned evasive and just spit it out."

"Well, this one caught my attention because, well, then I saw that a call went out of the same house to you—"

"Whoa. Whoa. Whoa. Wait a minute. Hold on. Stop. Back up." Colt held his hands in the air and then stood blinking like a bat in sunlight, too stunned to speak for a few long moments. "So...in other words... You were *also* doing surveillance on *me*."

She bit her lip. "Not exactly."

"What *exactly*, dammit!"

"Look. Something is going on and I—"

Colt walked away, shaking his head and squeezing his temples. "Geezuz chreest. I need to get out of here."

"No." She stamped her foot in frustration. "You need to trust me."

Colt jerked his head toward her, his eyes open wide. "Are you serious? Even though you don't trust *me*?"

A loud beeping sound interrupted the conversation.

"What's that?"

"It's the alarm at the gate. Someone wants to be buzzed in."

"Do you think we were followed?"

"No." She walked to the desk and touched the button to open the bookcase. "But when they came up empty-handed looking for you on foot, they probably figured out that you got a ride…"

"And dug up all the surveillance footage they could find."

"They might have seen my Jeep, but once we got outside of town, they have no way of knowing where we went." After turning up the volume for the barn-to-gate intercom, they heard, "Not without a search warrant you're not."

Joey smiled and whispered, "That's my stable manager."

"I'm with the Department of Homeland Security," a loud voice replied. "I don't need a search warrant."

"I don't care if you're the son of God." The stable manager sounded cool and authoritative. "As long as this property is located in the United States of America, you aren't getting onto it without a search warrant."

Joey looked up at Colt. There was no humor in her eyes. "It will take time, but they'll get a search warrant. We need to get out of here. I'm not sure where to go."

Colt thought about it a few seconds. "You have a farm truck—or better yet, a four-wheeler?"

She nodded. "Yes to both."

"Easy to get to?"

"Yes. We can go out the back and not be seen." She turned and looked at the bank of cameras, as the federal agents conversed outside the gate then turned and got back into their vehicles.

"Does your stable manager know what you do? And that you're here?"

Joey shook her head. "No to both. I told him I'd be gone a few days. He'll probably call me, though."

"Okay."

"You have a plan?"

Colt nodded. "I figure we're about fifteen miles from Phantom Force's headquarters."

"Less through fields."

"Right. If they're here, they've already been there."

"And then put it under surveillance—Valhalla, too," Joey said.

"Yes, but the house is miles from the main road. They can't see much."

"Then they'll get a drone."

Colt's eyes met hers to see if she was intentionally trying to talk him out of going to Phantom Force. "True, but it's pretty much all tree covered. Unless they have heat sensors, they won't see us."

They both watched the men from DHS turn their cars around and drive away.

"Let me grab some things." Joey left the room.

Chapter 26

Joey was only gone about five minutes, and returned with a backpack that appeared to be full.

"Looks like you're all ready to go."

"Mostly. I'll throw some water in yet. Here." She handed Colt a wide-brimmed cowboy hat.

"What's this?"

"It's a hat."

"I know it's a hat. What..."

"Just put it on. If they're looking from the air, they won't be able to see your face." She pulled another one out of the closet and stuck it on her head.

"You said the lines in here are secure, right?"

She nodded.

Colt picked up a phone and dialed.

"Phantom Force Tactical."

"Fury One, plus one, will be coming in by four-wheeler through the back." He glanced at his watch. "Forty-five minutes, give or take."

"Copy that."

He hung up and turned back to Joey.

After making sure she had everything she needed, she motioned for Colt to follow her. They went back out the way that had come, except that once they were outside, they cut to the left of the building toward a tractor shed. A covered porch on the house sat between the shed and the barn so they could not be seen.

"The key should be in it." Joey slipped her backpack onto her shoulders as she waited for Colt to climb on, then slid onto the seat behind him.

The engine turned over then quit. "Choke it, and let it run for a couple of minutes."

Colt did as he was told, and after the engine had warmed up, he pushed the choke in and hit the throttle. It stalled again.

"I hate this thing."

Colt turned the key again, and it started right up. He slowly pulled out of the shed as the four-wheeler shook and sputtered.

"When was the last time this thing was used?"

"Last spring, maybe?"

"Okay. Hold on." He squeezed the throttle again, causing Joey to grab him around the waist, and making him wince.

"Sorry, but you did that on purpose."

"I told you to hold on," he said over his shoulder.

He left her no choice but to do as he instructed as they took off through a field, heading toward a ridge of woods. Once there, they would be in and out of cover until they reached Phantom Force.

"I'm feeling a little bit like John Wayne right now." Colt had to talk loud above the noise of the engine.

Joey scrunched up her face. "Why? This isn't a horse."

"The hat, I guess."

Joey had to duck when they went under a low limb. "A little shout out would be nice."

"Sorry. You'd better keep your head down. More low-lying branches ahead."

Once they were inside the woods, Colt pulled the four-wheeler to a stop and looked at the compass on his watch. "Wish I could turn on my cell phone."

"We have to be getting close."

"I thought we would have run into the creek by now. Then I could get my bearings."

"Let's keep going."

He hit the throttle, and they headed deeper into the woods. The progress was slower now because there was no trail. Sometimes, he had to go around fallen trees, and sometimes, the multi-floral rose was so thick he had to detour for that, as well. At last, the sound of trickling water reached them.

"Want to take a quick break?"

Joey nodded. "Yeah. I wouldn't mind stretching my legs."

He pulled up to the bank and cut off the motor. "Should be just a few more miles."

Joey stood and rubbed her rear end. "That's good."

Colt lifted his leg stiffly over the seat, trying not to grimace at the pain the action caused. He'd tried to ignore it, but the ride over the rough terrain had been agonizing and exhausting.

Without looking down, he swiped his hand across his shirt to convince himself it wasn't wet with blood from torn stitches. Then with his head up, he listened for any sounds of aircraft overhead. That was the real reason he had stopped. He didn't want to lead the feds straight to Phantom Force if they were watching.

"Hear anything?" Joey seemed to be reading his mind.

He shook his head. "No, but that doesn't mean they're not up there."

"It will take them a little while to get organized."

"But we've pissed them off."

"And we're getting close," she said. "They're going to do whatever's necessary to stop us."

Colt sat down sideways on the seat of the bike. "Yeah. *Us.*"

Joey cocked her head and stared at him as if unsure whether he was being sarcastic or sincere.

"We're both on the same side, right?" He leaned in toward her, staring into green eyes that seemed to capture and reflect the sun even though they were sitting under trees.

"Yes. I'm sorry about the surveillance. I didn't know where the leak was coming from. I had to look at everyone."

"But we're on the same page now?"

She nodded. "Yes. We're on the same page now."

Chapter 27

Joey didn't want to hold on to Colt's waist, but the way he was driving, she had little choice. She attempted to keep her hands off his abdomen, which she knew must hurt, so grabbed on to his shirt, and then the belt loop of his jeans when that didn't provide enough support.

But even that method of trying to stay in the seat became useless when he steered into a field, so she wrapped one arm around his waist and tried to hold herself steady. With her cheek against his back, and her eyes closed, she tried to concentrate on what had transpired and the new obstacles that had been placed in their way.

"You okay back there?" He turned his head and yelled against the sound of the four-wheeler.

She put one hand out with the thumbs up sign, but continued to hold on for dear life with the other as they barreled over hills and around corners. It was obvious he was taking the most direct route, not necessarily the fastest—and definitely not the smoothest.

After they had stopped and taken a short break, Colt eased the four-wheeler down the bank to cross the stream, causing it to pitch precariously to one side. Joey bit her lip to keep from screaming. She hoped she hadn't unintentionally grabbed the site of his wound because she thought she felt him flinch again.

Stop being a little girl she told herself, just as she felt water covering her feet, then her ankles and almost to her knees.

Just as quickly, they were going up the other side, and not long after that, they burst across a short stretch of open ground and then went back into another patch of woods.

They crashed through underbrush and fallen limbs for about another hundred yards, and then someone yelled, "Over here!"

Colt gunned the throttle and headed toward a pickup truck. Joey wondered why he wasn't slowing down, and then saw that a ramp had been set up into the bed. She and Colt rode up the incline, and then he hit the brakes sharply, causing her head to slam against his back, and her hand to grab his solid, unyielding stomach again.

No one spoke, but everyone seemed to know what they were doing as if they had practiced this exact scenario a thousand times. Getting off the vehicle with shaking legs, Joey was immediately hoisted to the ground by two strong arms, and found herself staring into the straight white teeth of a smiling Wes.

"We meet again."

Before she had time to say anything, Colt had slid the ramp in beside the ATV and walked around to the passenger side door. "Hop in." He was all business.

Joey listened as Wes turned his attention to Colt and provided an update. Just as they had suspected, the police had been to Phantom Force looking for Colt and had come up empty-handed. But they had placed surveillance at the front gate, and were launching drones as they spoke.

Joey remained quiet as they traveled down an old tractor path toward a beautiful antebellum house, equally as stunning as Valhalla.

Colt exited the truck and waited by the door as Joey crawled out of the back seat. Just as she straightened back up, a woman with a bridle slung casually over her shoulder walked up a stone lane that apparently led to a barn. She was working on buckling a piece of leather strap so didn't see Joey or the truck.

"They have horses here?" Joey turned to Colt.

Her question was heard by the other woman, who looked up. "Yes, we have two. Do you ride?"

"Yeah. I'm Joey." She took a step toward the woman and held out her hand.

Colt sighed loudly behind her. "Joey, this is Caitlin Madison, my business partner's wife. Cait, Joey."

"Nice to meet you." Cait shook her hand. "If you want to come down to the barn, I'll show you around." All of a sudden, she got a funny look on her face, like she was both amused and surprised. "You here with Colt?"

Joey looked up at Colt to see what was so funny, but his face had anything but humor written on it. "Yes, she's here with me." He took Joey's arm and started guiding her toward the house. "On *business.*"

Joey looked over her shoulder toward Cait and waved. "Nice to meet you. Maybe later."

Cait smiled and nodded as Colt led Joey through a door into a large, cavernous room. There were tables set up with phones and computers, just like a command center for an emergency operation. When Joey walked through the door, an audible hush filled the room.

"This is Joey. She got me out of the little SNAFU I ran into today."

Joey gave Colt an appreciative glance that he revealed nothing more of her background, and then smiled at his use of the common slang for Situation Normal, All Fucked Up.

A dark-haired man, handsome, and about the same age as Colt stood from where he'd been seated behind a computer. "I'm Blake."

Joey nodded and stared into deep blue eyes that were commanding and comforting all at once. Like Colt, Blake had a square jaw and athletic build, and a gaze that indicated neither condemnation nor judgment. "Nice to meet you."

As he shook her hand, Blake's eyes turned a little more guarded. "Are you the Joey that contacted me about setting up an appointment with Colt?"

Colt answered for her. "Yes, but I think we have more important things to talk about today."

Blake turned to Colt. "You're right about that. You're quite popular right now—as in *wanted* very badly by authorities."

Colt ran his hand through his hair in agitation. "Yeah. Just what I need. Someone's going to have to take time to straighten this thing out."

"How do you suppose we're going to do that?" Blake stood with his hands on his hips. "It's not like you were jaywalking. It's a *murder* charge."

"Yes, but it's just a misunderstanding." Colt brushed it off. "It shouldn't take long to clear up."

Blake took a step toward him. "You mean you don't know?"

"Know what?"

"The bullet that killed Kelly came from *your* gun."

Colt laughed. "No it didn't. I have it right..." He reached into his holster and then remembered that the police had taken it.

"Okay. The police have my Glock, but the ballistics aren't going to match up."

"Dude, I'm telling you, they matched up—at least according to what they're saying."

"That's impossible. You know that."

"All I know is that, according to the police, you were standing over the body with the gun and told them she was dead."

"Well, that part is right."

"Look, they must have something, or they wouldn't have come out with this preliminary report so soon," Blake said. "Has your weapon been out of your sight at all, say in the last six months? Could they possibly have enough information to match it to a crime like this?"

"No. It's the gun I carry." Colt turned slowly and faced Joey, his eyes drilling into hers. "Hold on a minute. Yes, it was."

His voice turned so cold and emotionless so suddenly, it chilled her.

"Wait." Joey raised her hands when she read the look on his face. "You don't think I—"

Colt didn't say anything, but it was clear from the look of disappointment that his faith in their relationship and his trust in her sincerity had taken another drastic turn. The piercing expression of reservation and distrust aimed her way now squeezed her heart.

She turned her attention to Blake, whose conspicuous eyes studied her intently. Joey knew he'd been a homicide detective after retiring as a Navy SEAL, and felt like she was being analyzed and interrogated without any words. His steady, unflinching gaze seemed to impale her, yet his eyes did nothing to reveal what he was thinking. She could read nothing in them.

Blake didn't look away until Colt cleared his throat from beside her. Then he shifted his gaze to Colt and the two of them exchanged a look that Joey couldn't interpret, but she knew they had just communicated something significant between them.

"Okay. Wait. Let me think." She sat down on a chair and rubbed the bridge of her nose. "Colt's right. I had the gun in my possession."

"At all times?" Colt stood with hands on his hips, studying her intently. Wariness and frustration darkened his eyes with a brooding reserve, causing her mind to race with a jumbled puzzle of thoughts.

"No." She gazed up at him. "It was out of my sight one

time." She sucked in a breath. "No. Two times."

"Why? Where?"

"The debriefing right after the attack in the office building. I had a meeting in a SCIF, and had to leave it at the door. And then again a week or so later. Same place."

"Where was the meeting?" Colt stood with his arms crossed, looking doubtful. It wasn't unusual for people in her position to hold discussions in a Sensitive Compartmental Information Facility, but he still appeared unconvinced.

"Homeland Security."

Colt groaned and sat down. "So they called you to a debriefing, and had you leave the pistol at the door. Did you notice anything strange about it when you picked it up again?"

She shook her head. "No. Not really."

"Were you in there long enough for them to make a 3D copy?"

She gazed into space a moment. "No, but I suppose they could have switched out guns and done that later. I wasn't familiar enough with it to know one way or the other."

"And then they replaced it again." Blake rubbed his chin thoughtfully. His expression was unreadable, but the tone of his voice dripped with skepticism.

"Sounds far-fetched," Colt said, "but it provides another link that Rashad Alikhan is connected to this in some way."

"Rashad Alikhan?" Wariness and disbelief entered Blake's eyes. "From Homeland Security?"

Colt nodded, but his eyes never left Joey. "A call from his phone was placed to Kelly's house before the murder."

"How do you know that?" Blake's gaze darted from Joey to Colt and back again. Then he sat down and leaned forward with his arms resting on his legs. "Why don't you two fill me in on what's going on?"

Chapter 28

Joey nodded, giving Colt her consent to tell Blake what she had done. They were in too deep to stop now.

"Okay. Joey is in a position that allowed her to do some *extracurricular* surveillance."

Blake didn't make any comment, seeming to know better than to ask questions.

"She's been suspicious about some leaks and decided to check out the location of some phone calls that were made. When she drove by Kelly's house, it just so happened I was there at the time and in need of a ride."

Blake's eyes flitted over to Joey and then back to Colt. Joey couldn't tell if he believed what Colt was telling him—or believed she was on his side or not. He wore his usual hooded look, remote and unrevealing. The man was a blank slate.

"Hey, Blake," Podge said from behind his computer. "I couldn't help but overhear."

All three sets of eyes turned toward him.

"What's up?"

Podge stood with a piece of paper and handed it to Colt. "Not sure this is anything, but thought you might want to take a look."

Blake took a step so he could read over Colt's shoulder, then they both lifted their gaze to stare at Joey.

"What is it?"

"Were you aware that Rashad Alikhan had a half-sister?"

Joey shrugged. "No. Why?"

"Her name is Donya Abbasi. She's married to a Dennis Morgan and owns Bismillah Stables."

Joey searched her memory. She thought the name sounded familiar but couldn't think of how or where she'd heard it. When it finally registered, she let out a groan, then raised her eyes to see everyone staring at her.

"You know her?" Colt tilted his head.

"No." Joey stared at the ceiling a moment, as if that would help clear her foggy memory. "But I recognize the name. One of our intelligence analysts picked up a spike in explosive target compound sales in area sporting goods stores."

"You mean, like Tannerite?"

"That's the most well-known brand name, but he was looking at a whole range of products that are used to make targets explode during firearms practice."

From the concerned smiles on the faces of the men around her, Joey knew they had probably all had experience with Tannerite and similar products.

"What exactly do they consider a spike?" Blake looked at Colt and frowned.

"An unusual number of sales, and a large amount of high-volume sales—like fifty pounds or more at a time," Joey said. "And they were all paid with cash."

Colt began pacing. "So either we have a lot of major target practice going on in the area, or somebody wants to blow something up."

Podge spoke up. "It would be hard to trace who bought it since it's legal. It's sold at sporting goods stores everywhere. Not to mention online."

Colt agreed. "And it's safe to transport even after the two powders have been mixed together. It literally takes a high-velocity bullet to set it off."

"So, if it's legal, I'm assuming bomb sniffing dogs aren't even imprinted on it to notify their handlers when it's around."

"That's right. Certainly not the majority of them anyway."

"What does all of this have to do with Donya Abbasi?"

Everyone looked at Joey again. "Well, like you said, there is no way to track the purchaser, especially when they paid in cash. We pulled surveillance tape and were able to identify one buyer."

"Donya Abbasi," everybody stated at once.

"Yes. She was a little conspicuous since she drives a Mercedes. That's how they ID'd her."

"Why didn't you tell me about this before? Colt's voice had a slight edge to it.

"I didn't realize it was relevant until now."

"If someone that high up in Homeland Security is involved, we have to be suspicious of everyone we deal with," Blake said thoughtfully.

"Exactly." Joey shot everyone a look that said *I-told-you-so*.

"Well, did they follow up? Did Donya Abbasi check out?"

"A team was sent with a very specific search warrant and found that they have a shooting range on the horse farm."

"Nothing illegal—or even very unusual—about that."

"Right. Their official statement was that they only use it now and then for fun, but neighbors say it sounds like a battlefield on weekends."

"Regardless, it's legal, so there is nothing that can be done." Podge threw a pencil onto the desk and leaned back.

"They didn't see anything else suspicious, so that's as far as it went."

"Well, here's another little tidbit for you," Colt said. "Remember the rental truck that picked up the money from the mosque?"

Joey tilted her head and nodded. "The rental agreement was in Donya Abbasi's husband's name. And she owns the farm where the money was dropped and then picked up by the horse haulers."

Joey backed up against a chair and sat down. Hard.

She'd felt in her gut that Alikhan was involved. But to have a small piece of the puzzle fit into that logic made her almost sick to her stomach. The ramifications were too large to comprehend.

"It looks like maybe your instincts were right," Colt said, reading her mind.

"Somehow, that doesn't make me feel any better."

"This is bigger and deeper than we originally thought." Blake's voice took on a sense of urgency. "Anyone have any thoughts on who is behind it all? It has to be someone with money, power, and a pretty big vendetta against America to go to this much trouble."

A sudden expletive from behind them made all three heads turn toward another man at a computer terminal. He looked up as if just realizing they were waiting for him to explain. "I just received some new intel, Colt." He walked over to a printer and picked up a piece of paper. "You're not going to like it."

"Any intel is good intel at this point." Colt turned toward the man. "What do you have, Luke?"

"It's kind of sensitive." Luke's gaze traveled over to Joey and then back to Colt with a questioning look.

"Go ahead. She's got clearance."

"Okay. Great." His gaze ran across the paper again and he shook his head. "They traced the driver of the truck found in the pond to a Frank Clayton." He handed the paper over to Blake. "He's apparently drowning in gambling debts his wife didn't know about."

"So someone probably offered to pay him to give up the material, and he was going to live debt-free," Blake said, reading the paper.

"Except they killed him instead of paying," Colt added.

"Hmmm." Blake looked at the paper and his face took on a new seriousness. It wasn't just *someone*. He raised his gaze to Colt. "This is bad."

"What is it?" Colt snatched the paper.

"Police found a phone number on Clayton's phone." Blake spoke while looking at Colt. "It's a known associate of Arman Mohammad Sassani."

Joey felt a sudden current of tension pulse across the room and watched Colt's jaw tighten noticeably. In a split second, his entire expression darkened with an unreadable emotion.

Sassani was a name well known to her and anyone else in counterterrorism intelligence. He was a major player in the most dangerous terrorist organization on the planet—IJIN—the Islamic Jihad International Network.

She'd done her share of agonizing over his whereabouts and studying his habits, so had a personal connection to his terror network. She assumed this sudden strain by others was because they now knew who they were up against—and it was the worst possible scenario.

"You heard me." Luke handed them each another piece of paper. "Here's the latest." They all scanned the intelligence report while he explained the highlights.

"So we now have evidence that IJIN and the drug kingpin Carlos Valdez teamed up a while back." Colt shook his head as he read the report. "IJIN furnished weapons to Carlos's cartel and helped him distribute drugs in Europe and the Middle East."

Blake looked confused. "Okay. Carlos got state-of-the art weaponry and a wider distribution base for his drugs. What did Sassani get?"

"Right," Luke said. "On the face of it, it looks like Carlos was getting the good end of the deal. But Sassani was essentially using him and his network to position his own gang in the Western Hemisphere. He moved men into Mexico and used it as a staging ground, fundraising center, and operations base as a way to wage war against the United States."

"Asymmetric warfare." Colt stared at the wall, deep in thought.

"Correct," Luke agreed. "Basically, it's a two-pronged attack. By cooperating with Carlos's drug trafficking network, he was able to bring people and equipment into the U.S. Then, by sharing their tactics and techniques with the drug cartel, they encouraged and increased violence along the border."

"Which caused us to spend valuable time and money to protect it," Blake said as if thinking out loud. "And to top it off, all the drug money got funneled back to Syria and Iran to fund a terrorist organization that is more advanced than al-Qaeda and more dangerous than ISIS."

"The real concern about IJIN is their long-term goals. They want to radicalize Muslim communities and focus on infiltrating the United States with as many sleeper cells as possible."

"Hold up. I don't think I understand." Colt held the paper in his hands, his brow creased. "Sassani is sitting in Gitmo. How's he organizing all of this from prison?"

Joey cleared her throat and stood. "No. Actually, he's not at Gitmo anymore."

Colt had walked over to a nearby table to pick up a pack of crackers. His head jerked around, and the full intensity of his eyes were trained on her. "What do you mean he's not at Gitmo anymore? It's not a weekend resort where you come and go as you please."

The anger in Colt's voice, and the violent look in his eyes caused Joey to take a step back. "I'm afraid he was among those that President Sotero released right before he left office."

"No." Colt shook his head. "Impossible. I looked at the

list. He wasn't on there."

"I'm afraid there was a…" She paused as her eyes swept across the room. The tense expressions on all of the faces gnawed at her confidence. "There was, what they called, a *glitch*. They say the names got mixed up and he was sent to Omar in place of another prisoner. Of course, they kept it quiet."

"They call that a fucking *glitch*?" Colt threw the pack of crackers down, and everyone in the room shrank a little lower in their chairs. Joey had never seen such a look of anger and pain on a man's face, and found it even more unsettling to see it on the usually calm and composed Colt. This was serious.

"Releasing an American-hating terrorist leader to a country that condones killing all infidels is a fucking glitch?"

Startled by the ferocity of Colt's reaction, Joey glanced again at the faces of the other men. When her eyes locked on Blake, she saw that he wore a warm and apologetic expression now that seemed to say *he's not usually like this*.

Colt must have noticed the exchange. "Sorry." He turned his back, but his breath was heavy and rapid, and his hands were curled into fists.

Blake tried to explain. "Colt is the one who tracked this guy down. Almost got killed in the process."

"I know he's a dangerous man." Joey spoke while gazing reflectively at Colt's back. She'd read in a report that the guy who'd nabbed Sassani had been seriously wounded in the endeavor. She'd not known that man was Colt. "He was the deputy minister of intelligence for the Taliban, and is suspected of providing intelligence training to al-Qaeda for the attack on the United States on September 11."

"And that was just the beginning of his career," Blake said. "He went on to create IJIN by recruiting the most violent members of ISIS and al-Qaeda into the ranks."

Joey's heart hammered at the thought that this evil man could now be planning new carnage. "He was also suspected of being the mastermind for ambushes on our troops and bombings in other countries before he was captured."

"And hostage-taking incidents."

Joey glanced over at Colt because his voice sounded so different. It was cold. Emotionless. Strained. When she looked back at Blake in confusion, his eyes seemed to warn, *don't ask any more questions.*

She decided to switch gears. "So you're saying all this somehow ties into the current threat?"

"Unfortunately, yes." Blake sat down and pinched the bridge of his nose. "It's looking like our hunch was right that Cait's abduction was just the opening act of this thing."

"It's starting to look that way," Luke agreed. "He basically used Carlos. Planned it out so that it would look like a drug kingpin was behind it all."

"And all along, he knew Colt would eliminate Carlos for him, clearing his way to unite with *El Soldado*, and making it easy for him to plan an even bigger attack with no interference."

"Right, but when Colt showed up in DC, he had him framed for murder to keep him out of the picture." Podge nodded in agreement as they began to piece the puzzle together.

"Wait. I need to catch up here." Joey held up her hands. "So are you guys saying that Sassani knows Colt? They have a history?"

Chapter 29

The room grew deathly quiet for a few long, awkward moments. Some of the men put their heads down as if they didn't hear the question. At last, Blake spoke. "Sassani was behind a hostage incident that killed a close friend of Colt's."

Joey's eyes darted to Colt. He was staring at something on the wall, his eyes glazed over as if he were a million miles away. Feeling her phone vibrate, she pulled it out of her pocket and checked the message. "They've got a search warrant. They're in the house at Valhalla."

"Does it matter?" Colt was back to his old self, his face all business again. But it was clear he was holding a raw tension in check.

She shook her head. "No, they won't find anything."

"What about this call? They can't trace it?"

"No. Not the way I have it set up." She glanced at the phone again. "Dan says they've also set up surveillance on the house so it doesn't look like I'll be going back anytime soon."

"We have plenty of room here."

Joey looked up at Blake. "Thanks, but I'm not planning on sticking around."

Podge leaned back in his chair and threw his pencil onto the desk. "Who would have figured five years ago that we would have preferred dealing with al-Qaeda?"

"Yeah. Seriously. al-Qaeda is more shooting than thinking," Blake said. "A lot of desire but not a lot of training or tactical knowledge."

"IJIN is far more advanced," Joey agreed. "Their operatives are more skilled with weapons and more experienced with strategic planning."

"Sirs." A young man with a military haircut stood in front of Blake holding a piece of paper. "According to this, a warning bulletin for an imminent terrorist attack has been issued."

Colt ran his hand through his hair as Blake nodded his thanks to the young man and took the paper. He scanned it quickly and then summarized. "It says Homeland Security, Justice, and Defense agencies have all been placed on alert and instructed to aggressively work all possible leads and sources concerning this imminent terrorist threat."

"Why?" Colt walked over and read over Blake's shoulder.

"They've picked up chatter indicating a possible attack on the border."

Colt shook his head. "No way. That's too convenient. That's what they want us to think."

"The fact that the money has been laundered means somebody got paid for doing something," Blake said. "But who, and for what exactly?"

"If we go with our theory, then *El Soldado* knocked off the driver, stole the radioactive material, and ditched the truck." Colt sat down on one of the couches, and looked at Joey. "Do we have confirmation on that? Is the Cobalt gone?"

"Yes." She nodded. "Divers found the truck empty."

"So we can assume that *El Soldado* got paid a few million dollars for that part of the plot."

"And then the cartel promptly laundered the money by buying the three horses, which they can later resell, possibly for a profit," Joey added.

"That's all good information," Podge said, "but it doesn't help us to figure out what he's planning."

"Okay. Let's back up. Start at the beginning." Colt began to pace. "It looks like I was somehow the intended target of the attack in the high-rise outside DC. I don't even know how they knew I was in DC at that time."

"And even if they did find out that you were back east, how did Sassani learn you were going to be there at that specific time?" Blake turned to Podge with a questioning look. "Our Internet system is secure, right? The appointment with the informant was set up through email."

Podge nodded. "Absolutely. Everything is encrypted."

"Okay. What if you weren't the intended target at all?" Blake stood with his arms crossed, deep in thought. "Or what if the person on the other end of the email tipped off the bad guys?"

"Who would—?"

All eyes turned again toward Joey before he had even

finished his sentence.

"Wait, you don't think..." Joey's gaze swept the room and the accusatory look on each man's face.

"If the situation were reversed, what would *you* think?" Colt tilted his head slightly and studied her with a look that told Joey exactly what he thought.

"Look. You know what I do..."

"Actually, I don't." Blake raised his hand.

Joey ignored him. "I told you before that it was set up via email."

"Where? How?" Podge asked. "Your phone? Computer?"

Joey searched her memory, and then she swallowed hard. "My phone. I was on the road, and this was just a simple meeting." She sat down and put her head in her hands. "It was Rashad. All along, I thought it was someone with a vendetta against Colt. But now..."

"Why?"

"Rashad and I had a discussion—more like a confrontation—a few days before that. I made it clear that I thought something fishy was going on."

"You told him you suspected him of something?" Colt asked.

"No. Not outright." Joey shook her head. "But I insinuated it. Strongly." She bit her cheek while reflecting on the conversation. "It's beginning to look like he understood that I suspected something and wanted me out of the picture."

"And, I guess, he has the power and connections to trace your phone calls."

"Yes. Maybe not legally, but he has access to equipment

and people. He could have leaned on someone for a favor or could have done it himself."

"Is there a way to put surveillance on him? Follow him?"

"If we had a court order of course we could, but…"

"Damn." Blake sat down. "You'd think it would help to have a suspect, but it's only making things more difficult. If we overstep, or have the appearance that we've overstepped, we're the ones who are going to go down. They'll destroy us through the media."

Everyone nodded in agreement. Even if Rashad's involvement was something they knew, it was going to be almost impossible to prove.

"That's why I decided to check out his phone calls. Catch him in the act." She looked straight at Colt. "It was the only way to find out what is going on."

"Let's think this thing through." Colt ignored the dig. "Do you think Rashad Alikhan was groomed for this job all along? Or was he turned and radicalized after getting the position?"

"Or he could have been threatened." Podge had sat back down at his computer. "Sassani wields enough power that he could manipulate someone into doing his bidding."

"True. But what's Sassani's end game?"

"We have to start looking at the big picture." Blake sat down with a tablet on his lap. "What could they be planning? Let's make a list. Any ideas?"

"We were thinking the Monday night football game." Colt talked while skimming another report. "Big crowd and live coverage."

"Makes sense," Blake said. "Who's playing? Oh yeah, the

Steelers and Redskins." He looked at Colt and smiled. "As if my better half hasn't been talking about it all week."

"I'm not sure we should concentrate resources on a gut feeling, though."

"It's not just a gut feeling." Everyone looked at Joey. "Some of my colleagues have picked up some new chatter. No concrete evidence yet, but it's a good place to start."

"Should the public be alerted?" Podge looked up from his computer. "Should the game be postponed?"

"Not going to happen. The networks, the advertisers, and the football league would have a fit."

"Well, that's better than the alternative, isn't it?" Podge shook his head. "Let them if it prevents a massive terrorist attack."

"But we don't know that's the plan. It will be a little hard to convince them without hard facts."

"Great point." Podge agreed. "We can hardly cancel a game like that with no real evidence."

"So, basically, we just have to figure out what they're doing and prevent it."

"Yeah. That's all we have to do."

With a few taps on his computer keys, Podge changed the image on the large-screen television on the wall to an aerial view of FedEx Field.

"First thing we'll need is to make sure the Domestic Nuclear Detection Office is up to speed."

"That shouldn't be a problem. They can position Radiation Portal Monitors and use handheld survey meters for additional support," Colt said.

"That's a solid start." Joey chewed on the end of a pencil as she stared at the monitor. "But they possibly have a two-tiered plan in mind."

"What do you mean?"

"Like create some sort of disturbance or distraction—maybe big, maybe not—so that everybody's attention is drawn away from the real threat."

"True." Colt squeezed his temples. "That's pretty much their *modus operandi*. Start with a small explosion, and then shoot people when they run in the other direction."

"Which makes our job even more difficult. The distraction could even be miles away, to divert police and emergency assets away from the main scene."

"Let's assume for a minute, it's all planned for the stadium area. With the increased security, getting a weapon past the checkpoints won't be an easy task."

"Right, but we need to add a double—triple even—layer of security to make sure of that."

"I'm sure it's in the works," Podge said. "Once the Cobalt-60 went missing, the threat was raised for any major event. They're bringing in dogs from all over the country to patrol, as well."

"But with the missing cobalt, Sassani is going to figure that security will be tight." Blake shook his head. "He must have a plan that gets around that."

"With *El Soldado* involved, it could just be a squad of soldiers outfitted with bulletproof gear and carrying high-powered weaponry," Joey said. "They could simply go in with guns blazing."

"They'd get close, but they'd never breach the building," Colt countered. "Not without the element of surprise. And they don't have that."

"Okay, then what if they don't go through security?"

"What do you mean?"

"I mean like all of the things that make game day. Ice vendors, food trucks, supplies. How closely are they examined?"

"They're all vetted." Colt looked at Blake. "Let's give that another look, though."

Blake scribbled something down. "Okay, I'll get with DHS on that."

"Not Homeland!" Both Colt and Joey said the words at the same time.

"That's right. Rashad." Blake cocked his head. "They might be compromised, but it's a big agency. Are you sure we want to bypass them? This is what they do—Homeland Security."

"Let's leave them out of any of our plans," Colt said. "Call in our guys who are on standby. I'll stop by Langley and get them on board, too."

"You? How are you going anywhere? You're a wanted man, remember?"

Colt sat back in his chair and let out his breath. "Yeah. I forgot about that." He looked at his watch. "Which reminds me. I'm supposed to be at the White House."

"We have the horse trailer to transport you," Blake said. "But we need to get this figured out. I feel like we're missing something."

Joey looked at Blake with a confused expression at the

mention of the trailer.

"It's got a false compartment." Colt answered her question without it being asked. "We can have Cait take it out to drop off horses at another farm. They can search it, but they won't find anything."

"Only problem is, it's made for one person." Blake studied the two of them. "You'll have to decide who is going and who is staying."

"No. We'll fit." Colt looked at Joey. "We can stand close quarters for a couple of minutes. Right?"

"If you say so." Joey shot him a skeptical look.

"So back to the game. Do we also need to think about players?" Podge's statement made everyone stop what they were doing.

"Football players?" Blake looked incredulous. "You think we have terrorists on NFL teams?"

"Look, we have players that won't stand for the National Anthem."

That made everyone pause. The room grew silent.

"It's not something that should be disregarded. We've got to think outside the box." Joey defended the idea and the possibility. "If they can't get through the security defenses, they must be planning to infiltrate another way. I still feel like we're missing something."

"What about a drone?" Blake stood in the corner of the room with a cup of coffee in his hand.

"They will put a no-fly space zone in place," Podge said. "I'll check on that, though. Maybe we can extend it out to thirty or more miles."

"But what if someone launched a drone…say an agricultural size that was modified to carry and disperse something over a large area." Blake walked over toward the group. "They are stealthy and agile, and if flown aggressively could evade radar. How fast could it be brought down? And would that even be wise if it's carrying radioactive material?"

Everyone's eyes went back to the aerial view of the stadium.

"My agency has anti-drone technology."

In unison, everyone's attention turned toward Joey. It was clear they were all well aware of the new drone-stopping guns that could scramble the signal so the operator no longer had control. The gun could land the drone safely and prevent any detonation of harmful devices.

"Cool." Podge's eyes lit up. "Can you get a couple for us?"

"I wouldn't go that far." Joey smiled. "But there will be agents positioned around the stadium, so we can concentrate on other things."

Blake let out his breath. "Well that's one less thing we have to worry about."

"Speaking of which, maybe putting a sniper or two around the stadium wouldn't hurt." Colt turned to Wes who had just entered the room and was heading toward the coffee pot. "Wes can coordinate that."

"Did I hear my name?" Wes turned toward the group.

"Luke will fill you in." Colt walked toward the television and pointed. "All of the spectators and vendors should have to pass through a radiation monitor in addition to bag checks and metal detector."

"To be on the safe side, we should make sure they place

radiation detecting pillars in the parking lot, too." Blake stood with one hand in his pocket, the other wrapped around a cup of coffee. "Make all the cars drive through them to enter the premises."

"I'll double-check with DNDO on that," Podge said. "I have a contact who might lend us some prototypes of WIND technology for any of our guys going to the site."

"Excuse me?"

"Wearable Intelligent Nuclear Detection." Podge smiled. "Clothing that monitors the environment and alerts the user when nuclear or radioactive material is present."

"Sounds good." Colt's eyes remained locked on the screen. "What are we missing?"

"We need a break, a real lead," Blake said. "I don't want go into this and have it end up like…" He stopped himself and glanced at Colt.

Colt stared into space a moment, and then turned toward the door. "I'm going out for a smoke."

Chapter 30

Joey winced when the door closed loudly, and looked at Blake. "I didn't know he smoked."

"He doesn't."

"Oka-a-y."

"He's just going out to clear his head so he can think. He does that."

"If you say so."

Blake exhaled and studied her intently. "I'm not going to go into the detail, because if Colt wants you to know his history, he'll tell you."

Joey remained silent and waited.

"But long story short, he lost someone close to him during a mission in Afghanistan. *Very* close."

Joey cringed and looked at Blake. "And Sassani was behind it?"

"He wasn't there—just the mastermind. Colt didn't rest until he was caught. I mean, literally did-not-rest until he tracked the man down."

"And he assumed Sassani was still at Gitmo."

"Until tonight. Yes."

Joey swallowed hard and gazed over Blake's shoulder at the television screen, but wasn't really seeing anything. She was thinking about the time Colt had comforted her over the death of her husband, never mentioning his own pain. She felt a strange connection to him that was unexpected and unnerving.

"You look like you could use some fresh air, too."

Joey jerked her attention back to Blake and saw a mysterious glint in his blue eyes, one she couldn't quite interpret. As fearsome as his brooding reserve and unreadable mien had been earlier, this new expression put her at ease.

"I have some calls to make. We're taking a ten-minute break." He turned and headed toward a door on the other side of the room without another word.

Since everyone else in the room had gone back to what they'd been doing, Joey decided a breath of fresh air wouldn't hurt. As soon as she stepped outside, her gaze fell on Colt standing in the shadows of a tree. With his hands in his pockets, he stared at the landscape.

"You okay?" She walked up behind him.

"I'm fine." He sounded cold and unfriendly.

"You don't look like it."

He glanced at her and then went back to studying the sky. "It's nothing you can fix."

She took another stride toward him. "Are you sure?"

He seemed to hold his breath and then let it out slowly.

Joey realized how suggestive the question had been, so she

tried to lighten the mood. "I mean, I'm not a handyman like you, but I could give it a try."

"Blake told you?"

She swallowed before answering. "Not much. Just that you lost someone dear to you." She put her hand on his arm. "I'm sorry for your loss."

"It was a long time ago. Sometimes it seems like a lifetime ago." He looked down at her after a few minutes. "Sorry. I know I'm not the only one who's lost someone."

Joey cleared her throat. "And I'm sorry that I acted like *I* was." She peered up at him. "Really."

"Okay. Enough of the Debbie downer conversation." He threw his arm over her shoulder and gave her a sisterly squeeze. "We'd better get back to work."

"Wait." She stepped in front of him, her hands flat on his chest.

"You trust me, don't you, Colt?"

He gazed down into her eyes, unblinking. It took a while, but he finally nodded.

"Things are going to get...you know, pretty crazy out there." She hesitated, swallowing hard at the intensity of his stare, wondering if the same look was reflected in her own eyes. "And I just want you to understand that I..."

"Hey, you two ready to get back to work?" Blake stood on the porch with his hands on his hips.

They stepped apart and nodded.

"Yeah. We're coming," Colt said.

Chapter 31

Blake studied the two of them as they came through the door, but could read nothing from either face. He clapped his hands together. "Let's get back to business. I asked Cait to give us a hand. She's getting ready now."

"So we're probably good as far as getting searched at the end of the driveway, but how are we going to get into DC?"

"We just got that all worked out. Cait will drop both of you and one of the horses at Jubilee Farm. Even if they follow her and watch, she'll park where they won't be able to see you guys exit the trailer.

Then she'll go to another farm and drop the other one, which will hopefully keep them occupied. Meanwhile, we'll have other trailers coming and going from Jubilee, and you'll be in one of them going to Tagg's place in Fairfax. He'll have everything you need there including a change of clothes and vehicles."

The two of them looked at each other and nodded.

"Sounds like a plan."

"Let me go see if she's ready." Blake nodded toward Joey and pointed to a door. "There's a restroom. Colt can show you where to grab something to eat if you're hungry."

"Thanks."

Once Blake left the room, Colt walked over to a basket and pulled out a nutrition bar. "This might have to do for now."

"That's fine." Joey tore the wrapper and took a bite, while staring blankly at the wall.

"You okay?"

She brought her attention back to Colt. "Yes. It's just now hitting me that I have a bounty on my head."

"Oh, it's your first?" He winked to show he was joking.

"From a fellow American, yes—the first time I'm aware of."

"Well, it's not over. If anything, they're redoubling their efforts to find you." He cocked his head. "And now that you bring it up, maybe it would be better if you stay here."

Joey laughed and then stopped and stared at him. "You're kidding, right?"

"Does it look like I'm kidding?"

"No, but—"

Colt held his hand in the air and stopped her. "Believe me, your intelligence and technical skills could be put to use here. It's not like you wouldn't be actively working the case."

Joey took a step toward him, her green eyes sparking with emotion. "I'm going to pretend this conversation never happened. Okay?"

Colt held his hands up in the air in surrender at her expression. He'd learned his lesson about trying to argue when her eyes turned that color. "What conversation?" he said with a smile.

"You're a fast learner, Nick Colton."

Her voice had a hint of humor in it so he knew he'd successfully diffused a volatile situation, but the sound of his real name on her lips caught him by surprise. He pretended it didn't affect him, that he didn't want to hear her say it again.

"I'm going to go help Blake hitch the trailer. You can hang here."

"Okay." Joey poured herself a cup of coffee. "Let me know when you're ready."

Not wanting to disturb any of the men who were still working, Joey walked to the window and gazed absently at the large oak trees that lined the yard.

"Hey, Joey. Looks like I'm driving your getaway car."

Joey turned around to see Blake's wife, Cait walking toward her. "Sorry that you have to get involved in this."

"Oh, it's no problem." Cait grabbed two bottles of water from under the counter, and handed them to Joey. "You'd better take these along."

"Thanks." Joey took the bottles, and squeezed them into her jacket pockets.

"That's a beautiful ring."

Joey looked up to find Cait examining her left hand. "Oh, thanks." She gazed at the ring a moment too, as if just remembering it was there, then looked up. "I hope we can go riding someday. I have a couple of horses that need some time on the trail."

"That would be great. I'd love that." Cait pulled a phone out of her pocket, and checked a text message. "Blake says they're ready to roll."

As they headed outside, Joey struck up another conversation. "So just how small is this hiding space?"

"Oh, you're small. It's big enough for you." Cait skipped down the porch steps as the trailer pulled up in front of them. "Don't worry."

"But it's going to me and Colt."

Cait stopped walking and studied her with a funny look on her face. "You're kidding, right?"

"No. Why?"

"I didn't realize you two were that close."

"What do you mean?"

"I mean, it's going to be a *really* tight squeeze."

Joey shrugged. "Colt didn't seem to think it would be a problem."

Cait smiled. "Hmmm. That's not like Colt."

"What's not like Colt?"

Cait moved closer and talked like they were old friends. "You may have noticed Colt isn't exactly a people person—especially when it comes to close quarters."

"Yes, but I get the feeling Colt will do about anything if it means getting the bad guys."

"Good point." Cait laughed. "That's true. Absolutely anything."

Chapter 32

"Ladies first." Colt swept his hand toward the small compartment that was hidden in the dressing room of the horse trailer.

"No. I think you should go first, Colt." Blake stood with his hands on his hips. "Put your back against the wall and then Joey can stand with her back against you."

Colt hopped into the trailer and did as Blake suggested, followed by Joey. "Like this?" She leaned into Colt as Blake tried to close the door. "Tighter. I can't get it closed."

Colt wrapped his arms around Joey and pulled her in even more. "Try now."

Joey had to turn her head sideways, but the door finally closed.

"Don't take too long, bro." Colt spoke loudly enough to be heard outside the door and a good ways beyond. "Let's get moving."

Joey tried to take a deep breath, but she was squeezed in so tightly, there was no room for her lungs to expand.

"You okay?" Colt's voice was tender in her ear as the trailer began to move.

"Other than not being able to breathe, I'm fine," she whispered back.

He loosened his grip slightly, but her cheek was smashed against the door so it didn't help much. She relaxed into him slightly, but the feeling of his solid chest behind her did little to help her catch her breath. The man was solid everywhere even while relaxed.

After a few minutes of rocking and swaying over the dirt road, the trailer came to a stop, signaling that they were at the end of the lane and being questioned by the authorities. As the garbled voices of men came closer, Colt's embrace increased again. The outside door latch clicked open, swiftly followed by light seeping into their tight quarters. The trailer swayed as someone stepped in and inspected the interior with the sharp beam of a flashlight.

"Clear here." The door slammed shut.

After what felt like hours, the voices faded and the trailer began moving again. Colt fumbled around in the dark and released the latch. As soon as the door opened, they both fell forward and inhaled deeply.

Joey put her hands on her knees and continued taking deep breaths, sucking in air as if she were drowning.

"You okay?"

"Getting there. I'm really claustrophobic."

"Why didn't you tell me?"

"What were you going to do about it?"

He looked at her with a smile. "Good point." He squeezed

her arm. "And good sport. That had to be hard."

"It's all part of living the dream." She held onto a hook holding bridles as they rounded a turn, knocked off balance as much by the swaying of the trailer as the smile of approval she'd seen in his eyes. "I guess we might as well get comfortable." Joey lowered herself to the floor and stretched out her legs.

"Roger that."

It took a moment for Joey to realize that Colt wasn't speaking to her. He was listening to Blake through his earpiece. Then he talked to her as he slid down the wall to sit beside her.

"You hurt yourself?"

Joey realized she was absently rubbing the sore muscles in the back of her neck and shoulder.

"No. Just trying to get these knots out."

"Here." Colt patted the space between his legs. "Sit here. I'll loosen them up for you."

He didn't give her time to object, but practically picked her up with one arm and positioned her in front of him. "Just relax."

After a few minutes, Joey felt like her eyes were rolling back in her head at the feel of his hands on her neck and shoulder.

"Wow. You are really tight. I'll work on this knot right here."

Joey's head lowered another notch as he kneaded and rubbed the tissue. He seemed to know how to manipulate and soothe each muscle in a way that made her drowsy and comfortable.

"When was the last time you slept?"

"I don't remember," she murmured with her eyes closed. The tenderness of his touch was like a magical elixir that hypnotized and relaxed her. She felt heavy and warm, like her senses were drugged, yet she was still vaguely aware of the strength of his hands and the warmth of his flesh.

"We've got at least a fifty-minute ride." He pulled a horse blanket from a shelf above his head and threw it across her. "We'd better grab a soldier's nap."

That was the last thing she remembered until she was nudged awake. "We're about five minutes out."

With difficulty, Joey struggled back to wakefulness, blinking as she tried to remember where she was. When she opened her eyes all the way she was gazing into the smiling eyes of Colt. Somehow, she had ended up lying against his chest with her arms wrapped around him. "Sorry about that." She struggled to sit up.

"No problem." Colt helped her take a seat beside him. "But next time we sleep together, *you're* the pillow. Okay?"

The words were playful but the implication was not. Joey searched his face for a hint of his true meaning. Seeing nothing but humor in his eyes, she took his joke in stride. "As long as it's not in the back of a horse trailer you have a deal." She lifted her hand as she spoke and pressed on the back of her neck.

"Still hurt?"

She looked up, expecting to see humor again, but his eyes were full of concern and compassion. "No, as a matter of fact," she said, still probing her neck with her fingers. "It feels loose—like it hasn't felt for years. What did you do to me?"

"Magic touch." He smiled out of the corner of his mouth and held up his hands. "Remember?"

Joey nodded and stared at his calloused hands, wondering how they could be so strong and potentially lethal, yet so sensitive and gentle.

He had the reputation of being fearless. Intrepid. Daring. Yet the boyish grin he now wore caused him to appear sensually appealing—not deadly or dangerous. "If you ever go into the massage therapy business, let me know."

"Does that mean you'd hire me?" He leaned down close, his steely eyes staring straight into hers with an intensity that was unsettling. Joey tried to read the look, but took so long to analyze it that he spoke again, his voice tinged with disappointment. "I'll take that as a *no*."

She reached over and put her hand on his leg, then quickly removed it. "That means I don't think I could afford you." She laughed in an attempt to appear unaffected by him, but she knew she probably failed in the endeavor. "I'm broke, remember?"

"Special rate for you." He winked, but his expression was suddenly serious as he watched her face with absorbed attention. "Free."

"Now you're talking." Joey rested her head on the partition behind her and closed her eyes, partly to gather her thoughts and partly so he couldn't read the look in them. She tried to ignore the foolish hammering of her heart, and forced herself to breathe slowly and evenly so he wouldn't see her anxiety.

For the last ten years, she'd been perfectly content being a widow, the idea of being anything else not even entering her mind.

Suddenly, everything had changed.

His suggestive words knocked her off guard, sending waves of conflicting emotions washing over her. Was it *fear* causing her heart to pound so? Or *excitement?*

Joey scolded herself for reacting so impulsively—maybe even recklessly—because an attraction to a man like Colt could be hazardous. She couldn't afford to be distracted by impractical relationships or romantic notions.

Perhaps more importantly, neither could *he.*

A warning spasm of alarm erupted within her, as she realized the perils and problems associated with such thoughts. Yet his teasing banter touched her deeply, reaching into her soul and seizing her heart like an unseen hand. Instead of preparing herself for an extremely dangerous operation, she felt the urge to giggle like a schoolgirl.

This wasn't like her.

Joey tried to think of something else so she could fight the out-of-control emotions racing through her. Her thoughts turned to Scott, and his resemblance to the man sitting beside her.

Like Scott, Colt was ruggedly handsome, and had a persona that pulsed with energy. They were both commanding, confident men, and had a way about them that demanded attention and respect without saying a word.

But where Scott's eyes were deep blue and charismatic, Colt's were dark, almost black, and mysterious. They held an unfathomable depth within them that was compelling.

Captivating. She took a deep breath and let it out slowly. *Irresistible.*

Colt leaned over and pushed a tendril of hair from her face. "What are you thinking?"

Joey's eyes jerked open. So he could see it—or maybe he could sense it—or maybe he was feeling the same thing, too. Her gaze fell first upon his raven-black hair, which lay in alluring disarray, then shifted to his strong jaw, covered in stubble. When her eyes met his, she was surprised to find that his expression was more tender than sensual, but full of genuine interest.

His eyes continued to study hers with curious intensity, his stare so galvanizing she found it hard to think. His ability to seemingly read her mind added to her discomfort and confusion. "Umm, just trying to figure out what we're up against and how to handle it."

"Oh." Something flickered far back in his eyes—something like disappointment—before he rested back against the wall. A tense silence ensued as he became quiet and preoccupied— seemingly musing about some deep problem of his own.

Joey leaned into him and tried to lighten the mood. "What are *you* thinking about?"

He looked down at her and then away. "Nothing."

The amusement died from Joey's eyes as she searched his face for answers, but he was expressionless now, as if guarding a secret. Despite his tightly closed lips and shielded eyes, she sensed that he was troubled—maybe even angry—and felt a pang in her heart that she had done nothing to assuage his distress.

The atmosphere in the trailer had turned from light and humorous to electrically charged—and now to distant and detached. The brief moment of compassion and connection they'd shared was gone.

Joey didn't know if she should breathe a sigh of relief—or shed a tear of regret.

Chapter 33

Colt sat quietly beside Joey, getting jostled against her as the trailer inched its way up a pothole-filled lane to their final destination. They'd changed trailers at the first farm when Caitlin had dropped one of the horses, and were now arriving at a farm owned by a fellow operator who would provide gear, phones, and vehicles.

In the first leg of their journey, Colt had closed his eyes in a futile attempt to sleep, but when Joey had rolled over and laid her head on his chest, he'd been afraid to wake her. Despite his discomfort and his arm tingling with lack of circulation, he'd been content watching her get some needed rest.

"Fury One, you're at T-minus five." When Blake's voice had broken through the silence to alert Colt they were close to their destination, he'd gently nudged Joey awake. She'd gazed up at him confused, with sleepy eyes and tousled hair.

Colt was tempted to say, *good morning, sleepy head*, but decided instead on, "We're about five minutes out."

And here he was in the last few minutes trying to quash

the surge of emotions sweeping over him, and trying to extinguish the memory of the look he'd glimpsed.

Even now his thoughts drifted back to those green eyes gazing up at him, wearing the type of expression that made him ache, because he knew she was denying to herself that she felt it, too.

Snap out of it, Nick. His mind dueled and struggled over the necessity for discretion and the obligation of restraint. The responsibilities that lay upon his shoulders were too critical for any type of diversion, especially a female one. Her ties to the past and his commitment to his job were too strong to contemplate an association other than a purely professional one.

The logical part of his brain quickly resolved that she should never know how he felt—while the emotional side reeled with disappointment that she would not.

"You ever think you'd be sitting in the back of a horse trailer as part of your job?" Her voice interrupted his confused and chaotic thoughts.

"I've been in worse places." His tried not to sound too dismal.

"Yes. I guess this pales in comparison."

In the ensuing awkward silence, Colt stretched his legs out and then bent them back in to get the circulation going again.

"Is everything going as planned so far? Do you have an update?"

"We're right on schedule. They're going to have some clothes, disguises, new phones, and vehicles for us when we stop." He glanced over at her. "Stay in contact as much as you can."

Joey nodded, but Colt could tell her mind was on something else again.

"You having second thoughts?"

"No. I'm just hoping we're not being manipulated."

"What do you mean?"

"Sassani is a master at throwing down clues in one direction while doing something in another. And if he has Homeland Security working with him, it wouldn't be hard to mislead."

"True. But the cobalt *was* stolen. Would he go through all that just to throw us off track?"

Joey shrugged. "I don't know. I'm just thinking."

"Overthinking, maybe."

"Yeah. Maybe." She took an exasperated breath and looked the other direction.

"Okay. What else is bothering you?"

She gazed up at him as if surprised that he could read her so well. "Nothing's *bothering* me, I'm just thinking."

"Okay. About what?"

"What if we do such a good job of preventing a security breach that the terrorist's mission is compromised before the device reaches its intended target? They might try to detonate it rather than allow the plot to fail completely."

"A possibility, I suppose," Colt agreed, "but I don't see them getting anywhere near the stadium with the massive security procedures that are in place."

"I guess you're right. Just going through scenarios in my head."

"I think we've got all our bases covered." Colt downplayed her concerns, but he admired her commitment and tenacity.

She was good at what she did and took it seriously. He could see why she'd been recruited to such a high-ranking position.

"You know how I feel about Homeland Security, but you can trust the guys at TF2. I mean, if it comes to that." Her words came from out of the blue, and seemed tinged with ominous warning.

"But will they trust *me*?" He gave her an inquisitive look. "If it comes to that."

"I've put in a good word for you. And they've heard about your reputation."

"Which is?"

She smiled. "You mean you don't know?"

"No."

Joey didn't elaborate on his reputation. In fact, she ignored it. "The go-to guy is Ned. I want you to remember his number—just in case."

"Just in case of what?"

"Just in case...you know, of an emergency."

Colt studied her face a moment and then nodded. "Okay. What's the number?"

He repeated what she gave him, and then leaned his head back. "All set with Ned's number...just in case."

After a few minutes of silence, he looked down at her. "You're not planning on doing something crazy, are you?"

"Depends what your definition of crazy is."

"Silly me," he said. "Telling the woman who jumps four-foot fences on a twelve-hundred-pound animal for fun, not to do anything crazy."

Chapter 34

When the trailer came to a stop, the two of them waited for the door to open, and stepped out to find themselves in a large indoor arena. A man wearing blue jeans and a flannel shirt simply said, "Follow me," before walking away toward a gate.

He picked up a backpack from a trunk and handed it to Joey. "Bathroom's right there to change in." Then he turned to Colt and nodded toward a stall. "Your stuff's in there."

Colt found a security officer's uniform, sunglasses, and a hat. When he was done changing, he strode out and found the man handing Joey a phone and a set of keys.

"A Rav4 for you." He turned to Colt and handed him another set. "And a pickup for you. The phones have the other number in the contacts. You'll have to add anyone else, but keep it to a minimum."

Colt nodded and then took his first good look at Joey. She was dressed in a pair of skinny jeans tucked into cowboy boots. A ball cap that read, *News Corps* and a heavy turtleneck sweater completed the outfit. But it was her hair that drew his attention. Wisps of dark curls stuck out from beneath the hat. Her long blond hair had vanished beneath a wig.

"What's so funny?" She cocked her head as his smile.

"Nothing. You look…different. But I see you're still in the news business."

"Wait until I get my coat on." She held up a bulky coat that would no doubt make her look ten pounds heavier. "I don't think I'll be recognizable in this thing."

"Your vehicles are right outside." The man interrupted them. "Take a look at your ID's and paperwork on the seat, and get familiar with them." Then he turned and disappeared.

"I'm heading to the stadium." Colt swung a backpack of supplies over his shoulder and started walking toward the door. "Check in with me in sixty minutes."

Joey nodded. "I have something to look into, and then I'm heading there."

Colt stopped at the tone of her voice. "Care to share?"

She didn't respond right away.

"I'll take that as a *no*."

She shrugged. "I don't want you to worry."

"So *now* I'm worried."

Joey pointed her key fob at a blue Rav4 and pushed the button to unlock the door. "Since we're on the subject, you have to promise me something."

She said the words casually, but he could tell her indifference was forced.

"What?"

She threw her paperwork in the car and turned to face him.

"You're supposed to say, '*okay*.'"

"Okay… I *think*."

Her gaze locked on his. "We don't know exactly what we're up against out there."

"True."

"So I want you to promise you'll do what you need to do." Her green eyes glimmered with a strange vibrancy. "No matter what."

"That's a strange thing to promise."

"But you will, right?"

Unable to imagine a situation in which he would be unable to keep the pledge, Colt nodded. "Yep. I can promise that."

The conversation ended and an awkward pause ensued. Colt curbed an unexpected desire to wrap his arms around her or kiss her cheek. The thought of showing emotion was as unfamiliar and foreign to him as the feeling itself. "Stay safe, Josephine."

She held out her closed hand for a fist bump. "You too, Nick."

Chapter 35

Monday afternoon

Caitlin walked back up to the house after parking the truck and trailer, trying to decide what to do with herself for the next few days. The kids were sleeping over with friends, and Blake had left while she was still out. There was no telling when he'd return, but it didn't sound like it would be tonight. The house would be unusually quiet.

Her cell phone rang as she was going up the porch stairs.

"Hey, girl. What are you doing tonight?" It was her best friend Susan.

"I haven't decided yet. My schedule is pretty open."

"Well, I have something I think you'll be interested in."

Caitlin looked down at her phone when it started to beep, then put it back to her mouth. "Sounds good, but tell me fast. My phone is about to die."

"You're not going to believe this, but I scored two tickets to the game tonight."

"What game?"

"*The* game."

"You're kidding me!"

"I kid you not. And, of course, I want to take the biggest football fan in Virginia with me."

"Now I'm *sure* you're kidding me," Cait said. "You know they're playing the Steelers, right?"

"Of course, I know that. Do you want to go or not?"

"Yes. I want to go, but those tickets are impossible to get."

"Well, just so happens, I got a call from a friend who works at the bus company. They had two people cancel at the last minute. How soon can you be ready?"

"Wow. Give me at least an hour. I'm just getting done with barn work."

"Okay, but try to hurry. They're saying security is going to be unusually tight. The tickets come with a bus ride from Leesburg so we don't have to worry about driving."

"Count me in." Caitlin ran up the stairs as she talked and peeled off her clothes. "I'll drive to your house and pick you up for the trip to Leesburg."

"Great. You'd better hurry. The bus pulls out in less than two hours."

"I'm going to change and head out the door. See you soon!"

Caitlin pressed end and then quickly texted Blake. "I'm with Susan if you need me. Phone's almost dead. Stay safe."

She didn't bother to tell him she was going to the game. She knew he was working with Colt on something big—possibly a terrorist attack in DC. But she would be in Landover, MD, far enough away to be safe from any of that chaos.

She plugged in her phone while she got dressed, knowing it wouldn't be charged, but would at least have a little juice.

When she grabbed it and headed out the door, she noticed she had a new message from Blake. *Where u going? Plug in your phone.*

Cait smiled. Big bad Blake—Mad Dog Madison as he was known when she'd first met him—was actually a thoughtful, gentle worrywart. She couldn't blame him after what he'd seen during his tenure as a Navy SEAL and then as a homicide detective. But he was always worried that something bad was going to happen—doubly so now that she was pregnant. And she knew he still blamed himself for what had happened when she was kidnapped even though it was in no way his fault.

Shoving the phone into her pocket as she picked up her backpack, she decided to ignore the message. Her phone was almost dead, and she wanted to save what little battery life it had for a true emergency.

Anyway, Blake knew how to reach her if he needed to. There was no sense telling him where she was going and causing him to worry. He needed to be able to concentrate on what he was doing.

"Here it comes." Susan pointed toward the road at the small dot that grew larger as the vehicle drew closer.

Caitlin jumped up and down, partly to stay warm and partly from excitement. She couldn't believe she was going to a Redskins game—against her favorite team the Steelers, no less. This was going to be one for the memory book.

The bus came to a screeching halt in front of them, and they fell in line behind the others to board. Susan went first, but stopped when she was on the first step. "Oh, I thought

Hank was driving today," she said to the driver.

"He's sick."

Caitlin was close enough to see the man's face and dark eyes. They looked irritated at the question. Angry even. "Hurry up."

Once the two of them found a seat near the middle, Susan leaned over to Caitlin. "That's really strange. I just talked to Hank this morning. He's the one who called me about the tickets."

Caitlin looked toward the front of the bus and saw the driver was looking at them in the large overhead mirror. He was Hispanic. Clean-cut. A man she would consider handsome if not for the forbidding, angry expression on his face.

She looked away, too excited about the game to dwell on it. "It's going to be a long night. Maybe Hank decided he wasn't up to it."

Susan nodded, though she didn't look convinced. But once the vehicle started rolling, her apprehension seemed to fade as she and Caitlin caught up on what was happening in each other's lives.

They had met when they were both journalists—but worked at opposing newspapers. Despite the competitive nature of the business, they always chatted when they saw each other at press conferences or ran into each other during events. Once Cait had married Blake and left the field, they'd grown even closer.

When the conversation waned, Caitlin looked out the window and then glanced down at her watch. "What time are we supposed to get there, anyway?"

"Two hours before kickoff, I thought." Susan looked out the window. "Where are we?"

Caitlin leaned over and looked out, too. "I wonder why he's going this way. Seems like the long way around."

"Something doesn't seem right to me." Susan turned toward Caitlin and whispered. "Doesn't Blake always tell you to follow your gut?"

Caitlin nodded as her eyes went back to the driver. He appeared nervous now. His head darting back and forth as if looking for something.

Before she could respond, Susan pulled out her phone.

"What are you doing?"

"I'm going to text Hank. See where he is." She sent the text, sat back, and gazed out the window. "Traffic's heavy now. We're hardly moving."

Caitlin pulled out a bottle of water and took a drink. "Oh well, we're heading to a Steelers game. Life is good!"

Susan laughed. "Where's your hubby anyway? I'm surprised he let you out of his sight."

"He's away. Working on something. And the kids are at a sleepover, so your invitation couldn't have come at a better time. It was just me and that big old house."

"Glad I could help." Susan turned her attention to her phone as if waiting for it to vibrate—or hoping that it would.

"By the way, my cell's almost dead so I told Blake to call you if he needs to reach me."

"Girl," Susan said, frowning, "you need to keep that thing charged. What if there would be an emergency?"

"I know, but I'm old-school. I can't get used to carrying

one of those things around." She moved closer to Susan and whispered. "Did you hear back from Hank yet?"

"No. Do you think I should try calling?"

Cait nodded. "Yes."

Susan dialed and bit her lip as the phone rang. After a long pause she said, "Hey, Hank, I'm on the bus. Just checking in to see if you're okay. Call me when you get this."

She disconnected and looked at Caitlin.

"Something's definitely wrong."

Chapter 36

Once he was in the truck and on his way, Colt clipped his ID badge onto his uniform and glanced over his paperwork when he was stopped at traffic lights.

The name assigned to him would be easy to remember. Nick Carter, which was his first and middle name. Then he called Blake so everyone at Phantom Force would have the phone number in case something happened to the radio they were using.

"It's Colt. Anything new?"

"Yes." There was a long pause. "I'm at the federal command center. They're seeing spikes in chatter."

"So it looks like we're on the right track?"

"Affirmative. They're sending more assets to the game."

"Any talk of alerting the public?"

"It's been discussed. But Homeland Security is insisting that the hysteria created will be worse than an actual attack—and we're not one hundred percent sure a strike is imminent."

"People have the right to make up their own minds." Colt shook his head in exasperation.

"Since there's going to be an obvious police presence, they're going so far as to alert people that some threats have been received. They're downplaying it, though."

"Well, that's something."

"You on comm yet?"

"Affirmative."

Colt clicked on the mic. "Radio check. How do you read?"

"Lima Charlie," Blake said. "How do you read?"

"Lima Charlie."

Blake paused a moment as if reading something. "Let's not forget the possibility that Homeland Security might be more deeply involved in this than we even know."

"I got it," Colt said. "Make sure everyone on our team understands that the bad guys might have credentials."

"And weapons."

Colt didn't respond to that. He was thinking about the ease with which a person with a Homeland Security badge and credentials could walk around the complex.

"Every nuclear detection device for hundreds of miles is onsite or near it," Blake said. "There's no way they'll get something through."

"I know that. And you know that. And so does Sassani." Colt tried to ignore the tremor of warning creeping up his spine. "So what in the hell is he planning to do?"

Chapter 37

Monday
1600 hours

Arman Sassani walked back and forth in the room filled with computer screens and IT experts with his hands clasped behind his back and a smile on his face.

Today was the day he'd been waiting for most of his life. In a mere eight months, he'd turned this rented dilapidated farmhouse and outbuildings in northern Virginia into a state of the art control center—and now the time was at hand.

He could hardly believe his good fortune at finding this place. The elderly owners had died, leaving the fifty-acre property to their grandchildren—all of whom lived in New York and none of whom wanted the responsibility of upkeep.

Like most squabbling relatives, they couldn't agree on a price or even whether or not to sell, so they settled on allowing a local attorney to handle the details of renting it out. That arrangement gave Sassani room to do what he needed to do with no prying eyes or the threat of unannounced visits from nosy landlords.

Everything so far had gone smoothly, including his journey to America. The minutes and hours and days he'd spent sitting in a cell in Guantanamo Bay planning this operation were now bearing fruit. All of the naysayers who told him he was wasting his time, that he would never leave Gitmo let alone be able to pull off a massive strike in America had been proven wrong.

Yet he had to admit to himself that even during the planning stages, he'd never genuinely thought he'd be here. Organizing the largest terrorist attack ever to take place on American soil, step-by-step, piece-by-piece, had been more of a way to keep himself occupied and relieve his pent-up rage than anything else.

But when the Americans had called his name and he'd found himself on a plane to Omar, he'd known that *Allah* had indeed chosen him to do this great thing. Of course, none of it had been by accident—but the fact that it had all come together was a small miracle in itself. The radicalization of a high-ranking official in the Department of Homeland Security had been the icing on the cake.

Sassani had spent the next few months building and strengthening contacts in Mexico, including one Carlos Valdez. With the help of the drug kingpin, he was able to expand his operation quickly and begin to fine-tune his plans.

Although he was content to carry out the entire operation from Omar, the policy of the United States to accept refugees from war-torn Syria, had been too enticing to resist. After very little vetting, he'd been given safe passage to the United States.

How long will it take for American citizens to realize that their greatest asset—freedom—is our greatest ally?

Sassani laughed out loud at the thought of the vetting process. He'd been required to fill out some paperwork that included answering the question *Are you a terrorist?*

He'd responded to that query with no hesitation and without a trace of guilt, because in his own mind, he was not. He may have caused terror, yes. But so did the United States. Who were they to decide what kind of terror was evil and what kind was acknowledged as necessary?

Once on American soil, *Allah* had continued to shower him with good fortune.

Now, here he was, mere hours away from the big show. After all the hard work he'd put into the planning, it surprised him that he wasn't the least bit nervous. Excited, yes. But worried, no. He'd spent almost as much time misleading the U.S. government by creating false evidence trails as he had working on the real plan—so he knew the surprise would be complete.

Only one thing gave him pause and kept him from feeling completely confident—an old nemesis, Nick Colton. It was Colton who had tracked him and sent him to Gitmo after losing a member of his team in Afghanistan. The man had been relentless in hunting Sassani down to exact his revenge.

Now it is MY time for revenge.

Sassani felt his pulse pound with agitation for the first time as he thought of Colton. He'd just been informed by his men that they'd lost sight of him *and* the TF2 agent he was likely with, but he shrugged off the notion they could do anything to stop him. There were too many contingencies in place for him to fail.

Still, it irritated him that his ally in the Department of Homeland Security had failed to eliminate the TF2 agent once and for all when he'd had the chance. Sassani had more important things to concentrate on today than what these two were up to—and it bothered him that they were still around to create obstacles.

On the other hand, it would be the men from *El Soldado* who would be on the front lines today. They would be the ones going in with guns blazing, and they would be the ones whose blood would be shed.

Of course, they would also be the group blamed for the strike—and the group that would take credit for it. Sassani and his men would simply fade away into the fabric of American society, and live normal lives while planning the next operation.

During tonight's spectacle he would remain miles away from the destruction, sitting in this farmhouse watching the show. Thanks to the security feeds from Homeland Security, he would have the pleasure of watching many different angles, and thanks to the live reporting on television, there would no doubt be hours and days of entertaining coverage.

The door squeaked open behind him, but he kept his eyes on the monitors. "Is everything ready?"

"Yes. Everything is in place."

Sassani looked at his watch and then back up to the screen. It was still about three hours before the game started, but the parking lots were busy.

He looked over to a man typing on a computer. "How much longer?"

"Just a few minutes." The man did not look up or stop tapping on the keyboard.

As Sassani watched the young man work, a smile lifted the corners of his mouth. Albert was the product of America's penitentiary system and had used his prison term to his advantage. Sentenced to four years on a minor computer hacking charge, he'd devoted his time behind bars to networking with other computer geeks and learning new skills.

The government had even offered Albert a job upon completion of his sentence, but Sassani had offered him a much better salary. This assignment was a piece of cake for him—despite recent upgrades to the stadium's security system. And it was one of the most crucial components of the entire plan.

"Here we go." Albert pointed to a large television on the wall.

Sassani took a step closer and nodded as he viewed video footage of cars flowing into the parking lot. The screen was split into six different sections.

"There is no way the security teams will be able to tell the difference?"

"I'd say the chances are less than one percent."

"Very well. We are ready to begin." Sassani felt a thrill of excitement sweep through him. "Go ahead."

Albert begin to tap away on the keys again, his head bent low in concentration. In less than a minute he looked up and nodded. Sassani turned toward the rack of monitors in the front of the room that showed traffic moving into the stadium and the parking lots outside. The screen flickered for a split second and then resumed. Unless someone was watching closely, they would not have noticed the change.

He walked over to a table with two men on headsets. "Anything?"

They both shook their heads. "Nothing here. No radio traffic. No one seemed to notice."

The smile on Sassani's face grew larger. Step one had gone off without a hitch. On to step two.

Chapter 38

Blake sighed and paced in the command center. He'd rather be out walking the site with Colt, but they had both decided it would be better for him to serve here. He knew the assets they had and how to reach them with a moment's notice.

With a few minutes of down time, he pulled out his phone to check in on Cait. The call went straight to voicemail. Unlike most women her age, she hated carrying a phone and rarely used it. The few times she did remember to take it with her, the battery would be dead.

He hung up and dialed the number for the house instead, hoping he could catch her before she left with her friend. That phone too went unanswered, so he decided to shoot a text to Susan. He'd known Cait's best friend almost as long as he'd known Cait, so all he said was, *Wife check. Where you guys at?*

Putting the phone back in his pocket, he stared blankly at the wall trying to figure out what was gnawing at him. He'd served as a Navy SEAL for eight years and then as a homicide detective for another dozen, so when something didn't feel right, he tried to pay attention.

Was it just the situation he was in at the moment? Trying to stop a major terrorist attack before it happened? Or something more?

Blake shrugged off the gloomy feelings, attributing them to being separated from Cait. He felt guilty for having to leave—especially since he'd just promised her he'd never let her out of his sight again.

After being kidnapped by the drug kingpin Carlos Valdez, she'd been back less than two weeks before intelligence of a new terrorist plan had become more concrete and portentous. The scope and possible consequences of this strike demanded his onsite involvement.

Squeezing his temples in an effort to focus, Blake chastised himself. *Snap out of it. Concentrate.*

Never in a million years, would Blake have pictured himself standing in a tactical operation center with his mind concentrating on—and worrying about—a woman.

After a failed first marriage, he'd thought he was done with that stuff. But love has a way of changing hearts and minds. Even after a year of marriage to Cait, Blake still felt more like a love-sick twenty-year-old, than his real age of forty-two.

One of the men from Phantom Force interrupted Blake's musings by handing him a paper on a clipboard. He sat down to read it, but found it hard to concentrate. If he could just hear Cait's voice and be assured she was okay, he could get down to business and focus on the problems at hand.

"Are you okay?" The man stood beside him with his arms crossed, waiting for a response.

"Sure." Blake glanced back down at the paper. "Why?"

"It's just a food order, dude. What do you want?"

Blake lifted the menu without reading it and scribbled *cheeseburger sub* on the paper beneath, before handing the clipboard back.

"Thanks." The man started to walk away, but talked over his shoulder. "Tom wants to meet with you in thirty for an update."

Blake nodded, hoping he'd get a phone call or text from Cait before then. He'd kept his message on Susan's phone short and light so he wouldn't seem like an over-anxious husband. Maybe he should have made it more obvious that he was worried about his wife.

He pulled his phone out again, and contemplated sending a second text. But the thought of interrupting Cait in the middle of a fun afternoon with her friend made him stop. Yes, he wanted to talk to her, but his anxiety was as much from guilt as it was concern. They were expecting their first child together, and he'd given her less than a day's notice he was leaving.

Blake didn't put his phone away. Instead, he dialed the number of the person he always called when he needed a steadying force.

When Susan's phone chimed, Caitlin nudged her arm excitedly. "Is that Hank?"

Susan studied the phone. "No, it's your husband. He wants

to know where you are." She looked at Cait. "You didn't tell him where you were going?"

"I never had a chance before my phone died." Cait shrugged. "Anyway, I wanted it to be a surprise."

"Okay. Well, should I tell him now or do you want to keep it a secret?"

Caitlin laughed. "No, it's not a secret. You can tell him."

Susan sent a text and leaned back.

"What'd you say?"

"I told him I scored tickets from a Leesburg Lines bus driver and now you're living the dream, heading to the Steelers game."

"He's totally not going to believe it," Cait said with a smile. "He'll be almost as surprised as I am."

Chapter 39

ONE HOUR UNTIL KICK OFF

Colt answered his phone while walking across the busy parking lot. "What's up, buddy?"
"Just checking in," Blake said. "Hoping you have something."

"Nothing but a pounding headache." Colt stopped walking and squeezed his temples. "Which I'd be glad to give to you."

"No thanks. I have one of my own."

"You're just homesick—or maybe being-away-from-your-wife sick."

"Yeah. You've got that right. Wish I knew where she was."

"What are you talking about?"

"I got a text that she was going somewhere with Susan, but as usual, her phone is dead."

"Oh, well. She's a big girl. And Cait's not the type to go out for a wild night on the town while her husband's away."

"I know. I just don't like not being in contact."

"Give Susan a call if it will make you feel better."

Blake laughed. "I just sent her a text. I'm one step ahead of you. Speaking of making contact, you hear from Joey?"

Colt glanced at his watch, and saw it had been about ninety minutes since he had last spoken to her. "Now that you mention it—no."

He felt a warning thump in his brain that increased the strength of his headache, but didn't have time to dwell on it. A security vehicle with its lights flashing was heading toward him, and the driver had his arm out the window waving toward Colt. "Hey, I'll call you right back. I might have some news."

"What's up?" Colt walked up to the window.

"You Nick Carter?"

"Yes, sir. You have something for me?"

"Supposed to give you this."

Colt took the piece of paper and read it silently. "Thanks." He didn't show any emotion until the car had driven away, and then he said "holy mother-fucking shit," as he pushed the button for Blake on his phone. This wasn't something he wanted broadcast across the radio that he wore. "Hey, we have a problem."

"The bus?" The severity of the situation was clear by Blake's tone.

"Yes. You've heard?"

"It's just starting to come across. The info I have is that an employee at Leesburg Lines followed the sound of a phone ringing and found a dead bus driver in the closet. His ID and company coat were gone."

"I need everyone you have on standby ASAP." Colt went into full operations mode. "And I want some more firepower."

"It's on its way." Blake's voice remained steady and calm even though Colt could tell he was typing on a computer and sending messages as he talked.

"Put two of our guys with the police looking for the bus. If we can get it stopped before it gets here, all the better."

"Two snipers on the bus," Blake said, comprehending what Colt meant. "Got it."

"I'm heading toward the large vehicle parking lot now." Colt had reached his truck, but traffic in the parking lots was at a standstill, so he decided to hoof it. "Let me know if you hear anything." After disconnecting, he grabbed the rifle that had been stuck behind the seat for him and slung it across his back. Then he stuffed some extra magazines into his pockets and took off at a trot for the bus lot.

He hadn't made it far when his phone vibrated. Thinking it was Joey, he breathed a sigh of relief, and reached into his pocket without slowing his pace. "What's up?"

For a moment, all he heard was heavy breathing, then a voice, gravelly with fear and concern spoke. "You've got to stop that bus."

Colt was starting to breathe heavily himself from his fast pace. "What do you think I'm doing here, brother? Going to a picnic?"

"No, you don't understand—" Blake stopped for a moment as if trying to form the words. "I think Cait's on that bus."

Colt's first reaction was to stop running and ask if he'd heard correctly, but he ignored that response and instead ran faster. He knew Blake had already disconnected.

There was nothing more to say.

Chapter 40

With his mind intent on analyzing the situation, and his eyes constantly scanning the terrain for anything out of place, Colt continued in the direction of the bus lot. He was zigzagging between cars, trying to take the most direct route to his destination, when his phone vibrated again.

Finally. Joey must be checking in.

He pressed the *answer* button. "About time. Go ahead."

"Yes. Umm. Hello?"

"Who is this?" Colt pulled the phone away and looked at the number.

"This is Paula at the Stop and Go on Fleet Street. Someone dropped their phone."

"Oka-a-y?" Colt questioned, shaking his head as he took in the distance he still had to cover. "I'm kind of busy. What does that have to do with me?" He almost hung up without waiting for a reply.

"You're listed on the phone as ICE…the *In Case of Emergency* contact."

"What did you say?" Colt didn't give her time to respond to that question before he asked another. "Was it a woman?

What did she look like?"

"I'm not sure. But there was a woman in here buying coffee right before the phone was found."

"What did she look like?" Colt looked around, realizing he had yelled loud enough for everyone in the parking lot to hear.

"If it's the one I'm thinking about, she was kind of tall. Dark, curly hair."

"And boots? Was she wearing boots?"

"Yes. Cowboy boots."

"Where did she go? How did she drop the phone?"

"I don't know." Now it was the woman who sounded frustrated. "Someone found the phone in the alley and brought it in, and now I'm calling you."

Colt put his hand on his chest as he ran to hold his heart in its place. "Did you call the police?"

"For a lost phone?" The tone of her voice revealed that she thought he was overreacting. "No."

It took everything within Colt to shape a coherent thought and then express it through speech since most of his brain was preoccupied with warding off an intense emotional pain. "Call them. Give them this number as a contact. Tell them it's important. I gotta go."

Colt believed he'd known what Blake was feeling when Caitlin was missing, but he hadn't. This was like a shotgun blast to the chest, only ten times worse. He'd never felt so helpless—and mortal—knowing he could not be two places at one time.

Phantom Force had prepared for a worst-case scenario, but

this was shaping up to be the most ambitious terrorist attack on American soil since 2001—and perhaps, when all was said and done—all-time. He concentrated on breathing normally.

Facing bullets was nothing compared to this—and even this was nothing compared to the uncertainty of what the rest of the day would bring.

As this new and unexpected sense of urgency consumed him, Colt remembered the number of the TF2 agent that Joey had given him. He pulled himself together and dialed as he ran.

After two rings someone answered. "Go ahead."

"This is Nick Colton, I'm—"

"I know who you are. What's up?"

"It looks like there is a TF2 agent missing."

"We're aware, but she's not actually missing."

"Well, I just got a call that her phone was found…"

"Okay, but she's not *missing*." The man came across as calm—almost bored.

"I'm not following." Colt started to get a bad feeling in the pit of his stomach. He wanted to scream at the man and ask him what in the hell was going on, but held his tongue and waited.

"We just picked up a blip on the screen. We have a visual."

Colt tried to get his brain to catch up to what the man was saying. "You mean she has a tracker on her?"

The man was silent for a moment, as papers shuffled in the background. "Affirmative. Her wedding ring."

"So are you saying she did this on purpose?" Colt's voice cracked, but at least he got it out.

"She was tasked with helping abort a major terrorist attack..." The man did not bother to finish the sentence.

Colt remembered Joey's last words to him, and then pictured a roomful of men sitting calmly at a table, watching a screen. To them, it was a blip leading them to their target.

To him, it was someone he'd met by chance—and someone he'd fallen for by accident.

It was Joey.

Chapter 41

Trying to ignore the cold air being sucked into his lungs, Colt kept the phone to his ear, but had only run a few strides farther when the radio channel he was using to monitor the stadium's security crackled to life.

"Hey, I have a bus on Redskins Road that missed the lot. He's heading your way to go around. Over."

Without saying goodbye, Blake disconnected and stuck the phone in his pocket while yanking the radio off from where it was clipped to his pants. He was getting ready to respond when someone else yelled, "Turn it around!"

"It's just a bus of spectators, dude." The parking attendant replied, sounding tired and agitated. "Calm down."

"Turn it around. *Now*." Another voice came over the radio, loud but composed. "Don't let it come any closer."

"Nothing more I could do," the attendant snapped. "I don't think the driver speaks English."

Colt spotted the bus from across the parking lot and increased his speed. He wasn't sure what he could do to stop a thirty-thousand-pound vehicle full of innocent civilians, but with Cait on board, he sure as hell wasn't going to stand around and wait to see what happened.

Sassani watched the monitor with the correct security feed, his heart beating with anticipation. The man directing the buses into the lot waved his arms to slow the bus down, but just as he had been instructed, the driver held his hands up as if he didn't know where he was going.

When a second security person ran onto the road to get him to stop, he had already passed the bus parking lot entrance.

The driver opened the door and the man put one foot through the door, shouting over the noise of the bus. "What are you doing? That's the bus parking lot right there."

"*Si*. I go around," the driver said.

The man growled. "Okay. Get this thing out of the way. Go around and pull in that lot right there!"

The driver nodded, closed the doors and hit the gas. Sassani's eyes were focused on the row of monitors and his entire being concentrated on the scene as it unfolded. He was the director of this orchestrated concert of events and would be calling all the shots.

When the vehicle reached the stadium, the driver pulled the vehicle across both lanes of traffic and came to a screeching halt. Then, as planned, he opened the door and exited the bus.

"Now." Sassani spoke calmly through his headset to the sharpshooter, even though his heart was racing with anticipation. "Take your shot."

He could hear the people on the bus yelling at the driver and asking one another what was happening.

The gunshot and the subsequent explosion were

simultaneous.

The thirty pounds of exploding target compound and gallon of gasoline that had been placed in a portable bathroom right beside where the vehicle had come to rest sent shrapnel and flames high in the air. The concussion blew out most of the windows on the bus, and left the back end of it a mass of twisted metal.

Security officers and police who had been running toward the vehicle to get it moved were down on the street, and utter chaos ensued as pedestrians ran in every direction.

Chapter 42

Colt was still more than thirty yards away, but he could see the fire from the explosion was dangerously close to the fuel tank. He raced toward the scene, aware that he might be running into a radioactive area or that a secondary strike on those responding might be forthcoming.

But instead of inspiring fear, as the situation would have in normal people, it evoked angry indignation and outrage, and inspired him to run even faster.

"Out of the bus!"

Many of the occupants had already exited and bystanders were helping those who were too shaken up to move. One of the spectators pointed to a man. "What's going on? There goes the driver. What's he doing?"

Colt looked over his shoulder and saw a man in a black sweatshirt with the hood pulled up trying to look casual as he walked away. He turned back to the bus to find Caitlin grabbing his arm, crying. "I thought that was you, Nick. What is happening?"

He pulled her and her friend away from the scene. "I have to go." He held onto her shoulders and shook her lightly to make sure she was listening. She had a dazed look in her eyes, so he wasn't sure she could understand what he was saying. "Start walking. Don't trust anyone—even if they're in uniform—and stay away from crowds of people. Do you hear me?"

He gave her another gentle shake and looked over Susan. "Call Blake. He'll get you out of here. Now go!"

He didn't wait for an answer. He caught sight of the driver again and took off running.

It wasn't until he was about twenty yards away that the man apparently comprehended that someone was following him. He glanced over his shoulder, saw Colt, and took off running.

Colt talked into the stadium's security radio as he ran. "I have eyes on the driver of the bus. Black hoodie and pants. Northeast corner of the parking area." He saw the man turn around and winced when a bullet made a loud *ping* off the car in front of him. "Shots fired."

Taking cover behind a car and then crawling underneath a truck so he could be another vehicle closer, Colt saw the man standing behind a vehicle doubled over and sucking air in, trying to catch his breath. Colt crawled out, staying low, and crept a little closer. He swung his rifle around to the front, but didn't want to take a shot unless he had to. He wanted this guy alive.

The man started moving again, but continued looking over his shoulder and breathing hard. Apparently not detecting Colt's approach, he stopped at a vehicle and fumbled in his pocket for the keys.

Colt sprinted the last few steps. Before the driver could turn around, he grabbed him by the neck from behind and slammed his head into the car, hard. "Drop it."

Instead of obeying the order, the man struggled to turn around and fire.

"Buddy, you just made a *really* big mistake." Colt slammed the man's forehead into the car again, three times. By the third hit, the man released the weapon and his knees buckled. "Stop!"

Colt gave his head one more bang, then threw him onto the ground and straddled him. "If you want to live, tell me what's coming next."

"You're a security guard." The man sneered, looking at his uniform. "You can't kill me."

Colt yanked the man to a sitting position by the strings of his sweatshirt, jerked the hood off, and then slammed the back of his head to the pavement. "Wrong. I'm not a security guard." He lifted the man's head and slammed it down again. At the same time, he tightened the strings on the sweatshirt around the bus driver's throat. "And, wrong. I *can* kill you."

After seeing the confused look in the man's bulging eyes, Colt pulled a revolver from his waistband and held it next to the man's temple. "No one is going to rescue you. They're all busy. You have one more chance."

"Stop! Please! I don't know. They didn't tell me."

"Who is *they*?"

"I don't have a name." He struggled to breathe. "Just a number."

"Sorry. Bad answer." Colt lifted the man's head again, even

higher than the previous time.

"No! Wait!"

"Did you remember something?"

"Yes. Stop." He whimpered and groaned. "I might know something else."

"Start talking."

"The bus. It's a distraction."

"For what?"

"Something bigger."

"Are you trying to fuck with me?" Colt rolled him over with one movement, snatched a handful of his bloodied hair and slammed his forehead into the blacktop.

"No!" The man started sobbing as Colt snapped a zip tie onto his wrists behind his back. "Please. No more!"

Colt leaned down close to his ear. "Here I am, trying to be a nice guy by not cracking your skull open you filthy piece of scum." He elevated the man's head up high off the pavement again. "But if I don't know the plan in ten seconds, it's bye-bye mister nice guy."

"Ambulance."

"What did you say?" Colt pulled the man's head to within inches of his own.

"Ambulance. Armed men."

"How many? From where?" Colt dropped the man's head and let it hit the pavement. "Not fast enough. How many? From where?" He lifted him again.

"I don't know how many. Stop!" The man's mouth dripped with blood, and his nose and forehead were pulpy and raw. "Hopewell Transport. *El Soldado.*"

Just then, two security officers rushed up between the cars with guns drawn, one aimed at the man on the ground and one at Colt.

"This is the driver of the bus." Colt dragged the blood-spattered man up to a standing position. "He says they have an ambulance bringing in men."

"Sure they do, buddy."

Colt gaze slid from the face of the officer who had spoken, down to his badge and then back up. It said: *Homeland Security.*

"What's going on? What do you think you're doing?" One man spoke, but both men now had their guns trained on Colt. He saw their earpieces and radios, and realized he'd alerted them to his location.

"Me?" Colt looked casually to his right and then his left. "Actually, I think I'm getting the hell out of here."

He pushed the cuffed bus driver into the two of them and took off running, keeping his head down behind cars as the men gave chase. He thought he heard shots fired, but he was breathing too hard to be sure.

Colt keyed his mic for Blake. "Code Firestorm."

"Got it. Sending in the cavalry." There was a pause. "What's the situation there?"

Colt could hear the alarm in Blake's voice. He was trying to remain professional, but he knew his wife was in danger, and he was helpless to do anything about it. Colt crawled under an SUV and watched the two men run by.

"There's been an explosion." Colt whispered, trying to catch his breath. "I'm thinking it's only round one."

"A diversion?"

"Maybe. Redskins Road is now blocked. No way in or out."

"What do you mean Redskins Road is blocked? I'm looking at the security camera feeds as we speak. Traffic looks normal."

Colt jerked his head up and hit it on the top of the vehicle. "What did you say?"

"You heard me." Blake sounded like he was moving closer to the monitors as he spoke. "I'm seeing a line of cars. Blue pickup truck, then a white sports car, then a greenish-looking Jeep. They're moving. Barely. But moving."

Colt crawled out from under the car, and staying low, made his way to get a visual on the burned out bus and the crowd of people. Cars were at a complete standstill. None of them looked like what he was describing.

His heart hit the ground as he realized what had happened. Sassani had hacked into the stadium's security feed. The task force and security personnel who were monitoring the feeds were watching a line of vehicles flowing smoothly into the parking lot—possibly tape from an earlier game. They had no way of telling anything had happened unless they'd received audible communication—and Colt had no idea if that had been compromised, as well.

"They've hacked into the security system?" Blake phrased it as a question, yet his tone indicated he already knew the answer.

The ensuing silence was interrupted when another explosion ripped through the air. Colt knew without looking that another access road was now blocked. The terrorists were penning them in for the grand finale—whatever that was going to be. If he let them get their way, there would be no escape. No way for ambulances and fire trucks to get in, and no way for the spectators to get out. Already, people who had seen the first blast had run screaming to the opposite side of the stadium, only to be caught in another explosion.

This was Hell with the lid off.

"Have you seen Cait?"

"Affirmative. Had eyes on Cait." Colt had learned that good news required the same calm voice and composure as the tragic, but trying to sound indifferent and unemotional in this situation was the toughest thing he'd ever done. "She's fine and should be making contact." He felt, rather than heard, Blake's sigh of relief, and then remembered what the bus driver had told him.

"Get snipers on the ambulances."

"Come again? Ambulances?"

"Affirmative. Ambulances. Confirmed that Hopewell Transport is full of tangos."

There were more of them out there, and Colt still didn't know what they had planned. The mission was not yet done.

In fact, it was beginning to look like it had just begun.

Chapter 43

Colt grabbed his phone and punched the number for TF2.

"Do you have eyes on her yet? On the vehicle she's in?"

"A team is heading her way now. We had a little trouble with the satellite link-up. We're trying to catch up with a visual."

"What's the plan to get her out?"

"We have to see where this takes us first."

Colt remembered the camera and mics in the halters. "What about sound and video? She wasn't wearing anything for sound and video?"

His question was met with silence.

"What are you getting as far as sound and video?" he asked again.

Ned cleared his throat. "Nothing right now. It's black and mostly quiet. Just the sound of an engine. It's possible she's covered up or is maybe even in a trunk."

Colt considered another possibility. She wasn't moving or speaking because she was already dead.

In the silence, Colt heard the sound of a siren come through the phone. "Is that her mic recording that?" He pressed the phone closer to his ear.

"Yes, we're checking with emergency services now, to see what's been dispatched, based on where we're spotting the blip."

"Nothing has come over the scanner from there, sir." Colt heard a woman in the background report.

Then a man said, "Emergency services says everything's quiet in that sector."

"It doesn't sound like it's getting any closer or farther away."

"She's *in* it." Colt's heart started racing. "I've got credible intelligence that another wave of attacks is coming by ambulance. Hopewell Transport."

"Are you onsite?" Ned's voice increased in volume and urgency for the first time, but he didn't wait for an answer. "We need to take that ambulance out."

"I'm on it, but alert your men." Colt took off at a run to find a high vantage point. "I'll alert mine."

He disconnected and keyed his mic. "Code 2-1-1."

"I read," Blake said. "We have snipers on Hill Oaks and Garrett Morgan. We were assured Homeland was taking care of the others."

"I'll try to find a spot covering Bishop Peebles Drive."

Colt knew that was most likely the direction the next wave was coming from because it was the only one still open. After causing chaos at two of the other entrances, they now had an ambulance crammed with explosives or full of armed gang members—maybe even both—heading this way.

Colt's calves burned as he ran toward the road. When the siren from an emergency vehicle grew louder, he looked around for a better vantage point. A large box truck sat about three rows away. Without losing stride, he ran to the truck, placed one foot on the front bumper, then stepped up to the hood, and hopped up to the top of the vehicle.

A truck with a trailer even higher was parked about four feet away. He made the leap up and across without hesitation, and dropped to a prone shooting position to wait for the ambulance to come into sight.

Just as a speck of flashing lights appeared, he pressed the button on his phone to reconnect with TF2.

"I have eyes on the ambulance. I need double confirmation."

"There's no such thing as Hopewell Transport. Take it out."

Colt swallowed. Killing was part of the job. When behind a gun, he was paid to squeeze the trigger when it was called for. He'd spent most of his life in training to execute this one little act, and had accepted the responsibility of taking another's man's life on more than one occasion.

But he hesitated. All he could think about was how it felt when he'd lost Jennifer Griffin. *Please, not again.*

"Are we sure?"

"We're sure," Ned said. "Cleared hot."

Colt disconnected and put the rifle sights up to his eye to get a better view of the ambulance. He keyed his mic to Blake. "I have eyes on the ambulance."

"Hit it," Blake commanded. "Before it gets too close."

The vehicle was approaching a place where there were few cars and no civilians. Colt moved his finger to the trigger, but hesitated. "Joey might be in it." Even to his own ears his voice sounded husky and unnatural.

There was a short silence, but Blake said the words that Colt expected him to say.

"One life or a few thousand, brother. You know what you have to do."

Colt felt a drop of sweat slide down the side of his face. Losing her would be one thing...

Being the cause of it another.

"Listen to me. Take the shot. *Now!*"

Colt barely heard Blake. The words Joey had spoken continued to echo and reverberate through his skull. *Do what you have to do. Promise?*

Colt inhaled and released his breath in a slow, deliberate manner. One more deep breath, and an adjustment through his scope.

I promise.

He pulled the trigger.

Chapter 44

Colt's first shot caused the ambulance to veer crazily, and the second shot sent it off the side of the road into a field with the driver slumped over the wheel. As the doors opened and men began to jump out, Colt pulled the trigger a third time.

The resulting explosion sent pieces of the ambulance and body parts flying in every direction. The vehicle disappeared into a veil of smoke and fire, and the men disappeared into a thick mist.

Judging from the mushroom cloud that rose into the air, Colt knew he'd struck another cache of target practice explosive and gasoline hidden in the ambulance.

After the initial burnout, nothing but a black hulk emerged through the smoke. The front axle with one wheel attached was the only recognizable piece of the vehicle that remained.

Adrenaline-filled tension and strain quickly transformed into gun wrenching pain. Colt slid down the windshield of the truck to the hood, his body limp, his shoulders heaving with emotion.

From the hood, he slid to the ground, and dropped to his knees as soon as his feet hit the blacktop. With his forehead on the pavement, he laced his hands behind his head, and took deep breaths, trying to clear the images that ran through his mind. He didn't make a sound. He knew screaming wouldn't change the situation and crying wouldn't make him feel any better. He'd done what he had to do.

"Are you okay?"

Colt stopped breathing but didn't look up. He wasn't sure if he'd actually heard a voice or was just dreaming it.

When he felt a hand on his shoulder, he knew there was someone there.

He opened his eyes and lifted his head a few inches, just enough to see two cowboy boots standing in front of him.

Joey squatted down so her face was even with his. "You okay? You hurt?"

She no longer wore a wig and her face was smudged with dirt. Still, Colt didn't move anything but his eyes, which traveled to the site of the ambulance, still smoking behind her, and then zeroed back on her with a look of dazed disbelief.

"I'm here." Joey placed her hands on his face. "Not there."

Colt pulled her into him and closed his eyes, his head buried in her hair. He didn't know how she'd gotten there, but he didn't care. He was afraid if he let her go, she would disappear. *This can't be real.*

"You're suffocating me."

He felt her struggling against him. "Sorry." He pulled her out to arm's length, more shaken than he cared to admit as he struggled back to reality. "I thought you were…"

She placed her finger on his lips, and he thought he saw something more wistful replace the concerned look.

"I'm sorry. It's a long story and we have to go." She glanced over her shoulder at the burning wreckage, while taking his hand to pull him up.

"Go where?" Colt was vaguely aware of steam rising from his sweat-covered shirt into the chilly air.

Joey pointed to a chopper circling overhead. "That's our ride. They're pretty sure they know where Sassani is." She started walking away and talked over her shoulder. "I thought you might want to come along."

Colt took a few long strides to catch up to her, as a powerful sense of urgency washed over him. "You'd better believe it."

Chapter 45

Once they reached the field where the chopper had landed, Colt climbed into the seat beside her and put on the headphones.

Neither talked as they flew over the chaos below. The smoking remains of three bombs that had been left in portable bathrooms were still smoking, as was the ambulance Colt had blown up with his shot. Security teams were moving people in an orderly fashion to an area where they could be checked and released in a systematic and organized manner.

Colt looked over at Joey and keyed his mic. "No dirty bomb?"

She nodded and pointed to a circle of vehicles with flashing lights in the distance. "A drone. They brought it down with one of the anti-drone guns."

Colt leaned back in his seat and breathed a big sigh of relief. Innocent people had been hurt—some probably killed—but it wasn't the disaster it could have been. He turned his head and stared out the window again, wondering if he should feel some guilt for the sense of gratitude and exhilaration consuming him.

"So where have you been? And why didn't you check in

with me?" He turned to Joey. "And how did your ring get in that ambulance?"

"Whoa. Slow down." She looked at him with sympathetic shimmer in the shadow of her eyes. "Sorry about the lack of communication."

Colt exhaled slowly. The intense relief he felt at finding out she was safe helped to squash the anger he felt that she had scared him half to death—but barely. He turned his attention back to her as she began to explain.

"I passed an old garage on the way here and noticed an ambulance sitting in the alley with a nervous-looking driver behind the wheel. I needed a cup of coffee, so I parked about a block away and walked up the alley behind it to check it out a little closer."

She paused and took a long drink of water from a bottle someone handed her. "I thought it was even stranger that the windows were all covered, and since I had to get moving, I had no choice but to stick my ring on the bumper so TF2 could track it."

Colt just nodded for her to continue. "But your phone. How did you lose your phone?"

"Okay. Hold on. I'm getting to that." She looked at him with the slight glow of humor shining in her eyes. "It's these damn women's jeans. They don't have useful pockets." She shook her head. "I went and bought a cup of coffee at the store next door, and shoved the phone into my back pocket. By the time I came back out, the ambulance had left. I was in a hurry, so I didn't notice that my phone was missing until I needed to make contact. I was supposed to meet up with an operative from

TF2 to get a radio anyway, so I wasn't worried about it—but then things started happening and I didn't have time."

She gazed up at him with her vibrant green eyes. "Sorry if you were worried."

"Just a little," Colt said, curtly. He had to look away from her remorseful expression because it made him want to draw her close and never let her out of his sight again. Instead he just asked, "How do we know where Sassani is?"

"We're not positive, but a member of the task force went through some files of Donya Abbasi's husband."

"The attorney."

"Right. He recently handled the rental agreement of a secluded farm right outside of DC."

"Nothing real suspicious about that."

"No, it only rang alarm bells because the renter paid for a full year in cash."

"Okay. That *is* a little suspicious."

"Speaking of which, we should be getting close."

In the distance, they could make out the glow of flashing lights, and soon, they were over the scene. Emergency vehicles of every description were parked in a farm lane and some were still arriving, driving across fields from the opposite direction.

"Guess our arrival isn't going to be much of a surprise visit," Colt said dryly.

As soon as the chopper landed, the two of them hopped out and were immediately greeted by Ned. "I see you found our missing agent."

Colt nodded as his eyes scanned the setting. "No one has moved in yet?"

"No. We've been waiting for the electric company to cut off the juice." As he said the words, the light on the pole and everything near the house went dark. Ned lifted the radio on his shirt to his lips. "Kill all the vehicle lights."

Within a few minutes, the lights of the emergency vehicles surrounding the property had gone dark.

"We're going to proceed with caution in case of booby-traps," Ned said. "There's a good possibility all the buildings are jammed with explosives."

He'd barely finished his sentence when a large blast practically knocked those standing close by off their feet. Some men hit the ground and others hid behind vehicles as pieces of a nearby barn fluttered to the ground.

"Did one of your men set that off?"

Ned shook his head. "No. Maybe Sassani knew we were coming in when the lights went out and blew himself up."

"No way." Colt shook his head. "He's too big of a coward. He would never do that." His eyes continued to scan and study the layout of the land. "If anything, it's a distraction. He wants to lure a fire crew in closer."

He turned to Ned. "Tell your guys to be careful with any shots fired. There might be more target explosives in there that he wants *us* to set off by shooting at something."

"They've been warned."

"If it's okay with you, I'd like to go in."

Ned cocked his head. "Do you know what Sassani looks like? Can you identify him?"

"I know him like the back of my hand."

Ned turned to Joey with a questioning look. When she

nodded, he conceded. "Okay. Richard will get you set up with comm. You can get your equipment over there." He shook his finger at him. "My lead guy is in charge, though."

Colt went to the back of a truck where men were being outfitted with weapons and gear. Someone handed him a bulletproof vest and helmet. As he turned to put it on, he saw Joey suiting up, as well. "What are you doing?"

"The same thing you're doing."

"Negative."

"Excuse me?" Her countenance clouded over with confusion, swiftly followed by disbelief, and then irritation.

"I said, *neg-a-tive*." He leaned down so his face was even with hers. "As in, you're not going near that house." He used a tone that carried authority, and assumed he made it clear that the command was firm and final. As far as he was concerned, the conversation was over.

"Oh, really?" Joey reacted with a hostile glare and tilted her head in a way that indicated she did not plan to accept his demand. "And since when do I take orders from you?"

"Okay, how about this." Colt remembered his conversation with her friend Bev about working with headstrong horses. "I'm *asking* you not to go, instead of *telling* you." He slipped the vest over his shoulders and pulled the belt tight. "That's how they do it in horsey world. Right? Is that more agreeable to you?"

The answer came quickly. "No, it's not more agreeable. How dare you—"

"All right. I'm pulling out all the stops." Colt didn't want to be a smart ass, but he wasn't going to allow her anywhere near someone as evil and dangerous as Arman Sassani. Period.

He took a step closer and spoke in a purposefully low and seductive tone. "I don't throw this word around lightly, but here goes… *Please.*"

In response, Joey shook her finger in his face. "Do you have any idea how much training and experience I have?"

"Yes." Colt straightened back up and continued his preparation, slipping a helmet with night vision onto his head and buckling the strap. "Congratulations. But you're still not going."

The shock reflected in her eyes at his cavalier comment yielded quickly to full-fledged fury. She took a step toward him, and he almost took a step back. "Do you think you're the only one who dreams about killing Sassani every night?" Her voice broke with an emotion that was more like anguish than anger.

Colt's eyes searched her pain-filled face as the significance of the words began to register. Sassani had been behind the ambush that killed her husband. She'd never mentioned the connection even though her desire for retribution was clearly as strong as his own. The reason she'd been aware of Sassani's release from Gitmo was because she'd been in the process of tracking him down.

He put a calming hand on her shoulder. "I'm sorry… But…" He cleared his throat. "You're not going in as long as I have anything to say about it."

Joey bristled with defiance, making it clear that anger was the only emotion in control now. Her hands curled into fists and her face became a glowering mask of rage. Like Old

Faithful, she was getting ready to blow.

"Why in the world would *you* have anything to say about what *I* do or don't do?"

Colt had no desire to have this conversation in this place at this time, but he could see it was unavoidable. He took a deep breath, never removing his eyes from hers. "Because it's dangerous, and I don't want you to get hurt."

Seeing that his statement did nothing to appease her wrath—and perhaps did much to increase it—he leaned down close so that only she could hear. "And I think—"

He faltered. Even though he knew the words he wanted to say...*needed* to say, he found it hard to verbalize them.

"You think, *what?*" She stamped her foot in such a way that he knew it was now or never.

"I love you. Okay?"

Chapter 46

Joey took a quick, sharp breath, and then stood frozen, her sparkling eyes wide with astonishment. Colt tried to read the range of emotions that crossed her face as the surprise wore off, and kept his gaze locked on hers as she struggled to capture her habitual, cool composure.

If this had been a normal situation, Colt would have been content to stand and stare, soak her in, and kiss those uncertain lips, but he had work to do. "I'll see you in a bit."

Slinging his rifle over his shoulder, Colt nodded to the other men, and started toward the house, relieved that she'd offered no outright objections to his declaration.

He didn't throw *those* words around lightly either. One of the biggest regrets of his life was that he'd never said them to Griff.

His father had taught him to be straight-forward and frank, speak your mind rather than hold things in. The military had taught him that sometimes you don't get a second chance.

He wasn't ever going to let that happen again.

"No. Wait." Joey's voice broke through and he felt her grasp his arm. "You can't just walk away after saying something like that."

Colt looked at her, and then glanced back at the men still

making their way toward the house. "Sorry, but I kind of have to go."

Joey reached for his vest and pulled him close. "Be careful, Nick." She stood on her tiptoes and gave him a hurried kiss on the lips. "Do what you have to do, and come back to me. I'll be waiting. Okay?"

Consumed by an undefinable sense of rightness, Colt felt his mouth twist up into a lopsided smile. "Yes, ma'am. That sounds like a plan." He shot her a wink before lowering his night vision goggles, then turned back toward the men and trotted to catch up.

By the time Colt made it to the house, his heart rate had returned to its normal pace, and his mind was focused like a laser on the job at hand. He wasn't leaving here until Sassani was captured or dead.

He hoped to make it out alive, but if he didn't, he was going to die a happy man.

Chapter 47

Arman Sassani stood in the shadows of a small outbuilding wearing his own set of night vision goggles and watching the scene taking place near the emergency vehicles. A slow smile spread across his face as he observed the emotional display.

He didn't know how these men had tracked him down—but he knew the one bringing up the rear had something to do with it. Nicholas Colton seemed like an imaginary superhero that wouldn't give up and couldn't be killed. But tonight that was going to change.

Even though large parts of the mission had failed, Sassani was still in a position to take out a significant number of infidels. But at this point he didn't care about the numbers. As long as Colton was among them, he could claim victory.

He'd watched his plan crumble before his eyes on television when the drone had been brought down safely. The media had then scrambled to Homeland Security offices to broadcast Rashad Alikhan being led out in handcuffs, and there was a headline that other arrests were pending. Like a game of dominos, the authorities were knocking down his accomplices one by one.

Little did they know that Sassani was still in the game.

Dressed the same as the men who were coming to look for him, Sassani waited patiently for them to make their way down the farm lane. They were moving with an abundance of caution, obviously expecting a fight.

Once they surrounded the house and kicked in the door, Sassani nudged the man beside him and pointed to the woman standing alone by the vehicles. "That is our ticket to freedom. Let's go."

Once the point man had breached the door, the eight men who had been stacked in a line behind him, entered the structure and began clearing it room by room.

The living room was empty of targets, but full of possible intelligence. Set up like a command center, it contained tables of computers and electronic equipment lining two walls.

"Living room clear." Colt heard the transmission before he'd even entered the house. "No tangos."

The men began to break off in teams down a hallway, clearing the rooms on each side. When the officer in front of Colt kicked open a door on his right, he entered, swinging his rifle from three o'clock to nine o'clock. Finding the room clear, he squeezed the shoulder of the man, and they continued down the hall to the next room.

The process took a little longer than normal because of the tedious amount of time it took to look for booby-traps. Still, in less than twenty minutes the dwelling was clear. No Sassani.

Colt stood on the porch with the others, his eyes darting

around the property. The house had been under surveillance and, for the most part, surrounded for most of the day. There was no way Sassani got away, and Colt wasn't leaving until he found him.

The fact that the computers and other equipment had been left behind, proved that those involved had left in a hurry. They had to be here somewhere.

As the rest of the group went back toward the waiting emergency vehicles to figure out their next move, Colt lagged behind. He knew that a preliminary check of the outbuildings had been conducted before the search of the house, but he wanted to take another look. Maybe there was a secret room or an underground shelter.

Stepping off the porch, and heading toward a small wooden structure, he caught a slight movement in the tree line to his right. Lifting his gun, he shouted, "Don't move."

Not heeding the warning, a figure emerged, taking a hurried step out of the dark shadows as if being pushed from behind. Colt moved his finger to the trigger and began applying pressure. He blinked repeatedly, trying to identify the hazy green image he was seeing through his night vision goggles. Then he lowered his rifle. "Dammit, I thought I told you to stay behind."

Joey didn't have time to respond. Arman Sassani gave her another shove forward, and stepped into the yard. Her long hair was wrapped tightly around his left hand, and his gun was pointed at her head with his right. "We meet again, my friend."

Colt's rifle flew back into position. "Let her go." It was not spoken as a request. There was steel in his rasping voice.

Sassani's smile widened, as if enjoying the reaction. "I don't believe you are in a position to be giving orders."

Dressed like a SWAT member, complete with regulation boots and credentials, Sassani appeared relaxed and in control. It was easy to see how he had moved around the other men from different federal agencies so easily. Clean-shaven and outfitted as he was, he did not resemble the picture distributed to law enforcement in the least. Even Joey may not have recognized his altered appearance until it was too late.

"You Americans have the habit of being much too trusting." Sassani's words verified Colt's assumption that Joey had been deceived by the SWAT attire, but his taunting tone caused Colt to uncharacteristically lose his temper.

"We are also in the habit of only making war upon *armed men.*" The words rang through the darkness and then hung in the air as Sassani's respiration intensified to match his rage.

He became surprisingly—if not suspiciously---quiet, causing Colt to raise one hand in the air and attempt to sound more conciliatory. "Stop with the games. What do you want?"

In response, Sassani jerked Joey's hair, causing her to take a step back and meet Colt's gaze. Her expression reflected sympathy and regret, but not a trace of fear. She lifted her head another notch and seemed to be imploring him with her eyes: *Do what you have to do.*

"For now, I want you to drop your gun." Sassani's voice broke through the silence with an ultimatum that Colt knew would not be given a second time. He weighed his chances of getting a shot off before the terrorist could pull the trigger, and came to the conclusion that it was too much of a gamble to try. Under ordinary circumstances, he might have accepted the odds, but not tonight. He'd already been given one second chance. He could not press his luck and ask for another miracle.

Nodding his head at Sassani to show he was going to comply, he kept his gaze locked on Joey, and strove to conceal any signs of panic from his eyes.

In hers, he saw nothing but a strange glint of serenity, contradicting the inherent spirit of fight he knew lay beneath. Her deceptively calm appearance revealed the traits of a true soldier. It was clear she was relying on senses rather than thought.

Colt's heart kicked once at the sudden fear that Sassani would kill him in front of her. He'd witnessed Griff's death, and it was an image that had never been erased from his memory. If Joey survived, he didn't want her to relive this night for the rest of her life.

Just as he was getting ready to place the weapon on the ground, he saw Joey's eyes drift to something behind him, and then grow wide with alarm. By the time she yelled, "Colt!" he'd already spun around, firing with lightning-fast speed as he turned.

From that point on everything started moving in slow motion. Colt thought he heard other gunfire, but the flash of light that came from an instantaneous explosion blinded him.

He remembered lifting his hands to pull off his night vision goggles, but he didn't have time. The heat and rush of air from the blast struck him hard, sending him falling backward. It seemed to take a full minute to hit the ground.

Then everything went black.

Chapter 48

Colt didn't know if he'd been unconscious for a split second or several hours. He awoke to the sound of voices, and sirens, and flashing lights.

"Buddy, are you okay?"

He blinked at the face leaning over him.

"Talk to me. Are you okay?"

It was one of the men from the SWAT team. Colt wiggled his fingers and moved his legs, then nodded. "Help me up."

The man reached down and helped him to a sitting position. That's when he saw the medics surrounding the spot he'd last seen Joey.

He tried to stand, but ended up half crawling, half walking. "What's going on? What happened?" His words were not loud, but everyone within earshot heard the pain.

One of them held him back. "Give them room. Let them work."

"What happened?"

"We're still piecing that together."

"Let me through. I need to talk to her."

Someone patted him on the back. "She's going to be all right, buddy. Calm down." He must have noticed the wild look in Colt's eyes. "You need a medic? You were out cold for a few minutes there."

"I'm fine." Colt shrugged off the man's hand. "We...work together. What happened?"

The man whistled to one of the men standing close by. "Kent, come over here."

One of the younger men of the SWAT team walked over with a questioning look on his face. "Sir?"

"Tell this guy what you saw."

The man named Kent turned to Colt, and spoke with a noticeable Southern drawl. "Well, sir, I was standing right over there by that outbuilding and saw a guy coming up behind you. I couldn't get a shot, so I ran to about that fence post." He indicated his position, then turned back to make sure Colt was still listening. "When you turned and fired, the guy behind you fired at the same time. He missed you, but struck the hostage."

Colt listened while staring blankly at the scene in front of him. One of the medics held a bag of fluid high in the air, while others worked on getting an IV line going. They were working swiftly, but not frantically.

"Your shot took that guy down," Kent continued, nodding toward a man lying sprawled out on the ground. "But it went straight through and hit a cache of Tannerite and gasoline back there."

Colt looked over his shoulder at the bits and pieces of wood and glass that were strewn all over the yard. He remembered seeing a small structure there—about the size of an extra-large doghouse—where the explosive materials must have been hidden. A deep cavity in the ground showed how powerful the blast had been.

"What about Sassani?" Colt's voice was barely above a whisper. He dreaded hearing the answer because he knew he'd most likely gotten away in the chaos.

Kent pointed to a man lying face down a few yards away that Colt hadn't noticed in the dark. "He tried to run."

Colt's head jerked over to look at the lifeless form. "How—"

"Wouldn't believe it if I hadn't seen it with my own two eyes." Kent nodded toward Joey. "Sassani trained his pistol on you when you turned around to fire, but his shot went wild because that woman knocked his arm into the air. Next thing I know, she has the gun, and Sassani takes off running."

Kent ran his hand through his hair and stared at the ground as if watching the image replay in his mind. "Everything happened in a flash." He snapped his fingers. "I saw her body kind of flinch—I guess when she got hit—but she still got a shot off at Sassani before going down. I didn't even see her aim, but dang if he wasn't DRT." He looked at Colt, shaking his head with a look of disbelief and amazement. "Dead Right There."

Colt stared at the body. Sassani wore a Kevlar helmet and full body armor. From the amount of blood pooled around him, he'd been struck in the neck—about the only place a shot would have counted.

His gaze drifted back to Joey as they lifted her onto a gurney for transport. "Thanks, buddy." Colt spoke over his shoulder to Kent as he hurried forward and fell into stride beside the medics. Joey's head lulled from side to side as they traveled over uneven terrain on the way to a waiting helicopter, but she made no protest, no sound. Thick lashes rested on her cheeks, making her skin look pale in the dim light.

"How is she?" Colt tried not to choke on the words as he laid his hand on hers. He wanted to hear some hopefulness, or at least cautious optimism, in the man's voice, but his tone was unemotional.

"She's hanging in there," is all the medic said.

Colt gave her one last squeeze as they loaded her into the helicopter, but wished he hadn't. Her hand felt cold, lifeless. She looked so vulnerable. As the chopper began to rise, he turned instinctively away from the backwash, and walked toward a group of vehicles in the distance. He needed to find a ride.

As he covered the ground with long, purposeful strides, Colt gazed up at the blanket of velvet sky pierced by a million twinkling stars—but he wasn't really seeing. He was thinking about what had happened.

She was hit with a bullet meant for me. Colt raked his hand through his hair. *It should be me on that chopper.*

He'd gone into this mission perfectly willing to die. But for the first time in a long time, he wanted to live. When he felt his phone vibrate, Colt pulled it out of his pocket mechanically. "Go ahead."

"Good to hear your voice, bro," Blake said. "How's it going over there? I heard we got him."

Colt took a slow, deep breath, waiting for the ruling of his own will, waiting until his speech could be clear.

"Hey, you still there? You okay?"

"Yeah. I'm good." He cleared his throat so it wouldn't crack. "Joey's been hit."

"What? Bro, I'm sorry. Where is she?"

"They just medevacked her out. I'm getting ready to head to the hospital."

"I'm almost clear here," Blake said. "I'll meet you there."

"No."

"What do you mean, *no*? How bad is it?"

"I don't know. Bad, I think."

"Then I'll meet you at the hospital."

"No. Go home to Cait. She needs you more than I do."

There was a long pause. "I'll do whatever you say, but I'm here for you, buddy."

"I know you are. I'm okay. Do me a big favor and give your wife a kiss for me."

Blake took a deep breath and exhaled. "You sure?"

"Positive." Colt stared blankly at the night sky again. "Hold her tight. Tell her you love her. Okay? I gotta go."

Chapter 49

Joey floated on a sea of darkness, the waves lifting and releasing her, sometimes spinning her, so she always seemed to be in dizzying motion. She had no concept of time, no idea how long she drifted and floated, content to go wherever the water took her.

But that all changed in an instant. One minute, she was floating weightlessly; and the next moment, she was dumped like a discarded ragdoll onto a firm, unforgiving surface. The calming cadence of waves was replaced by an annoying beeping sound, and the darkness was replaced by light. Even the soothing sensation of water vanished in an instant, hijacked by sharp, throbbing pain.

"Hey. You awake?"

Joey forced her lids open and stared into the black, liquid eyes of Colt. His lips were pursed, and his face was stamped with weariness and concern. She said the first thing that came to her mind. "You look tired."

Colt leaned closer, his expression now tinged with a

mixture of relief and humor. "For future reference, that's not something you should say to a man who's been sitting by your bedside for the past thirty hours."

"Really?" Joey murmured, trying to smile. The effort made her eyes close again. "Don't you have anything better to do?"

"No." His response was so fast and firm, she reopened her eyes. The amusement that had flickered on his face was gone, replaced by a glint of longing. Joey tentatively raised her hand and ran the back of her fingers across his jaw. "You need a shave."

Colt's dark eyebrows arched. "For future reference, that's probably the second worst thing you can say to a man who's done nothing but grab a shower and watch you sleep."

Joey turned her head toward the beeping machines and gazed down at her arm. "Is that all I've been doing? Sleeping?"

"Pretty much. After surgery they kept you drugged for the pain."

"Oh. That explains the throbbing."

"Let me call the nurse back." He arose from his chair with alarm. "She was just here getting you cleaned up, and told me the medication was being decreased to see how you do."

"No." Joey smiled, trying to console him and ease his concern. "It's not that bad."

He bent down and swiped a tendril of hair from her face in an instinctive gesture of comfort. "Are you sure?"

She nodded, and reached up to run her fingers through her hair, assuming it would be a dreadful mess. Instead, she discovered it was neatly plaited.

"The nurse braided it." Colt must have read her questioning

eyes. "When I stepped out for a cup of coffee, she brushed your teeth, washed you up. You're all good to go."

"Good to go?" Joey examined her arm again. It was about ten times its normal size from the bandages. "I feel like the Michelin man."

"Do you remember what happened?"

Joey laid her head back on the pillow and closed her eyes as a contented smile began to form. "No. I don't remember anything after that kiss." As soon as the words left her mouth, she regretted them. Maybe her memories weren't memories at all—but a dream or a desire—caused by pain and drugs.

"Yeah. I have that effect on women." A smile broke through Colt's usual mask of reserve, but Joey didn't see any sign of devotion or any acknowledgment of the brief intimate connection they'd shared.

Maybe he hadn't really meant what he said—if he'd even said the words *I love you* at all. He'd been facing a life and death situation at the time. She couldn't blame him if he'd made the declaration prematurely or maybe even unintentionally.

His smile faded as he regarded her with a somber, thoughtful look. "But I have a feeling that trauma and blood loss triggered your memory loss—not me."

Is he trying to steer me away from the subject? Joey stared at the ceiling, trying to conquer the bewildering array of conflicting emotions pulsing through her. As casually as she could manage she asked, "Speaking of trauma, tell me what happened."

"You really want to talk about that right now?"

His forbidding tone and his reluctance to discuss the incident roused Joey's curiosity. She closed her eyes, trying to recall the events. After a moment, she jerked her attention back to Colt and her gaze swept over him. "You're okay? That man behind you was—"

He put a calming hand on her arm. "Thanks to your warning, I'm fine. He fired and missed me—" She watched his expression darken with an unreadable emotion "And hit you instead." His voice drifted into a hushed whisper, and a look of tortured pain crossed his face.

Joey's heart dropped at the look and the words—and what it all implied. "And now you blame yourself." She didn't state it as a question because it wasn't. An unspoken pain was alive and glowing in his eyes, proof that this bedside attention was caused by the burdensome weight of guilt—not affection— and certainly not love. It was clear from the look on his face that he felt responsible, was full of regret. That's why he hadn't left her side.

"Did I say that?" His black eyes flashed in protest.

Joey turned her head away. She didn't want to fall prey to his magnetic gaze. He had a way of stealing her resolve, holding her prisoner. "No. But I know you. What you've been through. It's understandable that you would—"

"Look at me."

"You can go," she continued, still staring at the wall. "I'm fine. I'm sure you have better things to do. Thanks for stopping by."

"Look. At. Me."

Joey wanted to refuse, but his voice was commanding and pleading all at the same time. She slowly turned her head and then raised her gaze to meet his. A strange, faintly impatient look shimmered in his eyes as she waited in silent expectation for him to speak.

Trying to remain expressionless, Joey concentrated on keeping her heart cold and still, even as his black eyes searched hers, unyielding and insistent.

Seconds ticked by. The silence continued. He seemed to be weighing an important decision—or perhaps bolstering his nerve. Joey had the urge to turn away, but without warning, his lips lowered onto hers.

This was not a kiss of apology or remorse. It was a slow and thoughtful caress of the lips that awakened Joey's aching soul, and stirred feelings she thought long dead. Her pulse skittered alarmingly, triggering a new high-pitched intonation on the bedside monitor.

Colt finally pulled away and buried his face in her hair. "Did that feel like regret?" he whispered into her ear with gentle intimacy.

"I'm not sure." She nudged him away so she could see his face. "Try again."

Joey wasn't surprised to see his mouth lift into a sensual smile, but the smoldering flame that flickered in his eyes startled her, causing any last trace of resistance to fade. She lifted her hand to the back of his neck and drew him to her, impelled involuntarily by her own emotions.

Colt's lips recaptured hers with more desire this time, and his touch, firm and persuasive, invited even more. Joey was conscious of the rise and fall of his chest against hers as he enveloped her securely in his arms.

"Is everything okay in here?" A nurse came rushing through

the door to check the monitor that seemed to be stuck in a loud, chaotic alarm mode.

Colt lifted his head long enough to say, "Can you turn that thing off?"—but did not relinquish his hold.

The flustered nurse stopped in her tracks, and then smiled awkwardly. Continuing toward the machine, she pressed some buttons and warned Colt. "I'll silence it for a few minutes, but it needs to be on." She shifted her gaze to Joey with a look of envy. "Take it easy. Okay?"

"Thanks, ma'am." Colt turned back to Joey, and started to lower his head. "Where were we?"

Joey held him back with her hand flat on his chest. "You were telling me what happened."

"No, I think I was expounding on the wonders of my magic touch." He moved closer.

Joey resisted by turning her head. "Just a quick summary."

Colt's warm, possessive smile faded and an uncertainty crept over his face. "What do you want to know?" She felt the muscles on his back grow tense.

As she tried to recall what would cause this reaction, Colt's gaze shifted to the fingers sticking out from her bandaged arm.

"I'm sorry about your ring." He winced, as if reliving the pain of that emotional scene.

The image of the ambulance exploding flitted through Joey's memory. "It was just a ring."

"But it was important to you—your wedding band." Raw hurt glittered in his depthless black eyes. "I wish there was some way I could replace it."

"No." She shook her head. "It doesn't need to be replaced. It was part of my cover."

Colt seemed momentarily speechless. "Oh." He stared vacantly, seemingly unable to process the emotions of going from pure dread to promising hope.

"I mean, I thought about Scott every time I looked at it... but it *was* just a ring." She reached up and touched his cheek, rough with stubble. "So stop blaming yourself for that, all right? You did what you had to do."

Colt seemed too engrossed in his own thoughts to offer a reply, but relief was evident in his expression. Joey cupped her hand on his face to get his attention.

"Maybe all of this happened to teach us both a lesson."

"What lesson is that?" Colt turned his gaze back to her, but she could see his mind was still busy.

"It takes more courage to let go than it does to hold on..." She blinked, feeling suddenly overwhelmed with emotion. "And when you let go, you can still be okay."

That got his attention. Colt leaned close, searching her face pensively. "Are you sure you're *okay*?" He questioned her in such a way that she knew he was asking if she was ready to let go.

She nodded, and returned the burning question. "Positive... Are you?"

They stared into each other's eyes, no tears or sorrow evident in either one—only a hint of the past each heart bore and a glint of eagerness for what the future promised.

Colt took a deep breath and let it out slowly, as an irresistible smile lifted the corner of his mouth. "I haven't been this okay for a long time."

His lips slowly descended to meet hers in another kiss that was tantalizing in its tenderness. When he pulled away, Joey ran her fingers through his hair contemplatively. "Who would have thought I'd fall madly in love with a plumber?" She shifted her humor-filled eyes to meet his.

"I'm not *just* a plumber." He sat back, pretending to take offense. "I'm a pretty good all-around handyman."

Joey closed her eyes in delicious contentment as her mind drifted. "Good. I have some things that desperately need attention."

"Then, I'm your man."

The deep vibrancy of his voice and the underlying proposition he implied by his words caught her off guard. Joey snapped her lids opened and stared into eyes that brimmed with desire and passion. She answered without hesitation, ignoring her thundering heart and reveling in this new, delightful sensation.

"Yes, Nick Colton. You're my man."

The End

BONUS MATERIAL

FINE LINE (Book 2)

Blake Madison reached for the alarm at the first ding so it wouldn't wake his wife.

"It's Saturday," Cait said sleepily, reaching for his arm. "Sleep in."

"I'm going for a quick run." He crawled out from under the covers, carefully moving Max's head off his legs. "It's a lot of pressure having a young trophy wife. I have to stay in shape."

She threw a pillow at him, but then reached over and ran her hand over his abs. "You're doing a pretty good job of staying in shape."

The comment made Blake smile. He had gotten back into a weightlifting and running routine shortly after getting married, and was in almost as good a shape now as he had been when he was a young Navy SEAL. Then again, Cait was pretty fit herself. She had taken over most of the barn chores, and actually enjoyed splitting and stacking wood. She was always amused when other women saw her toned arms and requested the contact information for her personal trainer.

Dressing as quietly as he could in a pair of sweatpants and

tee shirt, Blake headed toward the door.

"You forgot something," he heard from beneath the covers.

He went back and bent over her. "I know. But I was afraid I'd be tempted to crawl back into bed."

"Good answer." She reached up, grabbed a handful of his shirt, and pulled him down for a kiss, causing him to linger.

Sitting on the side of the bed, he leaned down with his hands propped on each side of her pillow. "Do you know how much I love you, Mrs. Madison?"

She grinned sleepily and pulled him close again. "Show me."

"I just did that a few hours ago. Remember?"

"Umm hmm." She drew the words out with her eyes still closed and a contented smile on her face. "But that was last night."

He glanced at the door, then back at the bed.

She must have sensed his hesitation. "I'm just kidding. We have all day. Go for your run."

Blake lifted her hand off the covers and kissed it. "We've been married almost a year. We need to start acting like an old married couple, not newlyweds."

"Are you saying you want me to become a nag?"

"Only if you nag me about getting back into bed with you."

He gave her another long kiss, and then stood and stared down at her in the dim light. She was wearing his NAVY tee shirt—or as she called it, her favorite negligée—with one arm lying on top of the blankets. His gaze fell on her wedding band, and then drifted to her tousled hair spread out on the pillow and her long lashes resting on her cheeks. He reconsidered his need for outdoor exercise.

"Bring me a cup of coffee when you get back," she murmured, pulling the covers up and rolling over.

"I won't be long, baby." He headed toward the door and patted his leg for the dog to follow. "I'll take Max so you don't have to get up and let him out."

"Love you."

His heart flipped. "Love you more."

Just as he started to close the door, she spoke again. "Don't miss me too much."

He grinned as the door clicked shut. She always said that when he left, even if they were only going to be separated for a few minutes. It had become a routine. Even the kids said it now when they left for school or went to visit a friend.

Heading down the stairs he turned off the security alarm and went out onto the porch, taking a deep breath of the cool morning air. After doing a couple of stretches, he sprinted down the lane with Max trotting along beside, his heart bursting with happiness and contentment.

These early morning runs were as much for his mental wellbeing as for physical training. He usually used the time to clear his mind and focus on his business goals for the day. But as he listened to the cadence of his feet hitting the dirt road and the sound of his steady breathing, his mind drifted to his upcoming anniversary instead. He wanted to come up with something really special to celebrate—something that would show Cait how much she meant to him and the kids. It had been on his mind for weeks, but now the milestone moment loomed just days away and he still didn't know what that something was.

Moving to the side of the lane to avoid a large mud puddle, his mind continued to drift and wander. He thought back to the day he'd proposed, causing the vivid memories to replay through his mind like a movie.

Cait had just finished testifying at a congressional hearing about Mallory and Senator Wiley, and was waiting for him by the Washington Monument. He'd snuck up behind her and grabbed her around the waist with one hand and the shoulders with the other. Drawing her up against him, he'd whispered in her ear. "Come here often?"

She'd tried to turn around and look up at him, but he held her firmly with her back pressed against him. "If that's your best pick-up line, you're going to be a lonely man," she'd said.

"Really? It works in the movies."

"Sorry. But, no."

"Okay. How about this?" He'd leaned down and whispered in her ear. "Hey, baby. Wanna ride in my truck?"

"Now you sound downright creepy," she'd said. "That's a definite no."

"Okay. Let me see… Close your eyes this time."

"All right. They're closed."

"Hey, sweetheart." He had let go of her then and backed away. "Are you free?"

"I don't know." She'd laughed, but continued to stand with her back to him. "When?"

"The rest of your life."

Whether it had been his words or the seriousness of his

tone he didn't know, but she'd turned around with a perplexed expression on her face—and found him down on one knee, with Drew on one side and Whitney on the other. All three held onto a sign that said, Will you marry us?

Blake smiled at the memory. Her surprise and the children's pure delight at being a part of the occasion had forged a memory he would never forget as long as he lived.

Bypassing the security gate and turning left at the end of their long driveway Blake continued toward the main road, his breath coming faster now and creating short bursts of steam in the chilly morning air.

The gate made his thoughts wander back still further, to when he and Cait had testified against Senator Wiley and Mallory. They'd tried to keep a low profile and return to their private lives, but the media attention and social media campaigns from political fanatics made that impossible. There had been lots of intimidating communication and a few death threats immediately following the scandal, so despite the home's isolation, Blake had taken the extra steps of installing an electronic gate to stop vehicles, and upgraded the security system in the house.

The addition of Max and the fact that his house was a sort of informal headquarters for his security firm, made him feel pretty secure and confident that his family was protected. There was rarely a day when at least one former Navy SEAL did not stop by or spend the night—and depending on deployments for his company, there were often half a dozen or more.

Blake inhaled the musty smell of dying leaves and contemplated the gold and red colors splashed like a painter's canvas all around him. It was Cait's favorite time of year, and was beginning to be his as well. They'd harvested the last of the vegetables and pumpkins from the garden, and spent any free time together stacking wood in preparation for the coming winter. Somehow it wasn't work when Cait was involved. It was pure pleasure.

Passing the two-and-a-half-mile mark he knew by heart, Blake slowed down. The image of Cait lying in bed turned him around before he'd made it to the main road. If the kids were still asleep, maybe he'd take a quick shower and re-join her.

Sprinting the last hundred yards, Blake was surprised when Max didn't follow him up the porch, but continued around the side of the house with his nose to the ground. The dog usually had a pretty hearty appetite after a run and wanted fed immediately.

"Where you going, boy? Smell a raccoon or something?"

Blake let him go and entered the house to find Whitney walking slowly down the stairs, looking disheveled, but looking wide awake. So much for going back to bed. "What are you doing up so early, young lady?"

He didn't hear her answer as he continued into the kitchen to make a pot of coffee. With the coffee starting to brew, he stood in the glow of the open refrigerator door, trying to figure out what to make for breakfast. Maybe he'd surprise Cait with breakfast in bed as an early anniversary gift.

Whitney shuffled into the room behind him and noisily pulled out a chair at the small kitchen table. "When is Cait coming back?"

"What, honey?" Blake continued staring into the fridge. Having just turned four, Whitney talked a lot, but didn't always make sense.

"When are they going to bring her back?"

Blake closed the refrigerator door slowly as a twinge of dread crawled up his spine. He turned to Whitney and knelt down beside her. "What men, honey? What are you talking about?"

"The mean ones that came." Her eyes brimmed with tears.

Blake didn't ask any more questions. He stood and turned in one movement.

Racing to the stairs, he took them two at a time and headed at a full sprint down the hallway to the master bedroom. He tried to open the door quietly, hoping to find Cait still sleeping, but he almost tore the door off its hinges in his urgency.

The bed was empty.

Order FINE LINE (Book 2) today!
Available wherever books are sold!

Visit www.jessicajamesbooks.com

Dear Reader,

Thank you for taking the time to read this novel!

Although the heroes in my books are fictional, they are not unlike those who honorably serve us every day while separated from their own homes and loved ones.

There is no institution in this world that commands more admiration than the United States military, and no other group of men and women who deserve our unwavering respect more.

For information on military-related charities, news, and recommended reading, follow me on Twitter and look for the hashtag: #WarriorReader.

JESSICA JAMES
HONOR COURAGE LOVE
www.JessicaJamesBooks.com

About the Author

Jessica James is an award-winning author of military fiction and non-fiction ranging from the Revolutionary War to modern day. She is the only two-time winner of the John Esten Cooke Award for Southern Fiction, and was featured in the book *50 Authors You Should Be Reading*, published in 2010.

James' novels appeal to both men and women, and are featured in library collections all over the United States including Harvard and the U.S. Naval Academy. By weaving the principles of courage, devotion, duty, and dedication into each book, she attempts to honor the unsung heroes of the American military—past and present—and to convey the magnitude of their sacrifice and service.

Connect with her at www.jessicajamesbooks.com.

Contact the Author

Email Jessica@JessicaJamesBooks.com

www.JessicaJamesBooks.com
www.Facebook.com/romantichistoricalfiction
Twitter: @JessicaJames
Pinterest: www.pinterest.com/southernromance
GoodReads: www.goodreads.com/jessicajames

Made in the USA
Middletown, DE
28 November 2021

53627209R00201